THE DEMON'S WRATH

"You dare use puny magicks against me? Against *me?*" Lenc strode out of the fire and brushed away burning debris from his shoulders and arms. "I will show you real magic!"

The demon clapped his hands. The thunder rumbling down the streets of Kolya deafened Kesira. She fell to her knees, sobbing with the pain lancing into her head. Even putting fingers in her ears failed to stop the hideous noise ripping away at her soul. And just when she thought it might be bearable, Lenc clapped his hands again.

And he laughed...

Other Avon Books by
Robert E. Vardeman

THE QUAKING LANDS: *Book 1* in **The Jade Demons**
THE FROZEN WAVES: *Book 2* in **The Jade Demons**
THE CRYSTAL CLOUDS: *Book 3* in **The Jade Demons**

Avon Books are available at special quantity discounts for bulk purchases for sales promotions, premiums, fund raising or educational use. Special books, or book excerpts, can also be created to fit specific needs.

For details write or telephone the office of the Director of Special Markets, Avon Books, Dept. FP, 1790 Broadway, New York, New York 10019, 212-399-1357. *IN CANADA:* Director of Special Sales, Avon Books of Canada, Suite 210, 2061 McCowan Rd., Scarborough, Ontario M1S 3Y6, 416-293-9404.

THE JADE DEMONS #4
THE WHITE FIRE

ROBERT E. VARDEMAN

AVON
PUBLISHERS OF BARD, CAMELOT, DISCUS AND FLARE BOOKS

THE WHITE FIRE is an original publication of Avon Books. This work has never before appeared in book form. This work is a novel. Any similarity to actual persons or events is purely coincidental.

AVON BOOKS
A division of
The Hearst Corporation
1790 Broadway
New York, New York 10019

Copyright © 1986 by Robert E. Vardeman
Published by arrangement with the author
Library of Congress Catalog Card Number: 85-90820
ISBN: 0-380-89801-2

All rights reserved, which includes the right to
reproduce this book or portions thereof in any form
whatsoever except as provided by the U. S. Copyright Law.
For information address Howard Morhaim Literary Agency, 501
Fifth Avenue, New York, New York 10017.

First Avon Printing, January 1986

AVON TRADEMARK REG. U. S. PAT. OFF. AND IN
OTHER COUNTRIES, MARCA REGISTRADA, HECHO EN
U. S. A.

Printed in the U. S. A.

WFH   10 9 8 7 6 5 4 3 2 1

This one's for Dick Patten and Peter C. Rabbit

Chapter One

THEY CAMPED at the base of the towering granite spire, tired in body and spirit. Kesira Minette dropped to the ground, almost forgetting to cradle the infant she carried so gingerly. So much had changed, she thought. So much. She brushed a dirty strand of brunette hair back from her eyes and stared down at the baby boy.

His pale gray eyes boldly met hers—challenged her. No trace of child existed, save in body.

"What goes on inside your head?" she wondered aloud. Kesira cringed, waiting for the baby's answering cry, but it did not come. Atop the mountain, she had met the jade demon Ayondela and had almost perished in the conflict. If it hadn't been for the baby's shrill, shattering cries that had disintegrated the demon like a dropped pane of window glass, Kesira knew that she—and the world—would have been ground under Ayondela's heel.

Not that the outcome proved any better for either Kesira Minette or the world in general. One of four jade demons still lived, and Lenc was the worst of the lot. More cunning, stronger, more insane, he ruled now without opposition. He had used Kesira and her companions Molimo and the *trilla* bird Zolkan for his own evil ends. Cat's-paws. They had fought and destroyed Lenc's enemies without even realizing what they did, and now the jade demon ruled supreme.

Even worse, the baby she held, the one who eyed her so sagely, the one whose slightest cry brought death and suffering, this little one had been sired by Lenc.

"True," sputtered the green-plumed *trilla* bird. Zolkan fluttered to a bare tree branch overhead. The crunching of his powerful talons into the wood beat a counterpoint to the soft sighing of wind through the leaves remaining on the tree's highest limbs. "Bratling is Lenc's spawn. Kill it before it kills us!"

"I . . ." Kesira stilled her rampaging emotions. "I can't," she said, swallowing hard. "The boy may be Lenc's son, but he is also half human."

"You call that charwoman Parvey Yera human?" Zolkan spat out a thick red gob of bark he'd been gnawing. "Lucky I am *trilla* bird. Filthy human."

"We owe it to her to tend her son."

"We owe bitch nothing!" screeched Zolkan. The bird turned one harsh black eye toward the infant, then broke the gaze. The *trilla* bird could not outstare the boy.

Parvey Yera had been driven mad by deprivation, and her husband had given his life aiding them in destroying another of the jade demons. Eznofadil would have slain them but for the man. If for nothing else, Kesira owed something to Raellard Yera, and she'd have to repay the debt by caring for the baby, even if this boy weren't his son.

"We owe her," Kesira said firmly. "And the Order of Gelya is not to be accused of turning away the needy. Never has one of my order wantonly killed a child."

"Not human child. Demon spawn!" squawked Zolkan. The bird settled down, hunching his sloping shoulders and pulling his wings up to shield his head. In a few minutes, he tucked his large head under the left wing and snored loudly.

Kesira busied herself making a small cooking fire. Now and then she turned to peer over her shoulder at the red granite massif that had held Ayondela's jade palace like a jewel in an emperor's crown. Clouds drifted slowly around the cap, alternately veiling and revealing silently. She shuddered. Ayondela had commanded those clouds to cut and slash. Kesira still bore dozens of deep cuts from the demon's crystal clouds and hundreds of shallower scratches.

"Ayondela is dead. So are Eznofadil and Howenthal," she said quietly, firmly, trying to convince herself that she had done well. In one respect, she had. No one else might have opposed the power of the jade for so long. Her fury at Lenc's destruction of her patron Gelya had fueled her quest for vengeance, at first, but now she felt only hollowness. So much of what she'd accomplished had been abetted by Lenc himself. The demon had needed Ayondela and the others to bolster his power until the jade totally dominated his body, as it did now.

Now Lenc alone ruled the world. His slightest whim had to be obeyed, in violation of the eons-old pact between human and demon. Kesira felt the ember of hatred being fanned back into full blaze at the unfairness of it all. Humans should rule humans; demons were supposed to tend to their own affairs, asking only for minor obeisances and tributes.

No longer. Lenc wanted everyone to worship him. Kesira clenched her hands into tight balls and ground her teeth together so hard it triggered shooting pains up and down her neck. Consciously relaxing, using the meditative techniques of her order, she eased the tension. But after doing so much, to find only ashes...

Soft footfalls caused her to turn. A tall, dark-haired, dark-eyed man of middle years worked his way up the small ravine over which she camped. Clutched in one hand was a rabbit, fat from a delayed summer's feasting. Molimo dropped the animal beside her, then knelt.

"Will one be enough?" she asked. Molimo pointed to his mouth and rubbed his stomach, indicating that he had already eaten. Kesira tried to hold back the tears and failed. Molimo reached out and touched her. She flinched away.

"I cannot help it," he wrote on a small tablet. "The changes are too strong now, since confronting Lenc. I am stronger, but so is the shape alteration urge."

"I'm sorry, Molimo. I know you can't help yourself." Kesira wiped away the tears and found dirty smudges where the salty drops had mixed with dust on her cheeks. Molimo, caught in a rain of jade, had been cursed not only with having his tongue ripped from his mouth but also an inability to hold human form. When he least wanted, he changed into a wolf, without the slightest control over animalistic urges. He had never harmed her or Zolkan, but Kesira knew that the intensity of the transformation into other-beast now overwhelmed Molimo.

"You can control it," she said. "You can, Molimo!" The man shook his head. For the first time she saw red sunlight glinting off silver strands. After the jade rain, when she had tended his wounds, Molimo looked hardly older than seventeen. Now? Kesira guessed forty. The nearness of jade had taken its toll on him, even as he regained physical strength.

"Does Lenc age this way, also?" she asked, before she could still her words. Molimo nodded, then wrote quickly.

She peered over his shoulder, reading, "The jade makes him invincible in human terms, but it also robs him of virtual immortality. He has traded longevity for power."

"But you're not a demon. The effect of the jade . . ." Her voice trailed off.

"I have been touched by the jade." He pointed at his sundered mouth. "Its mere presence makes me feel faint." Molimo pointed at the jade tusk thrust through Kesira's belt. His hand shook.

"I don't know why I took Ayondela's tooth," Kesira said. "The baby—he forced me to do it." The words grated and caused her almost physical injury, just uttering them. How did the baby influence her? He was Lenc's son; Kesira could offer no other explanation. "I don't want to keep it because I see what it does to you, but I can't get rid of it! I just can't!"

Her hand flashed to the six-inch-long fang. To prove her point, Kesira pulled it free and threw it as hard as she could. The baby watched impassively, the only indication he even noticed being the small upturnings of his lips in a faint smile. The green fang cartwheeled into the sunset, stopped and hung suspended in midair, then slowly turned and curved back. It landed in the dirt at Kesira's feet, sharp point in the ground. Struggle as she might, Kesira couldn't prevent herself from bending over and pulling it free. She thrust it back into her dirty yellow sash. Only then did the compulsion die and give her a moment's surcease.

She blacked out. When she came to, the sun had dipped behind the Sarn Mountain range and chill night breezes stalked her. Kesira pulled her tattered robe more tightly around her thin frame, then moved closer to the fire Molimo

The White Fire

had maintained. Of the man-wolf she saw no trace, but Zolkan still perched on the tree limb.

As if reading her thoughts, the *trilla* bird said, "Gone. He hunts. You are to eat."

Molimo had dressed and roasted the rabbit, but Kesira found she had little appetite. Zolkan flapped down and hit the ground hard enough to send him staggering. The *trilla* bird waddled over to her and shoved a portion of the meat forward with the tip of his long wing.

"Eat."

Silently, Kesira obeyed. The baby reached out and gripped her robe when she had finished, demanding his own dinner. She found a rent in the fabric and allowed the infant to nurse contentedly at her demon-kissed breast. Kesira sighed with the simple pleasure of the feelings inside her; the spot where the demon Wemilat's lips had touched her breast now burned with an inner warmth. Wemilat had died so that the jade demon Howenthal might also perish.

Death, always death, Kesira thought, suddenly bitter. Her patron Gelya had died, killed by Lenc. The jade demon had left behind his mocking sigil, the cold, dancing white fire that desecrated all it touched. Wemilat had been ugly and misshapen, but his spirit had been beautiful. He, too, had died. And so many others, both demon and human.

"Do not dwell on it. We have much to do," said Zolkan. "Long trip. Long and tiresome."

"Why leave?" Kesira asked. The listlessness fell over her like winter's first soft snow blanketing the forests. "With Lenc invincible, one place is as good as another. Or as bad. The Sarn Mountains have a beauty to them that appeals to me."

"More than your nunnery?"

"No," she said. "But what is there for me? Lenc's flame consumes Gelya's altar. Sister Fenelia is dead. Dana, Kai and the others—all dead."

She brushed dirty fingertips across the knotted blue cord indicating her sisterhood in the Order of Gelya, then traced along the once-gold sash proclaiming her to be the Sister of Mission. Kesira laughed without humor. She had become

Sister of Mission simply by being the last of Gelya's worshipers. The others had died or lost faith.

"Why do I still believe? Gelya is dead by Lenc's hand. Why do I continue? Why not stay here for the rest of my days? The land is rich enough. I could grow some vegetables and perhaps even start an orchard of fruit trees. Game abounds. Molimo finds no difficulty in hunting."

"You would allow Lenc to enslave everyone?" asked Zolkan.

"How can I stop him?" Kesira morosely poked at the fire with a slender twig picked up from the ground. "You say it wrongly, also. Lenc already *has* enslaved everyone. Even my rune castings were dictated by his whim." Her only talent had been revealed to her as a fraud, as signs sent by Lenc to guide her in the directions he desired.

"Are you so sure?" pressed Zolkan. "Why must jade demon speak truthfully? Lenc lies for agony it causes others."

For a moment, Kesira brightened; but the hope sputtered and died just as the fire in front of her did. She made no effort to rekindle the fire—or her faith.

"Feel sorry for yourself," Zolkan taunted. "If this is all Gelya taught, pah!" The *trilla* bird spat. A tiny, quivering column of steam rose from the fire's embers.

"I feel for the world," Kesira said softly, more to herself than to Zolkan. Then she said, "That's not entirely true. How can any mortal embrace all the world? I care for what has happened to me and those I know."

Her eyes darted to the peacefully sleeping baby. In repose he appeared no different from any other child—but no ordinary infant shattered the jade flesh of a demon and brought down an entire palace with a single outcry. Truly, he had to be the spawn of a demon. And so, even this small thing, this newborn life, this simple joy, was tainted.

Live according to the tenets, simply and well, Gelya had promised, and the future was assured. The universe had order and everything was in its place. She need never want. Obey the Emperor, worship Gelya, know her place in society and the world, execute her duty to the best of her ability, and life would be kind and good. Those were the things she had been taught.

The White Fire

Those were the lies.

"Go to Limaden." Zolkan waddled back and forth, his fluttering wings fanning the fire to new life. Kesira listened to the bird with only half an ear as her thoughts turned inward.

She had done much in the past few months. When she had returned to the nunnery from Blinn with the lamp oil requested by Sister Fenelia, Kesira had composed only a few lines of her death song. A few lines describing her parents' death at the hands of brigands and her loyalty to Gelya—and nothing more.

Since that ill-fated day when the skies rained jade and she found mute Molimo, much had happened that must be included. Kesira began composing the lines. When the death song was finished—and only she would know that instant—her life would end.

Kesira mentally wrought and turned and twisted the words to her own particular scansion, music finding its way between words and phrases to illuminate and lend substance and emphasis. New verses told of Molimo and Zolkan, of the jade demons, of despair and triumph, sacrifice and death, daring Howenthal's Quaking Lands, the frozen waves of the Sea of Katad, the crystal clouds cloaking Ayondela's final resting place. All those fell neatly into her death song.

Kesira's brown eyes again checked the baby. He slept soundly now, a smile on pink lips. She couldn't bring herself to compose the verses dealing with the boy. The rhymes failed; she became confused and even the notes turned flat.

"My time is not at hand," she said.

"Foolish human. You know nothing," grumbled Zolkan.

"There is no need to go to Limaden," she said. "The Emperor Kwasian is there. He of all mortals might be able to hold out against Lenc. But what is there for me in the Emperor's capital?"

"More than there is here."

Kesira shook her head; she felt dull with fatigue. To stay here . . . the land was favorable and the tranquility appealed to her. She had seen too much death and suffering—had caused too much by her actions. Kesira Minette wanted only to rest. . . .

Her eyelids sank like the setting sun, slowly, inexorably, and she entered a land where dreams were stalked by nightmares. Kesira sat upright, eyes wide, sweat pouring down face and body. Her fingers gripped harsh, rocky soil and she looked around fearfully.

"What is it?" she demanded of Zolkan.

The bird had again perched on the denuded tree limb. Even in the darkness she saw his beady eyes glistening.

"Molimo," the *trilla* bird said simply.

Kesira pushed herself to her feet, propping herself up unsteadily with the staff she had fashioned from a green sapling. She longed for her old, stolid stonewood staff, but even that—Gelya's sacred wood—had been destroyed. Since then, she'd had scant opportunity to season a new staff. Not for the first time she cursed Gelya's prohibition against using steel weapons.

Unbidden, her hand went to the jade tusk sheathed at her belt.

"What trouble has Molimo found?" she asked, fighting down guilt as she fleetingly hoped Zolkan would not answer and that she could go back to sleep.

"Humans do not tolerate other-beasts. Bands of your kind hunt those like Molimo."

Kesira flinched as if the *trilla* bird had physically struck her. Never before had he used phrases like "your kind" to indict the men and women trying to cope with the afflictions brought by Lenc and the power of the jade the demon had ingested. In doing so, Zolkan put her in what she had unconsciously always considered an inferior group.

"Where? Maybe I can help him."

"Why bother?" the *trilla* bird squawked. "He goes on to fight Lenc. He must. You have chosen another path."

"Molimo's in trouble. Curse you if you won't help!" Kesira cocked her head to one side and strained to hear the slight sounds that had awakened her. A wolf's mournful yelpings were drowned out by the ululation of what she thought at first to be a pack of animals. Then the noise became clearer: human voices. A hunting band, seeking out the other-beasts, planning to vent its collective rage and frustration on the poor creatures trapped between human and animal.

Like Molimo.

"Watch after the boy," she said, getting her feet firmly under her now. She didn't even pause to see if Zolkan would obey. It hardly mattered. The boy had proven he could take care of himself. Hadn't he destroyed Ayondela?

And who would ever threaten the son of Lenc? Kesira pushed that from her mind, beginning the settling exercises that had given her tranquility through much of her life. Gelya had taught that fear sprang from uncertainty; tenseness was caused by fear. She relaxed. Slowly, muscles unknotted and confidence returned. While Kesira knew she was no match for a trained fighter, she could more than hold her own against a peasant brandishing a crude spear or a hay fork.

Her sisters in the Order of Gelya had never taken vows of nonviolence, nor had Kesira ever believed such pacifism possible. Gelya preached that violence spawned violence. Kesira tried to avoid conflict, would not initiate the attack if she could prevent it; but often, especially in these times of death and disorder, violence was the only saving response to violence.

Kesira crashed through low shrubs and made more noise than a dozen marching soldiers for a few hundred feet, until she was sure that those in the hunting pack had heard her approach. Then she changed tactics. On feet as silent as if she'd swaddled them in cotton, Kesira advanced, staff clutched so hard her forearms began to knot with the strain. She forced her muscles to relax. Over and over she went through the litany that would give her the needed mental and physical tranquility to react with maximum speed. Only when the nun was sure of herself did she begin circling.

Eventually Kesira found a rocky perch overlooking a sandy pit. Molimo snapped and yelped and dashed about inside a ragged circle formed by the hunters.

"Filthy beast," snarled one man in a voice more animal-like than the wolf's howls.

"It's an accursed other-beast," shouted another from the far side of the circle. He took the opportunity to poke Molimo in the side with a spear. The man-wolf spun; his strong jaws clamped on the spear's haft. The loud *snap!* as it broke echoed through the night, reverberating off stony buttes and down lonely canyons.

For a moment the men stood, stunned, as if it had never occurred to them that the other-beast they chevied might prove truly dangerous. Kesira almost cheered; but before she could, the men stiffened their resolve and surged forward as one, intending to overwhelm Molimo.

The wolf ducked under their probing spears and sticks, found a fleshy thigh and ripped. The man's screams did nothing to deter the others this time. If anything, it goaded them on. Red stripes crisscrossed Molimo's gray fur as they swung spear and knife, stick and rock at him.

"Stop!" Kesira shouted, rising up on the rock. They had heard—and forgotten—her noisy approach. Now they drew back fearfully to appraise this new danger.

"What do you want? Get you gone!" shouted the man with a large, jagged scar running diagonally across his face. Even in the dark, the cicatrice seemed to glow with an inner light.

"Where did you get the scar?" Kesira asked, deliberately pitching her voice lower to give an air of authority. She softened her words and spoke so that all had to force themselves to hear.

"Ayondela!" the man shouted. "She cut me with jade!"

The others nodded and murmured. They'd heard the story, no doubt told many times around the communal fires. And who knew? Kesira thought that the man might speak truthfully. The scar's odd inner light indicated no ordinary wound.

"She cut you? With one of her tusks?"

"A fingernail," the man said, almost as if this were an admission of cowardice.

"Let the wolf go."

"It's an other-beast," someone shouted. The leader with the scar motioned for silence.

"Aye, that it is. An other-beast. They steal our children and slay our women. They were touched badly by the power of the jade. They must be destroyed!"

"Let him go or you'll feel the true power of the jade." Kesira pulled the tusk from her dirty gold sash. Clutching

The White Fire 11

it like a dagger, she held the jade high for all to see. The tusk's faint glow brought instant silence.

Then, "She's a demon!"

"No!" Kesira shouted. "I am no demon. But I killed Ayondela, and this is her tusk. This other-beast aided me. Molimo, join me."

The men milled around, uncertain. For a fleeting instant Kesira thought she and Molimo might escape without further argument. But the jade-scarred man brought the others around too quickly.

"She lies to save the other-beast! You, Cord, didn't you lose wife and two children to the shape changers? And you, Exas, what of your mother? Doesn't she hobble on one leg because of the other-beast that attacked her?" The knowing, fearful mutters convinced Kesira that she had lost control.

"Molimo, hurry!" she shouted.

The men attacked again just as the wolf leaped to the rock beside her. Kesira had the advantage for a few seconds, and her staff cracked open several foreheads and broke some exposed wrists. But there were too many of them, and her arms quickly became leaden. She had been through too much, with little rest and even less food. A strong, meaty hand gripped her ankle and pulled her to the sandy pit.

She had replaced Molimo as the object of their hatred. Spears gouged and rocks pelted her. Kesira doubled up and tried to pull away, but she quickly realized that if she tried only to defend herself, she would die.

"No!" Kesira roared. She rose, spinning her staff so fast it became a virtual wall of green sapling encircling her, knocking away spear thrusts and bony fists.

When one man knocked the staff spinning from her hands, Kesira stood defenseless. Again she withdrew the jade tusk from her sash. Now it glowed a vibrant green. Wielded like a dagger, it didn't do much harm—but it *was* Ayondela's tusk. The men backed off.

As they retreated, Molimo attacked, biting and snarling. And from above came a green rocket bursting noisily above Kesira's head. Feathers floated down around her as Zolkan's pinions cracked under the strain of his dive and the sudden midair stop. Talons raked and the *trilla* bird's sharp beak ripped at exposed flesh. The threefold attack, by nun and bird and wolf, drove the men back.

"Run!" shouted the scarred man, when he saw his companions fleeing.

The men crashed off into the brush, and eventually the sounds of their boots against rocks and scrub faded away.

Kesira sank to the sandy ground and cradled her head in shaking hands. There could be no rest, not while even one of the jade demons walked the land.

"Zolkan," she said in an uncharacteristically weak voice, "how far is it to Limaden?"

"Far," the *trilla* bird replied. "Very far."

Kesira didn't know whether Zolkan meant in distance or in what they must endure. It hardly mattered either way. If the land of her birth was to again find peace, she must confront Lenc and destroy the remaining jade demon.

That was her fate; that was her accursed destiny.

Chapter Two

THE OTHER-BEAST hunters dogged their steps like a carrion eater waiting for its intended dinner to finally die. Kesira couldn't remember feeling more driven, more tired, less able to cope with the pressures of such dogged pursuit. But somehow she kept on moving toward Limaden, although she had no idea what lay in the Emperor Kwasian's capital for them.

"If these ignorant peasants are so vehement about killing unfortunates like Molimo," she asked Zolkan, "why won't the citizens of the capital seek his hide, also?"

"Might," admitted Zolkan. The bird fluttered and swooped and finally came to rest on her shoulder. Kesira didn't exactly wince when the *trilla* bird's sharp talons dug in; but she sagged from physical exhaustion. They had spent four hard days a'trail after fighting off the other-beast hunters. While they hadn't encountered another band as large or as determined, the nibblings of those smaller bands were almost as deadly: A cut here, a reopened wound there, and strength fled.

Strength none of them had.

"We should be glad we find only farmers," Zolkan remarked. "Nehan-dir and his Order of the Steel Crescent would make fine dinner of us. They eat *trilla* bird meat." The large bird shuddered hard enough to unbalance Kesira. She regained her stride, but with even less confidence. What Zolkan said was true.

Nehan-dir and his mercenaries had been left on the far side of the Sarn Mountains engaged in mortal combat with a small company of the Emperor's Guard. The Order of the Steel Crescent would sell its loyalty to whatever patron offered the greatest chance for power. Nehan-dir, as leader, had selected poorly. Their original patron, Tolek the Spare, had sold them to another demon for cancellation of a gambling debt. Even among the demons, with their extremes of emotion, desires and angers and loves many times magnified over those of humans, this unseemly behavior had brought only scorn. The Order of the Steel Crescent had abandoned its new patron in favor of another offering more raw power—the jade demon Howenthal.

Kesira had been responsible for Howenthal's destruction, again leaving the Steel Crescent without a patron. Going with the gusty winds of change, they had sought out Ayondela. Now that their newest patron had perished, Nehan-dir commanded that they worship Lenc.

This time Kesira thought they had chosen well. Lenc could grant them infinite power—or sudden death. But whatever the jade demon commanded, he would not simply cast them off or trade them in payment of gambling debts. She allowed a faint smile to cross her lips. A chance existed that, for a third time, she would personally rob Nehan-dir and the Steel Crescent of a patron. Howenthal and Ayondela had become jade dust on a devastated palace floor; she might still find a way to destroy Lenc.

The woman realized, even as she smiled at these wondrous thoughts, that they were sheer fantasy. When every footfall threatened to be her last, when her body ached and wounds burned with gelid fire and her own kind sought her death because she consorted with other-beasts, what chance did she have of destroying the last jade demon?

"Do you anticipate Nehan-dir finding us?" she asked Zolkan. The bird didn't answer, but Molimo dropped back from his position as scout. The man—he had stayed in human form for almost two days now—pulled out his tablet and wrote quickly.

"If Lenc informs the Steel Crescent of our whereabouts, we can expect visitors at any time," Kesira read.

"Can't we use the underground transport system?" she asked. Molimo had revealed a marvelous magical-powered cart that shot through tunnels dug with cruel power. They had dipped under the Sarn Mountains and reached the very base of Ayondela's cloud-capped stronghold in the wink of an eye. Zolkan had later remarked that this array of tunnels extended throughout the Empire and that one terminus lay less than an hour's walk from her destroyed nunnery in the foothills of the distant Yearn Mountains.

"Lenc destroyed it. He was angered after we used it to reach Ayondela," explained the *trilla* bird. Not for the first time Kesira wondered how Zolkan came by these snippets of information. He was seldom out of her sight. His occasional flights to reconnoiter and to scout for food provided no chance to exchange such data with others. But Kesira's lethargy prevented her from again questioning Zolkan. The bird always ignored her direct questions or cleverly turned the topic to one less interesting.

"How much farther to Limaden?" she asked.

Molimo wrote, "We go to Kolya."

"What? Why? Zolkan was adamant about going to the capital. He said that Emperor Kwasian would be the focal point for resistance against Lenc."

Molimo nodded. His dark eyes retained some of the blazing green highlights they took on when he altered form. Kesira shivered, even though the afternoon wasn't yet chilly. Every time Molimo's eyes shone green, he found it harder to keep human shape, and he took a little longer to shift back after he became a wolf.

"Kolya holds our destiny. We either destroy Lenc there— or not at all."

"May all the demons curse you forever!" Kesira shouted, anger animating her. "You and Zolkan prattle on and on about these things. How do you *know?* Tell me your source of information. Don't keep me ignorant. Haven't we shared enough for you to trust me?"

Kesira was shocked speechless when Molimo stared her directly in the eyes and slowly shook his head. His stride lengthened and he outpaced her, leaving her with the *trilla* bird weighing her down.

Before she could protest, Zolkan cut her off. "Do not ask. There are matters too dangerous for you to know yet."

"Yet? You mean one day you'll deign to tell me? What am I? Your servant? Your toady doing all the menial chores?"

She glared at the green-plumed bird. Coldness gripped her soul when she read the answer in the bird's unblinking beady eye.

"That's all I am to you—and to Molimo," she said in a stunned voice.

"You are more. Always," the bird said. "One day you will know. One day."

She clutched the baby closer to her breast and stumbled along in the dying afternoon light. She hadn't believed such cruelty existed in the world as this just shown her by Molimo and Zolkan. Kesira had taken the *trilla* bird in and nursed him back to health after he flew into the nunnery's sacristy one wintry night. And Molimo? She had kept him alive after he'd been caught in the jade rain. What did they refuse to tell her after all they'd shared?

The sounds of another pack of other-beast hunters drove these thoughts from her mind. Her pace quickened, and they were soon free of their pursuers.

Kolya lay nineteen days' travel to the west.

Kesira Minette entered Kolya, uneasy at the crush of people around her. It had been many months since she had seen such crowds, and she had never frequented cities larger than provincial Blinn while at her nunnery. Zolkan's head swiveled around as the *trilla* bird took in the exotic sights and sounds that made Kesira queasy.

"Good place," the bird pronounced. "Not like cities where they eat *trilla* birds."

"How can you tell?" she asked. "There might be stalls over in the central market."

"I know." Zolkan's smugness told her that he was probably correct. How he could know with such certainty was another of the mysteries surrounding the bird.

Kesira pulled her tattered robes around her ankles and moved through the crowds, unsure where she headed. The paved streets felt unnatural to her after having trod so long on dirt roads, but the lack of dust rising to make her sneeze and cough soon offset any discomfort from the hardness of the surface.

She cradled the baby closer when a parade pushed its

way through the populace. Two small platforms carried by well-dressed servants sported altars. Behind each platform walked a priest with head bowed low, chanting incomprehensible words, censers pouring out noxious fumes. Kesira was well versed in worship of most patrons, this having been a required portion of her education at Sister Fenelia's hand, but this ceremony did not seem at all familiar.

"What patron do they worship?" she asked an onlooker. The woman turned and glared at Kesira, leaving without speaking. Contempt and even suppressed hatred radiated from her as she rounded the corner and vanished from Kesira's sight.

"Not one of their followers," Kesira guessed. "If we find out what patron they worship, we might be able to invoke aid and..."

Her words trailed off when she saw Zolkan shaking his head sadly, as if she were the village fool.

"They worship Lenc," she said, understanding bursting upon her like the blooming of an ice flower.

"Who else remains?"

Kesira sank to the paving, pulling her legs up close. The baby protested by reaching out an unnaturally strong hand and tugging at her robe. She ignored him. The world swung around her in crazy circles, the people stumbling over her and going on, muttering about derelicts. Kesira closed her eyes and tried not to cry. Every turn presented new and more fruitless paths to follow; all led to Lenc.

"Seeds of rebellion need nurturing in Kolya," said Zolkan so low that only she could hear. "You can stir them against the power of jade."

"Why bother? A pitiful rabble waving pointed sticks will not topple Lenc from his lofty throne. He is invincible now. He rules with an iron grip." Kesira smiled mirthlessly. "I should have said that he rules with a jade grip."

"He cannot be in all places at same time," Zolkan said. "Kolya is ripe for uprising against him. Few like yoke he places around their necks."

Kesira fought her way to her feet and stood with tired back against a cool stone building. A hint of autumn entered the city on the soft summer wind and chilled her. Summer had been delayed because of Ayondela's curse. Once she had broken the demon's curse, summer arrived quickly, but the natural roll of seasons now shortened the warmth and promised bleaker winter.

"We must find a place to stay. The night will be cold without shelter."

Kesira looked around, trying to locate Molimo, but the man had disappeared into the crowd. She shrugged this off. He'd have to be careful. The slightest hint of shape change would bring down the wrath of Kolya's citizens, of that she was sure. All across the plains on the way from the mountains they had seen roving bands of marauders intent on slaying other-beasts. Some even offered generous bounties for other-beast pelts. Kesira knew that this served only as an excuse for the brigand bands to pillage and rape as they had always done, but the general populace now believed these lies.

That bespoke a real fear on the part of ordinary people concerning the other-beasts.

"Molimo," she said softly.

"He scouts. He will return. Shape change will not overtake him. He fights it hard in city."

"I hope you're right." Kesira walked aimlessly down the main streets, through alleys to lesser thoroughfares; and finally she located the quieter residential sections of Kolya. She saw a small inn with neatly swept walkway, freshly painted sign and the air of caring about it.

"There," squawked Zolkan. "We stay there."

"You take to wing. They'd never allow me in with a *trilla* bird on my shoulder."

"Bigots," the bird grumbled, but he leaped and quickly flew to the peaked roof, where he perched to glare down at Kesira.

Kesira's purse hung limp and empty. Getting a room and food would prove difficult even without the big bird's presence. With him, Kesira didn't want to consider the problems.

The interior of the inn proved as neatly kept as the exterior. The low wooden tables had been waxed laboriously and shone like mirrors. The flagstone floor felt cold beneath

The White Fire

her feet but better than the dusty trail that led to Kolya. At the back of the small public room ran a waist-high counter laden with foods that made Kesira's mouth water. She took two quick steps toward the banquet before her fingers brushed over her empty purse again. She stopped and simply stared in longing.

"Help you?"

Kesira spun guiltily and faced a portly man with a scarred, florid face. "I did not mean to sneak in like this. I . . . I saw the food and I am very hungry after long days on the trail," she finished weakly.

He studied her with practiced eyes, taking in the robe and its tears, the brutalized flesh beneath, the knotted blue cord and dirty yellow sash, the staff, the baby quietly suckling at her breast through one of the tears.

"Been awhile since you ate?" he asked.

Kesira nodded.

"You got the look of a nun about you. Which order?"

"Gelya," she answered simply. Kesira felt no need to add that Gelya had been slain by Lenc. Most of the patrons who had perished were killed by the jade demon.

"Rough times, eh?"

"They are, good sir."

"You willing to work around here for your meal?"

"And a place to sleep? We just arrived. Traveled through from the Sarn Mountains."

"You and the youngling crossed the plains what with all the brigands running free and wild?" The innkeeper appeared skeptical at this, but Kesira's condition finally convinced him. "You're a tough one, tougher'n me. Never leave the boundaries of Kolya these days. Used to roam free, I did. No more. Too many willing to cut your throat just for the sick thrill it gives 'em."

Kesira cared little about the man's past or his philosophy. His food drew her as a lodestone pulls iron, however. He saw, and waved her to the counter. She put the baby down behind the counter in a blanket-swathed box intended for a pet, sat and devoured the simple food until she felt ready to burst. Kesira leaned back and smiled.

"You eat like there's no tomorrow," the man observed.

"And who knows, you may be right, what with Lenc visiting his anger on us all the time. Not a fit place for a man nor beast—nor other-beast—these days."

"Lenc personally comes here?" she asked, surprised.

"He does. What he finds in Kolya is any mortal's guess." The innkeeper turned grim. "Would that he go away for all time." The grimness metamorphosed into fear, as if Kesira were Lenc and would still his hammering heart with a single pass of a jade hand.

"Lenc killed my patron," she said. "I have no love for the demon."

The man nodded as if his head bobbed on a rubber cord. Three men entering the inn claimed his attention; he put on a happy smile that Kesira knew had to be insincere.

The innkeeper spoke briefly with the three men. Finally, the man seated farthest from the entryway gestured to Kesira. She sighed. This wasn't the first time she had acted as servant. Her first five years at the Order of Gelya had been spent waiting on the elder sisters. They were harsh taskmasters; now Kesira was glad for that. Any customers in this placid inn would seem tame by comparison.

"What's your pleasure?" she asked the small, slender man. She stared at him boldly, not liking what she saw. He had a head that was too thin and a face like the nicked edge of a hatchet blade. Dark, cruel eyes studied her even as she stood waiting for his order. A tiny mustache, hardly more than a dirty smudge, disgraced his upper lip. In the shadowy interior of the inn, Kesira couldn't tell if that mustache hid a deformity. She thought that it did. Quick, jerky movements told of the man's inherent nervousness. He tapped fingertips against the table in front of him.

"Sit. Join us, my dear," he said in a tone both oily and edged in cold steel.

Kesira glanced at the innkeeper, who nodded. Kesira sat, stiffly erect and waiting.

"You've come from the Sarns?" the thin man asked. Kesira didn't speak. He wouldn't have asked if he hadn't already known the answer. "How did you avoid the hunting bands?"

The White Fire   21

"There are only so many of them. With enough agility and cunning one can avoid them."

"There's more," he said. "I know there's more. *How* did you come to be on the plains?" He leaned forward eagerly, fingers drumming in wave patterns on the shining tabletop.

"The jade demons forced the trip upon me," she said, wary of revealing too much. "Ayondela perished high atop her mountain. The power used by Lenc forced me to flee. We came to Kolya because there was nowhere else for us to go."

"You and the baby?" The man frowned so hard his head turned into a land more rutted than any farmer's prized acreage.

"The pair."

"You weren't touched by the jade? There are those in the city worried over Lenc's son. The demon claims this bastard spawn will one day rule Kolya and all the rest."

Kesira turned icy inside. No matter how she turned, Lenc blocked her escape. Such tales spelled not only her death but that of the baby as well. She moved so that the folds of her robe hid Ayondela's jade tusk. No one had noticed it yet; Kesira wanted to keep it that way.

"People always worry," she said simply.

"You avoided both jade demon and brigand?" The man's gaze turned harsher, more accusing.

"I am not in league with Lenc. He killed my patron. But the innkeeper's already told you of this." The way the portly innkeeper flushed showed the truth of her words. Kesira also saw that they were not satisfied with her explanation about avoiding the bands of homeless hunters on the plains.

Kesira knew that she dared not tell these men of Molimo. They looked no better than the hunters they'd already avoided. Speaking of Zolkan seemed safer, but still she hesitated. Kesira picked the one thing most innocuous.

"I can read the rune sticks," she said. "This allowed me to pass among the hunters unscathed."

The men sat back, eyes wide. They quickly recovered their senses and huddled, muttering among themselves. Finally, the thin man with the dark mustache turned back to

Kesira and said, "My name is Kene Zoheret. I represent a small group of citizens who, uh..."

"Get on with it, Kene," snapped another. "Tell her. If she can cast the rune sticks, she'll be able to find out."

"You," cut in Kesira, "are part of a group opposed to Lenc." They stared at her as if she were Lenc himself. Kesira laughed at their shock. "It takes no reading of the runes to figure that out." These men were rank amateurs in intrigue. She saw no purpose in joining with them, but then, where else might she turn? Even a sorry rebel might be better than none at all.

"We do take ourselves rather seriously," said Zoheret. "But you can read the runes?" Kesira silently pulled the carved box out from under her robe and opened it. The gleaming white engraved knucklebones spilled forth and rattled noisily against the hardwood table. Zoheret pointed, then demanded, "Read the cast."

Kesira swallowed hard and wiped the back of her hand across her mouth. Lenc had sent her the visions before, had used her, had made her believe she possessed powers only a handful do in any generation. Now that her usefulness had passed, the skill had to be lost.

But Kesira felt the wellings of a force deep inside similar to those she had experienced before. Visions flashed before her eyes, behind and in her head. She reeled a little, gripped the edge of the table for support and finally settled her mind in the ways taught by Gelya.

Clarity of image came then.

"You control some meager magicks," she said in a voice unlike her natural one. "You, Zoheret, are a minor adept at spells of fire. There is more." Kesira fought against an inky cloud veiling a profound truth about the rebel.

"That's enough," he said, shaking her arm and pulling her from the reverie. "You've convinced us. We need you to aid us in what we attempt this evening."

"What?" Kesira sat in a mist of confusion, her mind unable to snap back from the intensity of the vision. Always before she had just *known*. This time it was as if she watched reality unfolding at an accelerated pace. The *texture* of the rune casting seemed alien to her, different and—friendly.

"We will attack Lenc's temple," Kene Zoheret said with ill-disguised eagerness, misinterpreting her reaction. "We will storm the gates, burn them down, set fire to the priests—show the people of Kolya that resistance is possible!"

"You will only provoke Lenc. Killing his mortal pawns does nothing to weaken him."

"Something *must* be done," Zoheret insisted. "The tyranny of the demon is intolerable. Right?" He hastily checked his companions. They all agreed. Zoheret rushed on. "You can't know how terrible it is in Kolya. Lenc rapes our women, then tortures them to an agonizing death—and forces us to watch. His power holds us enthralled. We watch as he mutilates our children, destroys crops and stores with the pass of his hand, and we are powerless.

"Individually," Zoheret said with passion, "we are helpless. Together we can make a stand. We *must* fight him. We *will!*"

"Do you have alliances with those who follow other patrons?" Kesira asked.

"Why bother?"

"They might be in a position similar to mine. Their patrons dead by the hand of the jade demons. They might bring needed abilities—gold—to your rank."

"You can foresee the future. *That* is a skill we desperately need," said one of the other men.

Kesira didn't try to explain that she had no control over her visions. Ever since dealing with Ayondela, the feeling of power within had grown stronger, but it had died when Lenc told her haughtily that he had sent her the rune readings. Now, she didn't know. It felt right, but Lenc's insidious lies had, also.

"We have her approval for what we do this night," crowed Zoheret. Before Kesira could protest, say that she had seen nothing of their venture, the men slapped their hands ringingly on the table and stood. "To the staging area. We attack in one hour!"

Kesira grabbed Zoheret's sleeve as the man started after his two friends. "I saw nothing of your success—or failure—in this. Even without the rune cast, I can tell you it is a mistake. Attract Lenc's attention and he'll destroy you!"

"We strike for freedom!" Kene Zoheret's expression came closer to a sneer than a smile. Kesira edged away from him. "Come and watch us in our victory," the man went on. "See how we strike fear into that bastard's jade heart!"

"No," Kesira said, shaking her head and backing away.

"I'll tend the child," said the innkeeper. "It's needed for you to aid us. What few patrons are left to us must have sent you. Please." Kesira looked into the innkeeper's eyes and saw only sorrow there. In a low voice he said, "Lenc took my w-wife. Elounorie was one of the f-first he u-used. My daughter was the next."

"I'll go," Kesira said. She turned and followed Kene Zoheret.

"Soon, very soon," Zoheret gloated. He hunched over the crude map he'd sketched in the dust on the warehouse floor and stabbed his finger down at a spot marked with an X.

"This strikes me as pointless," Kesira protested. "So you kill a few of his loyal followers. So what? Has it ever occurred to you these priests might perform their services because they're more frightened of Lenc than obedient? That you might recruit them for your own purposes? A mortal spy in his confidence could provide more than a few dead priests who only mouth platitudes."

"They are the symbols Lenc uses in Kolya to keep us in check. Destroy them, and we show the citizens there is a rebellion against the demon!"

Zoheret's words rang hollow in Kesira's ears. She studied the thin man and worried about his motivations. He couldn't be swayed from this suicidal attack, and he kept his pitiful band of followers firmly in line with promises of the adulation and support they would receive after the night's activity.

"I can conjure just well enough to bring down the entire temple. The use of my burning spell will show Lenc he's up against more than a few sickly old women waving sticks at him."

Kesira had listened to Zoheret's stories of how Lenc had marched forth on the Plains of Roggen and destroyed the

Emperor Kwasian's entire army with lightnings drawn down from the sky, jade bombs that burst inside the commander's skull, turbulent storms that swept cavalry from their saddles. General Dayle had perished and left the army—or the fearful few who survived—in the command of a junior captain. All other officers had died hideous deaths.

And Zoheret thought to frighten Lenc with petty vandalism?

"Now, we must go now!" Kene Zoheret insisted. The fear had become a miasma cloaking the room, but none of the men dared admit he lacked the courage to venture forth on this mad escapade. She knew that the slightest sign of resistance would send these would-be rebels racing for the safety of their homes. Not a one had the courage that marked a real warrior. She thought about those she had seen who had this courage: Rouvin, now dead; Molimo, somewhere in the city; Captain Protaro of the Emperor's Guard, left behind in the Sarn Mountains. They were fighters to be trusted.

Kesira closed her eyes and settled her seething emotions. Somehow, even the most advanced meditative techniques refused to quell the hammering of her heart. They were going to their deaths, and only she seemed to understand it.

Single-file, they slipped from the dingy warehouse and into a square facing the temple Lenc had ordered constructed. Bits of jade sparkled in the night, illuminating the front steps leading up to the massive carved wooden doors. Kesira's anger rose when she saw that the doors were hewn from stonewood, the substance sacred to Gelya. Even in forcing others to worship him, Lenc mocked the other demons.

Zoheret motioned for the men to split into two groups, one circling to the left and the other going right. He and Kesira stayed in the square, directly in front of the ominously silent temple. Zoheret dropped to his knees and began the magical incantations needed to produce the fire spell. Kesira felt the air stir around her as the magicks condensed behind the guard spell holding them in readiness.

Zoheret clapped his hands and a minuscule fireball burst

forth to crash into the stonewood doors, which shed the fire in a molten cascade. Zoheret launched a second fireball but this one was even smaller than the first. Already his powers waned.

As weak as Zoheret's magicks had become, fate worked against those within the temple. Just as Zoheret's last, pitifully small magical fire sped through the night, a priest opened the door to peer out into the square. The fireball hurled past the priest and into the temple, to smash against fringed tapestries on the back wall. Kesira saw orange tongues of flame begin licking their way up the walls. Frantic shouts came from within. The priest in the door rushed out to find the public watering tubs.

A dagger found his heart before he got ten paces. Those of Zoheret's band who had lain in wait now jumped up brandishing their pitiful weapons. The other priests rushed outside and died on the points of those inexpertly used weapons.

"Now what?" asked Kesira. Her stomach churned with nausea at the sign of the wanton killing. It was bad enough when demon slew human. For one human to kill another defeated the purpose of any rebellion against the jade power. Didn't these men have families who would mourn their passing—and demand revenge on those responsible? How could a man, in good faith, join with those who had killed a friend and neighbor in the name of peace?

Perhaps this was Lenc's plan, to turn one human against another. Kesira knew the demon might find infinite pleasure in the petty squabblings and vendettas. Such misuse of the power Lenc controlled would not seem wanton to a demon befuddled by jade that slowly perverted him to its own mysterious ways.

"They're dead, they're all dead!" cried Zoheret. He danced around like a madman made even eerier by the shadows from the flames leaping twenty feet and more into the nighttime sky.

Kesira edged out of the square and pressed herself into an alcove of a small dry-goods shop. Because of their celebration, not one of the rebels had noticed the odd coloration of the flames engulfing Lenc's temple. They had begun as a normal orange. They now turned a deep green and changed from insubstantial gases rising into the darkness to a form she know all too well.

A form of the purest jade.

Unwittingly, Kene Zoheret had summoned Lenc.

Chapter Three

MOLIMO PURPOSELY left Kesira behind. The woman struggled through the thick crowds along Kolya's main street, trying to keep strange shoulders from crashing into the baby's head, dodging those moving slower, failing to keep up with Molimo's long-legged pace. Molimo made a quick right and ducked into the portal of a coppersmith's store. Kesira blundered along a few minutes later, looking lost. Zolkan weighed her down and, seeing Molimo, shifted a heavy, green-feathered body to prevent the woman from spying him.

Molimo held back a pang of regret at treating Kesira in such a cavalier fashion, but her presence would only prevent his doing the distasteful tasks that lay ahead.

Kesira spun around, vainly looking for him. She stamped her foot and started off down a side street Zolkan indicated. Molimo had to smile. The *trilla* bird proved his friendship repeatedly. Molimo waited until he no longer saw the dirty brown top of Kesira's head and the flashing green of Zolkan's feathers before he left his post.

Heaving a deep sigh, he looked up and down the street. Molimo closed his eyes and almost staggered under the imponderable force emanating from the center of Kolya.

Lenc's temple. No other explanation matched the facts. He had led Kesira to this city because Lenc had decided to make this his final battleground. If Kolya fell, so did all the world. Limaden meant nothing after Lenc's defeat of General Dayle and the Emperor Kwasian's entire force on the Plains of Roggen. Molimo concentrated and saw the march of ghost battalions before him. The entire battle fought through in only a few minutes, but speeding it up gave

Molimo the chance to see the errors made by the human commanders. Dayle was good—had been good. But never before had he faced a demon of Lenc's power.

Even the jade demon could be slain. The deaths of the other three proved that. Lenc might be the strongest, but the jade made him more vulnerable than any human thought—even Kesira.

Lenc had traded virtual immortality for power. Molimo choked down the incoherent cry of anger rising within his throat. He might outlive Lenc now, because of the adverse effect of the jade on Lenc's longevity, but even so, Molimo knew that the other demon might live for hundreds of years. Far too long for Molimo to continue suffering the indignities heaped upon him. If Lenc wanted supreme power, he was going to have to fight for it.

Molimo flexed his muscles. Many women passing by, and not a few men, watched enviously; but Molimo knew that his real strength dwelt within. For a human, he was well muscled, but his real power derived from force of character. It was that power the jade rain had stolen from him, and only now, after these long months, did he regain a significant portion of what had once been his.

He turned and stared into a small windowpane at his reflection. A man a score of years older than he remembered peered back at him. The healing had taken its toll and added enervating years to his appearance. Molimo brushed one quick-fingered hand through his hair and came away with strands of silver. When Kesira had found him, he'd been scarcely more than seventeen. Now? Twice that and more.

But he had healed.

Molimo made sure his sword hung freely in his sheath, and he skirted the center of town, heading for the far side of Kolya. The crush of the market fell behind. His pace quickened. The streets narrowed and the houses brushed along his arms. Only occasionally now did he sight another. This was the sorriest section of Kolya, that part no one spoke of in polite company. Molimo had entered the Festering.

Rubble filled the small walkway, forcing him to climb up and over, but his sense of direction remained secure. He unerringly followed the twisty, turning path through the slum region until he came out into a small courtyard.

Molimo paused when the quiet rattle of small-link chains echoed down the tight streets. He fingered the hilt of his sword but did not draw as eight scrawny youths crowded into the small area. One, wearing an elaborately embroidered eyepatch with a shining gemstone sewn in the center, stepped forward.

"You're a well-fed-looking one, now aren't you?" he called out to Molimo.

When Molimo failed to answer, the youth stepped forward and swung a short length of silver chain in a flashing figure-eight pattern. "You can make it easy or you can make it hard," the youth said. "Not that we care. In fact, fool, we haven't been getting enough excitement in our lives down here in the Festering. Certainly not with the likes of you."

Molimo pointed to his mouth and tried to indicate that he lacked a tongue. The leader of the scavenger pack seemed not to care.

He motioned, and two others joined him, one on the left and the other on the right. They held short, wicked daggers.

"Now, the boys and me, we been wondering about how you rich folks live over in—what would you say? In Quo? Genrer? Maybe near the Slurries? It might all be part of Kolya, but we never see it. We're stuck down here puking out our guts and starving to death and getting the rots.

"Think he'd like to make a small donation to charity, my good men?"

The two on either side of their leader moved with practiced coordination. Molimo didn't draw his sword. In the confines of this tiny courtyard, its length would be a hindrance. He waited. When the one on the left feinted, Molimo moved right. His fist traveled only a few inches, but connected squarely with the boy's solar plexus. The scavenger turned green and spiraled to the ground, gasping for air. Molimo half turned and lightly backhanded the other. The youth slammed with impossible force against the wall, then toppled forward like a felled tree. He lay facedown on the dirty pavement, unmoving.

"Stay back. This one be mine," the leader said. His chain whistled with menace. Molimo let him attack. The chain wound itself around a brawny wrist, then began to smoke. When molten droplets of the steel chain dripped to the pavement, the gang leader's eyes widened in horror.

"It's Lenc!"

He bolted for a side alley, but a flash of green intercepted him. Strong talons caught the back of his tunic and lifted until his kicking feet were inches above the pavement. Molimo motioned, and Zolkan twisted mightily in midair, slamming the youth hard against one wall. The bird's strong wings pulled the half-dazed youth around and smashed him into the opposite wall. Only then did he drop his victim.

"Prefer not to eat this one," Zolkan said contemptuously. "Take too long to clean."

You saved me a footrace, friend. This is the urchin I sought. The communication flashed between Molimo and Zolkan without words, touching the surface of their minds, imparting eddies of thought that never shared a verbal counterpart.

"Turn him loose and let me hunt him down again. I need practice. Being with Kesira has turned me into a pigeonshit carrion eater, not a hunter."

The youth heard Zolkan's words but not Molimo's silent reply. He jerked away. Molimo took two quick steps and caught him.

"You got me wrong, good sir," the scavenger leader stammered. "We meant you no harm. Just a prank it was. A prank!"

Ask him where I can find it.

Zolkan fluttered down and landed on the boy's arm, talons gripping so tightly they drew tiny pinpricks of blood. "We seek the Order of Lalasa. Where is the priestess?"

"Lalasa?" he stammered. "I know nothing of demon doings."

"Lenc will eat you if you don't answer," Zolkan promised.

Molimo scowled at the crude threat. But it worked. The floodgates of information opened and the youth babbled, telling them all they needed to learn between pleas not to feed him to the jade demon.

Have him lead the way, Molimo ordered. *I do not trust him. I read deception in his every movement.*

"He is good friend. He would not think to lie." Zolkan's talons closed until the youth winced at the pain. "Lead us, good friend. Lead us to Lalasa's place of worship."

"All other patrons, save for mighty Lenc, are outlawed. We can be punished mightily for seeking out Lalasa."

Tell him he'll die here and now unless he obeys us.

Zolkan didn't have to translate for the youth. The expression on Molimo's face bespoke the threat more eloquently than any words. With servile bobbings of his head, the youth turned and scurried off, motioning for them to follow. Zolkan fluttered along warily, but Molimo strode without fear.

As befit a demon.

"It is long since any came to our worship," the frail old woman explained. "We cannot keep the shrine in proper repair." She smiled, showing broken yellow teeth. "In fact, we prefer it in the Festering. Only the most faithful seek us out—and we have ample opportunity to decide to whom they are faithful as they wend their way here."

She patted the scavenger leader on the arm. He pulled away and held it; Zolkan had clawed him several times as he tried to escape.

"The boys are loyal enough. They do not seek gain by turning us over to Lenc."

"He has served purpose. Send him on," said Zolkan. The youth smiled weakly and looked at the old woman. At her gesture, he left.

"He will die before another year passes," the woman said sadly. "The Festering does not permit long life."

"Nor does Lenc. We come to seek others who share our concern."

The old woman peered myopically at Molimo, then lightly brushed calloused fingertips over his arms and chest.

"He is no meat in market," protested Zolkan.

"No, that he isn't. He is much more. He seeks Lalasa?"

Tell her I want any of the demons still actively opposing

Lenc to come. We must forge an alliance if we are to defeat the jade-wielder.

The woman seemed to understand before Zolkan could put the thought into words. She said, "Lalasa is far distant, in Limaden conferring with Emperor Kwasian. Lenc has dealt the Emperor a severe setback militarily, and they must regroup if they are to defend the capital. She is a kind patron, but not good at military matters."

"Other demons," Zolkan pressed. "What of them?"

"So few," she said, sighing heavily. "So very few remain. They always were a distant lot, but now they are fearful, too. The Time of Chaos is truly at hand." She emitted a sigh that sounded like a volcanic fumarole venting its noxious gases.

Not kindly disposed to us, is she?

"With good reason," Zolkan said. Louder, to the priestess, the *trilla* bird said, "We desire a room where we might summon them and meet with those answering the call."

"Lalasa cannot come. I do not know if others will."

"We must try. Only here—and in Limaden—is there a shrine still consecrated. Lenc is thorough in destroying other patrons and their worshipers."

"That he is." The priestess muttered some curses as she led them to a tiny chapel. A small block of dark orange *tulna* stone served as the altar. To the left in a red clay pot adorned with mystical symbols grew the fern sacred to Lalasa. On the other side of the altar stood a triptych carved from a rich oak, the wood most beloved by Lalasa. Somehow, in these settings, in the center of the Festering, the pathetic trappings inspired pity rather than reverence.

"I will leave you. I have no part in such a gathering." She bowed low and left. Zolkan fluttered around the tiny room twice before coming to rest on the back of a pew.

"Will any come when you summon?"

We can only find out by trying, Molimo indicated. He sank to his knees in front of the altar, another supplicant. But the force building around him could belong to no mere worshiper. The power grew, surged out, became directed, hidden from Lenc, aimed at any other.

For hours Molimo knelt before the altar. Zolkan watched

and worried. His friend lacked time sense when he entered this state. The *trilla* bird had seen him vanish within himself for weeks on end. If Molimo hadn't roused himself now and again for food, he might have starved. This particular body carried frailty to the limit, but the jade rain had locked Molimo within it, just as it had stripped him of his power and robbed him of his tongue. The bird began to seriously worry when Molimo stirred.

Lalasa will not come. Not immediately, Molimo reported. *But there are others.*

"How many?"

Too few. Four, possibly five. None I know well. A tear beaded at the corner of Molimo's eye, threatening to run down his cheek. He did nothing to stop the salty flood when it finally occurred. So few demons still lived—Lenc and his allies had slaughtered legions. And those who had survived possessed only minor abilities, insufficient to fight Lenc. The jade demon kept these few around for his entertainment; any true rivals had long since been eliminated.

A tiny *pop!* sounded. Zolkan swiveled his head around and peered at the tall, emaciated demon. Zolkan finally recognized him, and spat the gobbet of red pulp he had been chewing onto the demon's unpolished boots.

"What an unmannerly oaf you are!" protested the demon.

"I spit only on those I despise," Zolkan answered. "Of all demons, I should have known Tolek would live. Cowards and wastrels prevail, in any climate."

"One gets by however one must," Tolek said, feelings hurt. "I don't even know you or this knave abasing himself in front of Lalasa's altar. Who are you and how is it you can summon a demon?"

"A pathetic demon," snapped Zolkan. "Once I bore messages for only mightiest of demons. Now I must greet the likes of you." Zolkan spat again; Tolek had to dance away to avoid a second red-staining gob.

"That's no way to speak."

"When you gambled away your worshipers, you spawned Order of Steel Crescent. Caused countless miseries throughout empire as a result. I loathe you for that."

"The debts were staggering, bird. The trade seemed fair

to me. A few idle worshipers of no intrinsic value, in exchange for expiation and a rather nice island, too."

"Nehan-dir seeks only those patrons able to give Steel Crescent power. They worship power because of you."

"Oh, really. Not *because* of me. Don't try to blame the failings of mortals on *me,* bird. And don't try to change the subject. Who is this knave who managed to summon me so handily? He seems vaguely familiar, but..."

Another entrance silenced Tolek the Spare. A demon with arms thicker than ale kegs loomed in one corner of the room. Misshapen and immensely strong, the demon lumbered forward, knuckles dangerously close to the floor.

"Who calls Baram?"

"Welcome, friend demon. A moment, and all will be explained," said Zolkan.

A final *pop!* produced a dwarf with too-short arms, a head twice that expected for decent proportions, and a bulging forehead that settled into a bony ridge over his deep-set gray eyes.

Welcome, Noissa, greeted Molimo. *And you, Baram, and even you, Tolek.*

"Who are you, mortal? You speak as we do, but I do not recognize you." Noissa stepped back fearfully, hiding behind the orange stone altar.

We all have changed, Molimo said. *Most of all I. The jade changed me—luckily.*

"You are not Lenc," growled Baram. The massive demon knocked over a row of pews as he carved an area to hunker down in. "Only Lenc has contact with the jade."

I am aware of that. Eznofadil, Howenthal and Ayondela exist no more. I have aided the Sister of Gelya's Order in this. When I fought Lenc I was unprepared for the strength given him by the jade. He thought he destroyed me, but the jade altered my substance instead. I found myself trapped— disguised—in a mortal's form.

Molimo paused. *After all I have endured, I* am *a mortal, doomed to live out a short life in this form.*

Noissa edged around the altar, still fearful. "This might be a trick. Lenc is cunning."

"No trick, no trick," insisted Zolkan. "You know me. I stand by those words."

"Aye, you are familiar. You are the *trilla* bird who delivered messages and arranged for trysts." The dwarf relaxed visibly. "You even passed a note along to darling Leoranne for me."

"Your wife is still healthy?" asked Zolkan.

"For a mortal. Her days are limited but our joy still grows."

"Then listen, if you want more days for joy to grow. Listen well to him."

Molimo stood. He had hoped for a more auspicious turnout of demons. He found it almost impossible to believe that only these three—four, if Lalasa was counted—remained of those who had once frolicked and debauched with such abandon. Baram, for all his physical prowess, lacked real mental capacity. Noissa, on the other hand, was all intellect—and fear. For Tolek, Molimo had nothing but contempt; he expected no help from the lean demon. Any patron who traded his worshipers for a gambling debt deserved more than a *trilla* bird spitting on his boots.

But they were the survivors, the ones Lenc had permitted to live.

We must fight Lenc and kill him. The power of the jade will do that eventually, I know, but before that happens his evil will ruin this world.

"So?" asked Tolek. "We've had scant contact with the mortals for thousands of years. Why the sympathy for them now? Let Lenc do his worst. As you say, the jade destroys him daily, even as it augments his power. Let it burn him out like a guttering candle." Tolek produced a small flame dancing on one fingertip. "We can wait until he is snuffed out." The flame vanished in a twisting column of black smoke. The demon looked inordinately pleased with his minor magicks.

The Time of Chaos is at hand, Molimo communicated. *We must deal with this. To survive, we must prevent the coming of the new gods.*

"Superstition," rumbled Baram. "No puny god will replace me!" He picked up the one long pew he hadn't destroyed and crushed it to splinters in his meaty hands.

"This we must consider, Baram," said Noissa. "Perhaps the old legends are more. Perhaps the myths speak truly. Gelya seemed to think they did."

"All myth. Nothing more," roared Baram. "I do not die. I am demon!"

But Molimo had begun to think, as had Gelya. The world had formed from void and light, air and water decorating the surface of the planet. From these grew animal life. Humans came to coexist with animals, and their offspring were the demons, all human and animal traits magnified a hundredfold. Strength and weakness permeated the demons, and they lived apart, different from both animals and humans. The humans came to worship that which was strongest in their patrons, but few of the demons deigned to come into contact with the world beneath them.

So said the myth of creation. The myth of destruction told of mating between demon and human to produce true gods possessing only the finest traits of demon and human. And surrounding this birth whirled the Time of Chaos, the war in which demons perished and the gods flourished.

The Sister of Gelya's Order, Kesira Minette, Molimo continued, *carries a boychild that Lenc claims for his own son. There is indication the infant was born of a coupling between Lenc and a peasant woman named Parvey Yera. Do any know of this for certain?*

"Vague rumors only," said Noissa. "Lenc boasts his bastard son will carry on the rule of jade and found a dynasty stretching down through the eons."

He knows the jade robs him of life?

Noissa shrugged. "Perhaps. Perhaps he only says these things because they are more understandable—and thereby more frightening—for the humans. Without them, whom can he rule? He *needs* the mortals, lest he rule a world populated only with memories."

The boychild must be destroyed, Molimo replied.

"Kesira will never allow it!" cried Zolkan. "She thinks of the bratling as her own."

Lenc has deluded her. He uses her as a surrogate mother

until the child grows large enough to accept his role as Lenc's heir. We must convince her of this. The baby must die!

"So, kill the pink worm," said Tolek. "Why the discussion? If this is something you must do, then do it." He settled down, frowning at them. Baram flexed his muscles until joints snapped like breaking twigs. Tolek refused to let his fright show—too much.

For a mortal, Kesira Minette possesses profound powers. She casts the rune sticks and accurately reads them. Not even Lenc's lies can cloud her vision of the future.

"She sees the Time of Change upon us?" asked Noissa, shaking like a leaf in a whirlwind. The dwarf shrank back to the protection of the altar.

I know little of what she sees. It is blocked to me. Until I regain my full power, I cannot force her to do anything against her will.

"Why hasn't Lenc destroyed you? After all, you were the strongest of the lot of us," said Tolek.

The jade altered my form and robbed me of the power Lenc might trace to me. Only slowly have I recovered. And, Molimo communicated grimly, *others of our rank have given their lives to aid me. Toyaga died after giving me a spell of non-noticeability.*

"*That* one?" scoffed Tolek. "No one is fooled by it. You don't even vanish from sight. You just make yourself harder to see."

When Lenc and the other jade demons did not expect to find me at all, thinking me long dead, Toyaga's spell worked well enough.

Tolek only shrugged disinterestedly.

Are we agreed? We'll band together to destroy Lenc?

Baram grunted, then vanished without giving a definite answer. Tolek tried to hide the fear that illuminated his face.

"Don't be ridiculous. Lenc won't harm us. He could have slain us at any time. Since he's let us live . . . well, he must like us." Tolek smiled weakly, then vanished.

Old friend—Molimo turned to Noissa—*you do not believe that, do you?*

"I believe only that attracting Lenc's attention also draws

his wrath. You have not seen what he's done to the others. Not Baram and Tolek, but to Berura-ko and Roas and all the others." Noissa cringed, tiny arms unconsciously rising to protect his misshapen head. "He tore them apart. He tortured them horribly. He used the jade power in ways that made their agony last for an eternity even as they died in a split second. What he does to humans is a pale imitation of what he has done to those who opposed him in our ranks."

"You do not join with us?" asked Zolkan.

"I agree that the boychild should be destroyed. But this will anger Lenc. Perhaps... after my beloved, all-too-mortal Leoranne is no more... perhaps then I might be of some assistance."

But she might live for fifty more years! protested Molimo.

"Perhaps that long. I hope so. Please be careful—you always were the most impetuous among us. Now you are no match for Lenc."

Noissa disappeared as the other demons had. Molimo, shaking with frustration, sank to the floor once again and growled deep in his throat. The power that had returned to him was worthless unless he could use it—and he still wasn't strong enough to face Lenc alone. If only there had been other demons able to help!

"Your shape," cautioned Zolkan. "You change. Fight it, fight it!"

Halfway through, Molimo managed to stop the transformation. Sweating, straining, he forced his reluctant body back into its human form. The jade had hidden him from Lenc, but the cost had been so great. If he couldn't control his own form, how could he possibly defeat the other demon?

The path to Lenc's destruction must lie in the infant Kesira wet-nursed. Destroy the boy and Lenc's dynasty died also. A faint hope, but Molimo knew he had to nurture it.

We must find Kesira.

Zolkan said nothing as he perched on Molimo's shoulder. The *trilla* bird knew better than his master the danger in trying to separate Kesira from the boy. Even Lenc's wrath would pale in comparison. But Zolkan said nothing.

Chapter Four

THE LICKING TONGUES of flame coalesced into the figure Kesira Minette knew and feared. Lenc stretched out long green arms in a mocking embrace and threw back his head. Chilling laughter drowned out the crackling fire consuming the temple. Lenc's hands clenched into tightly balled fists, and his head lowered to study the small square in front of his ruined place of worship.

"Who dares oppose me?" he boomed. Kesira pressed deeper into shadows made less inky by the firelight. She summoned her courage and held her position. To run would reveal her to the jade demon.

Kesira let out her pent-up breath and tried to relax. Tenseness brought error; so taught Gelya. She watched in mute horror as Lenc pointed his finger and made stabbing motions. Every time he affixed his attention on some poor wight, he died. Those who had gathered around Kene Zoheret perished, one by one. Of the rebel leader Kesira saw no trace.

"You dare use puny magicks against me? Against *me?*" The demon strode out of the fire and brushed away burning debris from his shoulders and arms. "I will show you real magic."

The demon clapped his hands. The thunder rumbling down the streets of Kolya deafened Kesira. She fell to her knees, sobbing with the pain lancing into her head. Even putting fingers in her ears failed to stop the hideous noise ripping away at her soul. And just when she thought it might be bearable, Lenc clapped his hands again.

And he laughed. How the woman hated that mocking, tormenting laughter!

Kesira fought to clear her head, to keep control of her fear. It would eat away inside her and force her into view if she didn't conquer her emotions. The sight of Kene Zoheret scuttling away helped her find the focus for her hatred. That weasel of a man had created this maelstrom of death and destruction; now the craven ran from it.

Kesira edged back and watched Lenc run amok. The demon tortured those unfortunate men he found. When he used his prodigious, jade-driven might to rip off the roof of a house and drag forth a poor woman for his sexual satiation, Kesira ducked away and ran in the opposite direction. She allowed fear to rise up within her now, to lend speed to her flight, to show her heels to the one enemy in the entire world capable of intimidating her.

Out of breath, she rested against a cool wooden door. Sweat stained the wood, then began trickling down in a rivulet. She pushed back her lank hair and wiped her forehead, clearing it of the fear-sweat. Kesira opened the door and entered the inn. Zoheret had already arrived and sat in the far corner, clutching a mug of ale with two trembling hands. He spilled more than he got into his mouth.

"You left them to die," Kesira accused. "You launched the magical fire spells, then you ran, leaving your friends to be slaughtered by Lenc."

"I didn't know the demon would appear. How could I? I thought it would be a symbol, a gesture to show all Kolya that we could fight back and win."

"You turned it into disaster. As soon as word of what actually happened gets out, no one will dare oppose Lenc. Your action cost us the chance of any effective move against the power of the jade."

"You," snapped Zoheret, pointing a trembling finger, "did nothing to aid us. You read the runes wrong. You promised victory. You let this happen!"

"Now then, Zoheret, she did nothing of the kind." The portly innkeeper came out and perched on the end of one of his polished tables. "If'n I remember a'right, you stopped her before she read more than a few simple things about you. Not once did you ask if she saw victory this night in her castings."

"You two are in this together!"

Kesira snorted in contempt and sat heavily in a chair. The innkeeper brought her a small mug of the ale, but Kesira barely tasted it. Her mind was working to find a way to salvage a victory from this monumental blunder. With Lenc's attention drawn to the city's feeble rebellion, it wouldn't be easy.

She downed the ale in one long gulp, when her thoughts turned to the baby. Had Lenc somehow managed to detect his son? Was this the reason for the demon's presence? The burning of a single temple would hardly anger the jade demon so much. Whatever he did, he did for a reason. He *chose* to come to avenge the blasphemy.

Kesira couldn't put the coincidence of Lenc's presence and her own in the city to rest. Gelya had said that facts were stubborn. Kesira had been well trained in not assuming luck and ability were the same—she could change the course of all that happened, if only she proved smart enough to find the proper path. But to find that path required the knowledge of why Lenc had appeared now.

"Zoheret," she called over to the thin rebel leader, "what are your plans now? Most of your men died this night."

"I have a few more. And word has come that the Emperor Kwasian will support us with his personal troops."

"Soon?"

"Soon enough to count. We will regain Kolya. I feel it." The man, his hands shaking, sloshed more ale into his lap and didn't even seem to notice. And this was the mage Kesira had half hoped would provide the impetus to a real uprising against Lenc.

"Is the baby all right?" she asked the innkeeper.

The man nodded, but his expression changed as he asked, "Is this a normal child? He never cries. And his eyes..."

"What of his eyes?" demanded Zoheret. "Are they the green of jade?"

"No, quite the opposite. They are pale, almost colorless. But the boy's expression is so... so old. It's as if he's seen the world and knows it all, for a fact."

Zoheret shot to his feet and rocketed across the small public room to peer over the counter. Kesira followed a step behind. Before Zoheret could reach out and touch the child, Kesira grabbed the rebel leader's arm and spun him around. Her own normally soft brown eyes hardened into daggers.

"Leave the child alone." Her tone brooked no challenge. Zoheret stepped back in fright, startled at her vehemence. He recovered his wit slowly.

"What makes you so defensive about your son? He *is* your son, isn't he? Or is he of another's flesh?"

"He is an orphan."

"And his father? Might his father be the demon? Did Lenc spawn this miserable little worm of pink flesh?" Zoheret shoved Kesira out of the way and vaulted the counter. He landed heavily in a crouch. Before he could reach out to touch the child, Kesira hurried around the counter and clamped her hand firmly over the infant's mouth to prevent him from crying out.

Not only might Zoheret be killed—and the innkeeper and perhaps even herself—but that cry would draw Lenc's attention. The jade demon sought something in Kolya. What else could it be except his son?

"The innkeeper said he never cries, and yet you stifle him. Why?" Zoheret's curiosity got the better of him.

"The sound of an infant crying annoys me. I know how to discipline him to prevent his cries. And," Kesira said, rising and shoving Zoheret away, "you do not want to annoy me. Perhaps I do more than simply report what I see in the runes. Has it ever occurred to you that I might be able to affect the future through the rune readings I give?"

"But . . ."

"Is it death I see for you? Or something else? The casting was not sufficiently detailed to tell. Do you want me to do another?" The panic on Zoheret's face startled and pleased her. She had found the lever to move him to her will, but why the fear? Was the soft spot fearing his own death, or fearing what her rune casting might reveal?

Kene Zoheret rounded the counter and went to sit where his spilled ale frothed on the table. Kesira nursed the boy, and fought down her own feelings of panic at his calm acceptance of everything around him. Nothing disturbed the infant. The only hint that all was well came in the warmth of the spot where Wemilat the Ugly had kissed her breast. The lip print left by the hideous, kindly demon reassured her that no evil came from feeding the baby.

"We can attack again, burn down the monster's strongholds. He can't stop us," muttered Zoheret. "I can get the entire underground movement together for one huge strike. Even the Emperor's soldiers can take part when they arrive. Yes, that's it. One big attack. Lenc'll never recover!"

Still mumbling to himself, Zoheret left the inn.

"He is doomed to failure, and he'll bring down Lenc's wrath on everyone," Kesira said.

"You see this in the runes?" asked the innkeeper.

"I need only logic, not magic. Zoheret's spells are few and weak. He cannot hope to match Lenc. And to mere force of arms the demon is invulnerable." She paused, thinking about this. Was Lenc truly invincible? Would a sword thrust end his jade-driven life? He had forsaken virtual immortality for power.

Kesira stopped trying to wrestle with imponderable questions. It was futile; Gelya would not have approved. She must find the actions that'd be most productive, then follow that course to the end.

To the end...

It sounded too final for her to appreciate. Kesira called out to the innkeeper, "Is there anything else you want of me before I turn in? The place looks spotless. Not much business this evening?"

The man stared at her in disbelief. "After all you've been through this awful eve, you ask about polishing and cleaning?"

"I am Sister of the Mission of Gelya. I made a promise to trade work for room and board. Never have I gone back on a promise made willingly. Whether I am tired matters little. For what is given me I will work." Kesira waited. The innkeeper waved her toward the back of the public room.

"There's a fine little cot for you in there," he said. "You can sleep out of the cold and elements for the night."

The way he said it indicated he now considered her a liability. Kesira didn't blame the innkeeper. He'd lost wife and daughter to Lenc. Even allowing her to stay under the same roof might anger Lenc further. After all, she had taken part in the abortive attack on Lenc's temple and had drawn the jade demon back to Kolya. She began to appreciate the idea of being the small mouse, doing nothing to draw the tyrant's gaze, and possibly escaping harm.

But to live in fear at the same time?

Kesira picked up the baby, went to the room indicated and settled in. Before she had lain down, her mind had fixed firmly on the concept of never bowing to a tyrant's whim. She might play the mouse, but for her own reason: to muster her forces, take advantage of any chance, however slim, to defeat Lenc. Living in the dark shadow of fear for the rest of her life held no appeal. The test of courage was in the living, not the dying.

Kesira tossed and turned on the cot, unable to sleep. The more she tried to relax, the tenser she became. Finally yielding to insomnia, she rose and paced the tiny room. This soothed her; the room reminded her of the first cell she'd been given when she arrived at the nunnery so many years ago. As she'd grown older, she was allowed a larger room and a few possessions.

But her only true possessions were those she carried within her breast and spirit. Everything else could be stripped from her—and had been. Even Molimo seemed to have abandoned her, and of Zolkan she'd seen not so much as a pinfeather.

Idly, Kesira pulled out the box containing the carved knucklebones. She opened the hinged lid and tapped the bones out onto the cot. They fell softly, silently, like snow on a cold winter's eve.

The pattern confused Kesira for a few minutes. She had never seen this precise alignment before, and almost picked up the knucklebones to make a second cast. But she stopped before touching them. Closing her eyes, Kesira began to meditate, to seek out every morsel of information that had ever been imparted to her. Sinking down within her own mind produced the result she'd hoped for.

Unbidden, the single name rose to her lips: Lalasa.

Louder, she called, "Lalasa, your rune appears in my

casting. I need you—we need you." Kesira cast a hesitant glance in the direction of the sleeping baby. He lay with eyes tightly screwed shut, thumb in his mouth. If she hadn't known differently, Kesira would have thought he was simply another infant.

A human infant.

"Lalasa," she said a third time, "I would speak with you. Give me your counsel."

The air shimmered and turned mirrorlike. Stirrings like bugs crawling along autumnal leaves moved the length of the room, returned, became more distinct. Kesira felt her pulse racing. Never before had she summoned a demon.

"You are Kesira," the demon said. The shimmery curtain slowly faded to reveal a tall woman lavishly attired in purple velvet and a soft, delicate, lavishly expensive white fur. The demon's face was the feature, however, that startled Kesira the most.

Lalasa possessed no overwhelming beauty. If anything, Kesira would describe the demon as plain. And yet she consorted with rulers and advised Emperor Kwasian on the running of the empire.

"You have suffered much, but you hold up well. There is a chance," said Lalasa. "One I would have ignored previously, but seeing you, one I now endorse wholeheartedly."

"You will help us destroy Lenc?"

"Of course," Lalasa said impatiently. "Everything I have done since he, Eznofadil and Howenthal first placed the jade within their mouths has been directed to his defeat. You cannot know the agony of the jade. I have watched friends become greedy and turned into monsters capable of any perversion to satisfy the urges of the jade."

Kesira's anger flared. "*I* do not know the agony caused by the jade? My patron, Gelya, died. My order was destroyed. I have battled those demons and Ayondela—Ayondela who lost her son because of the power of the jade and was then seduced by revenge. It has ruined my life and my world, and you say I know nothing of the agony?"

Lalasa sniffed contemptuously. "Touch that jade tusk hidden in the folds of your robe. Go on, touch it." Kesira did. The tusk felt cold, quiescent. "It does nothing to you because you are human. If I were to touch it, the sensation might overcome me. I might follow Lenc. I might go insane—many demons did over the past thousand years. They thought to rule as Lenc has done, but they lacked whatever lies within his breast. The jade destroyed them instantly."

"Lenc it destroys slowly. Over the span of years, he grows insane."

Lalasa nodded.

"What aid can you offer?" Kesira asked. "The rune sticks gave no hint."

The tall female demon pushed both hands through her long hair. She crossed the small room in two strides and seated herself on the cot next to the rune sticks. She studied them for a few seconds, then shook her head.

"I read nothing in them to aid either of us."

"You didn't send this message to me?" asked Kesira, startled.

"You have the gift. Why do you ask?"

"Lenc told me that he sent all the readings."

At this, Lalasa laughed until tears rolled down her cheeks. "And you *believed* him? Demons can influence, but the talent is human. No demon casts the runes and foresees the future. I can read, but the casting skill is denied me. In that lies most of the ability."

Kesira considered this. Her flagging spirits began to rise as she realized her power was crucial in defeating Lenc. How she would stop the jade demon, she didn't know. But she would!

"I was called by another, but chose to speak with you. The other's meeting was futile," said Lalasa.

"Other demons will aid us?"

"Perhaps the greatest," said Lalasa. "But those few remaining in our rank provide him scant support. Baram is physically powerful, but lacks even a small human child's intellect. Noissa, brilliant in his way, is but a coward who flees his own shadow. Afraid of the dark, suspicious of the light—he can do nothing." Lalasa's expression turned to one of extreme distaste. "Tolek is another."

Lalasa's eyes crackled with hatred, and Kesira felt a sense of loss. She had learned of Tolek's perfidy long ago, even before entering the Quaking Lands to do battle with Howenthal. That such a coward should be among those left in demonic rank stripped away the veneer of confidence she had felt.

"I see you know of dear, precious Tolek," Lalasa spat.

"But if none of these can help us..."

"There is still Merrisen."

"But Merrisen died!" cried Kesira.

"What? When? I recognized his call only minutes ago. Rather than speak with him, I sought you."

Kesira shook her head. "He and Lenc fought months ago. Lenc turned Merrisen into jade and then shattered him. The rain of the shards preceded the destruction of my order. It severely injured a friend of mine caught in the rain. He even lost his tongue because of the shower of fragments."

"Merrisen lives," Lalasa said firmly. "I know the... the *feel* of him. I cannot describe it to a mortal."

"He will help us?" Kesira sat cross-legged on the floor like a new acolyte listening to her master's every word. A weight lifted from her shoulders. Zolkan always spoke so highly of Merrisen. The handsome demon would return and do battle again with Lenc. He *would!* Lalasa guaranteed it. This time there would be support for his fight. She would provide it!

"He must. Without him, we are lost. I can do nothing against Lenc. Even before he took the jade, I presented no threat to him. Now?" Lalasa shrugged.

"What are your powers? Zolkan tells me every demon has some human trait but magnified a hundredfold or more."

"True," the female demon said. She settled the velvet gown about her thin shoulders and stroked over the fur collar as if this soothed her. "Tolek is more venal than any mortal, Baram physically stronger, Noissa more knowledgeable, Wemilat kinder—and I am possessed of inherent ability to be a diplomat."

"You can make people agree?"

"Come to mutually agreeable terms." Lalasa's smile was wan. "With Lenc, there can be no negotiation. I am helpless against him. Instead of fighting him directly, I use my power to hold Emperor Kwasian to the throne, to keep the factions in the Empire welded into a unified front. Even though physical means are as nothing, still I make the attempt."

"But Merrisen?"

"Merrisen is the most balanced of all demons. He has no single outstanding talent. Every demon outshines him in one area, just as he outshines them in all others. Merrisen is unique. Only he saw the danger Lenc posed, only he had the power and wit and courage and selflessness to try to battle him."

"Merrisen still lives? How do I contact him?"

"I will find him and have him come to you. He is, after all, in Kolya. It was from my temple that his summons came." Lalasa stood. "Let me get Merrisen and bring him here."

"Wait, before you go," Kesira said, tugging at the demon's velvet gown. "I must know. Why is Kolya important? Emperor Kwasian makes his stand in Limaden. Why does Lenc come to *this* city?"

Lalasa looked at her with pity in her eyes. "All threads of power end here. Life, death—all."

"I don't understand."

"Lenc comes here because you are here. And because his son is with you." Lalasa looked at the sleeping baby, fear and loathing fleetingly shown on her face.

"He won't get him! I won't give the child over to Lenc!"

"Do not worry on that score. No one wants Lenc and his son reunited. Like the other demons, I want them both dead!"

Lalasa vanished behind the shimmery curtain, leaving Kesira staring at the cracked plaster on the back wall. Everyone wanted the boy dead—even the demons she had counted on for aid.

Kesira Minette sat and cried—for her dead patron, for herself, for her baby.

Chapter Five

KESIRA MINETTE slumped forward onto the cot where Lalasa had sat, head cradled by her crossed arms, and cried until the sleep that had been denied previously claimed her.

But the sleep wasn't peaceful. It seemed as if Lalasa visited her dreams to reveal the horrors wrecking the Empire. Kesira seemed to float a thousand feet above the Plains of Roggen, watching the antlike creatures moving about below. A quick swoop, much as she imagined Zolkan making, brought her breathless and excited to a spot less than a hundred feet over the heads of Emperor Kwasian's soldiers. General Dayle rode along their rank, nodding, pointing out minor infractions, generously heaping praise on officers and foot soldiers alike.

The world tore apart in a crazy kaleidoscope. When it reformed, Kesira saw the battle lines marching forward, spears lowered, grim expressions on every face. A shout went along the front line and the soldiers broke into a run, sprinting for a hillock where Lenc stood.

With amused superiority, the jade demon watched the thousands of men advancing on him. A casual pass of the hand sent his fireballs tumbling amid the ranks. The gaps caused by his wholesale destruction closed with new troops. Lenc again released the destruction with a nonchalant gesture, as if he did nothing more than swat an annoying insect buzzing around his head.

General Dayle attempted a retreat. It turned into a rout.

Kesira turned away, but only found herself staring at another aspect of Lenc's cruelty. She saw cities aflame, women ripped apart by the demon's huge jade penis, men blasted apart when fireballs appeared inside mouth and

51

belly—and what Lenc did to small children caused bile to rise into her throat. She choked back the burning vomit.

Spinning through space, she found herself on a circuit of the empire. Limaden with its majestic streets and noble rulers might have been a city deserted for a hundred years. No commerce crowded the markets; caravans camped at the fringes, not daring to move; and the citizens peered out from behind locked windows with a fearfulness that brought tears to Kesira's eyes again.

Limaden no longer presented a face of confidence to the world. Lenc had broken the empire's spirit.

"Oh, Gelya, how I pray for you." Kesira hardly dared to voice the thought that came on the heels of her involuntary outcry. "You are the lucky one, Gelya my patron. We who yet live now have to face this horror."

Over the Yearn Mountains she flew. Blinn no longer existed: the small town nestled in the foothills smoldered as cold, dancing white flame consumed stone and dirt and bone and flesh. Just a few miles farther she saw her nunnery. No one had entered since she had left so many months earlier. The front gates still hung awry and the altar was still desecrated by Lenc's mocking sigil: white fire. That cold light had eaten away the altar to half its original size.

When Kesira forced herself to look away, all she saw were graves covered in the yellow wildflower sacred to Gelya.

"My sisters." To release the anger rising within her, Kesira shouted, "Lalasa, why do you show me this? Why?"

Kesira's breath was taken away by the sudden transit to the Quaking Lands. Those once undulating plains now stretched quiet, inert. Farmers even dared run their furrows and plant along the extreme edges. The magicks brought to the terrain by Howenthal had died along with that jade demon. A solitary spire of rock rose in the center of what had been earthquake-tossed land. Sparkling green dust caught sunlight and reflected it to Kesira.

"You are gone, Howenthal. Along with Wemilat, you are gone." For Wemilat the Ugly, she mourned. No such gentle emotion reminded her of Howenthal.

Kesira blinked. Waves lapped across a sandy shore below

The White Fire 53

her feet. A gull sounded its mating cry; another swept back its wings and plunged seaward, snaring an incautious *gnar* fish. The Sea of Katad had never been more majestic, even when it had vanished under the frozen waves brought by Ayondela's curse of eternal winter.

The spire rising where Kesira had met and bested Eznofadil was no more. Lenc's cold fire had destroyed it totally.

The huge granite peak where Ayondela had perished replaced the seascape. Nothing remained of the demented female demon, not even the cutting clouds of purest crystal she had used as her weapons against humanity. High winds had whipped up the powdery dust of her shattered body and spread it over the Sarn Mountains. The land she had cursed now accepted her substance willingly.

The land, the sea, the air—Kesira had met the jade demons and defeated all in their strongholds.

She jerked back, surprised to find herself once more in the tiny room at the back of the inn. The blanket on the cot had become soaked with her perspiration and tears. Kesira stood on shaking legs. She had traveled around the empire and seen the destruction wrought by Lenc—and the destruction she had wrought on the jade demons.

"Thank you, Lalasa," she said, hoping the female demon could hear. "I understand now. I *have* mattered."

Kesira silently promised both Lalasa and Gelya that she would not stop in her attempts to defeat Lenc. She had no inkling how it could be done, but then she'd had no idea how to slay any of the other three jade demons before she did so. Wemilat had aided her, Zolkan and Molimo with their sudden insights, the baby with his destructive screams—all had made the difference between victory and failure.

She had not anticipated any of them. They had been there when she needed them. Lalasa had shown her that continued struggle against Lenc need not be futile, that she had to oppose the power of the jade until the proper instant.

But the one thing she would not do, not for Lalasa or Lenc or Kene Zoheret, was forsake the baby. She picked the boy up and allowed him his breakfast. The infant might be Lenc's son, but she would fight to the death to prevent any harm from coming to him.

Pale eyes stared up at her, knowing. The smile on his tiny lips both chilled and relieved her.

Kene Zoheret sat in the corner of the public room with a half-dozen conspirators. Kesira despaired at the snatches of their talk she overheard. Zoheret passionately urged another foray against Lenc's temples, something she saw as futile and self-destructive.

They refused to face the issues Kesira considered most vital. How were they going to act on their own and accomplish anything? Change of any meaningful sort could only come from concerted effort, in harmony with the others in the city. The Emperor Kwasian ruled because he commanded respect—and because he earned it through his wise orders and caring for those in the empire. Kesira had no doubt that the Emperor agonized every night over the fate of so many of his subjects, not because they had died, but because he had failed them.

Zohert addressed none of the real issues. He insisted on acting secretively, alone; on being in charge when others seemed better suited to the task. His sole claim to planning lay in his minor uses of magic. The pitiful fire spells had failed against Lenc. Kesira saw no reason for them not to fail a second time, yet Zoheret continued with his earnest, if misguided, planning.

"...all Kolya will notice us and rally around," Zoheret finished, smashing his fist into the table and looking at the small group.

Kesira frowned. Something struck her as amiss in the way Kene Zoheret spoke and acted. Not only did he violate the social strictures that had allowed the the empire to exist, he was openly contemptuous of the Emperor.

Zoheret acted as if he held back some vital fact. Kesira began to distrust him more and more.

"More ale!" he called. "We have made our decision. Now let us toast it!"

Kesira silently carried a tray of frothy mugs to the table. The men stared at her oddly, as if Zoheret had spoken of her in slighting terms. They took the ale and drank deeply, quickly finishing and scurrying off like rats afraid to face the sunrise.

When only Zoheret remained, he motioned her over to the table. "Sit," he said, as if he were the Emperor offering her the greatest boon imaginable. "That child with you—"

"I have no wish to discuss it." Kesira moved to leave. Zoheret grabbed her arm and jerked her back roughly enough to keep her at the table.

"It is Lenc's spawn, isn't it?"

"He is an orphan. I told you that already."

Zoheret eyed her, then released his grip. Kesira rubbed the spot where his fingers had cut like steel bands into her flesh.

"You must look into the future and scry it for me. We expect the Emperor Kwasian to send reinforcements soon. We must know when they will arrive."

"The Emperor sends troops?" This puzzled her. She had seen—Lalasa had shown her—the destruction wrought by Lenc on the Plains of Roggen. Why did the Emperor dare send forth even a small band away from the defense of his capital? Limaden had to rank more highly in the hearts and minds of the empire than Kolya. It was a symbol of unity as much as anything else.

"Not many," confided Zoheret. "A few. A company at most. But they will be adequate."

Kesira didn't ask "adequate for what." She had the idea Zoheret meant adequate for his own purposes. He was no better than Lenc, plotting and scheming for personal gain rather than for the betterment of all citizens.

"I'll cast the runes," Kesira said. She saw surprise cross Zoheret's face. He had expected her to refuse, but she had her own motives. There were too few soldiers left for the Emperor to dispatch even a company to Kolya's rescue. These had to come from somewhere else—and she thought she knew. The reading from the rune sticks would confirm her suspicions.

Kesira retrieved the bone box from under her gray robe, and flipped open the lid. Zoheret fell silent as she tossed the knucklebones onto the table.

Kesira settled her mind and let the images well up from

deep within her. Lalasa had claimed that this was a true talent, one having nothing to do with Lenc. The jade demon had lied to her, or had only influenced a few of her readings. Kesira Minette had the talent.

Use it, she told herself.

Images twisted and turned into more solid pictures. A soldier covered with scars and glory came riding from the Sea of Katad at the head of a squadron of men, numbering fewer than twenty. But the set to their leader's face, the familiar lines and planes, told Kesira what she needed to know.

"Captain Protaro comes," she said.

"The Emperor's Guard?" Fear and anxiety intermixed in Zoheret's question.

"A small detachment. They have been patrolling along the seashore. They met opposition with Nehan-dir and his mercenaries."

"They fought the Order of the Steel Crescent?"

"Yes."

"The outcome. What was it?" Zoheret shook her so hard the images blurred and went away. Kesira blinked; the public room replaced the vision of Protaro astride his mangy horse, leading his pitiful band to Kolya.

"Captain Protaro prevailed," she said simply.

"Nehan-dir is dead?"

Kesira stared at the rebel leader. His interest in the mercenaries following the Steel Crescent's banner seemed out of place. As if realizing he'd shown unseemly curiosity, Zoheret quickly said, "I need to know. The mercenaries are strong in this region. We must know if they are to be a factor in our fight."

"Nehan-dir lives. The battle was of little consequence, except that Nehan-dir was forced to retreat. Little damage was incurred by either side." Kesira considered lying to Zoheret and telling him that Protaro had completely eradicated the mercenaries. It might be instructive to see the man's reaction. But out of long habit, she told only the truth.

"When does this Protaro arrive?"

"By sundown. He rides on the outskirts of Kolya already.

He will circle the city before entering to find needed supplies and potential escape routes."

"He plans to show his heel and run like a craven?"

"Not at all," Kesira said, tiring of this. "He is a good soldier and scouts out strong and weak points. If he must retreat, he will retreat to a position of strength, not weakness."

Kene Zoheret nodded quickly, rose and left Kesira alone in the inn. The innkeeper was nowhere to be seen, so Kesira went into the back room. The baby lay in his makeshift cradle. She picked him up and rocked gently, more to soothe herself than the boy. Protaro's arrival would not be good for her, not after she had killed his sergeant and disobeyed the Emperor Kwasian's direct order to go to Limaden.

Kesira might have argued this latter point successfully. After all, she *was* heading in the direction of the capital. Zolkan had urged it, and so had Molimo. But of the sergeant's death as the guard pursued her in the mountain passes above the sea? Kesira would never be able to placate Protaro. Those two had been more than friends; they had been comrades in arms.

She rocked, and the baby drifted off to sleep. Kesira wished her own view of the future allowed her such peace.

"Where are you, Zolkan?" she cried out loud. Kesira paced the small room that had become more like a prison to her. The evening crowd had already left the inn. A pair of exceptionally thirsty customers stayed, but the portly innkeeper tended them. In fact, when last Kesira had glanced out into the room, the innkeeper had joined them. She doubted many coins slid into the till from that party. The innkeeper had relieved her and told her to rest.

Kesira needed the break. The strain of watching the colors change outside from bright day to ruddy sunset to ebony darkness had taken its toll on her nerves. Captain Protaro would arrive soon. Not only had the rune sticks foretold his coming, she *felt* it deep down.

And it frightened her. In ways Kesira couldn't put into words, she knew that Protaro's coming would trigger events in Kolya that no mortal could control.

"Where are you, you filthy, featherbrained bird?" Zolkan had vanished on their first day in Kolya and she had not seen him since. Calling out his name had drawn only strange stares from passersby in the street. And contacting Molimo was impossible. She had tried.

Kesira settled her rising panic the best she could and tried to sift through what she knew. Lalasa had told her that one demon who might aid them all had survived: Merrisen.

Kesira began meditating, working her mind around in such a fashion that an unspoken prayer went out to wherever Merrisen might be. At first, Kesira had to push away the sensation of being foolish. What if Merrisen were dead? She prayed for succor from a dead demon.

She realized then that she had done the same with Gelya, even though her patron had perished. This eased her mind. She concentrated, and allowed her thoughts free rein. A curiously disconnected feeling overwhelmed her. Kesira fought it, then encouraged it.

"Merrisen!" she called out. With that name went her hopes and fears, her need, the need of all in the world to be free of Lenc and to return to a normal, well-ordered society.

Feathery tickles brushed her soul, but no firm contact was made. Sweaty, tired, she sagged forward onto her cot. Kesira wiped her forehead and stretched out. Something soft touched her hand, causing her to jump.

"Trouble. Hurry, hurry," squawked Zolkan.

"Where have you been?" she cried. "I've been worried about you. Don't just go off like that again."

"You cast me out. You said no way to get room here if ugly, awful *trilla* bird like me came along." Zolkan sniffed and turned his head to one side, trying to look hurt.

"Don't be like that. Where have you been? Is Molimo all right?"

"I have been digging through trash to find small scraps of food to keep me alive. Horrible," the bird declared. "Ruins the oil on my feathers. So hard to preen when you are covered with garbage."

Kesira looked closely at Zolkan. The plumpness and glossy condition of his feathers put the lie to his statements.

The White Fire

Whatever he had been doing for the past few days, it hadn't been digging through refuse.

"Where's Molimo?"

"Around. I have come to tell you of the guard captain's arrival. Protaro enters city even as we speak."

"We must reach him before Zoheret."

"Zoheret?"

"He's leader of a band of rebels. He wants Protaro to aid him in some foolish scheme to burn down all Lenc's temples."

"Not bad plan, if you roast your dinner over flames," said Zolkan. "Otherwise, why antagonize Lenc to no purpose?"

"I see you share my sentiments in this, Zolkan. I hope we can convince Protaro not to throw away any real chance he has at defeating Lenc."

"One soldier—even Protaro—cannot defeat Lenc."

"He can fight. *We* can fight. And joined, we might be able to do an even better job. But after our last brief meeting, I doubt Protaro will listen to me. What do you suggest?"

Zolkan let out a loud, wordless squawk. "You ask me, an outcast from polite society?" The *trilla* bird craned his neck around, taking in not only the small room but the public room beyond.

"Stop it!" Kesira snapped. "There's no time for petty squabbling."

"Always time," Zolkan muttered. Louder, he said, "Protaro bivouacs a half-hour's walk outside Kolya. Should I inquire as to the captain's intentions?"

"A half hour?" Kesira considered. "I'll go personally. The distance isn't too far. If I hurry, I can be back here before dawn."

"Why bother?"

"The innkeeper has been good to me. I promised to work for my room and food." A twinkle came to her eyes, and for the first time in days, she smiled. "You have me to thank for placing all that succulent garbage outside for you to dine on."

"Fool's errand," said Zolkan, scowling at her. He shook

his head and caused a minor snowstorm of bright green and blue feathers. "Protaro aids only Emperor Kwasian."

"Our goal is the same—defeating Lenc."

"Sooner you start, sooner you find out how wrong you can be," said Zolkan. The heavy bird perched on her shoulder as if daring her to brush him off. If anything, the familiar weight and nearness comforted Kesira. She picked up the sleeping baby, slipped out the back way and, following Zolkan's earthy directions, found the road on which Protaro camped with his men.

As she walked in the night stillness, Kesira noted that no one shared the road. Even at night Kolya had bustled with activity, and the night wasn't old enough yet for all citizens to be in bed.

She grew increasingly uneasy as she walked. Finally, Kesira said to Zolkan, "Where is everyone? I . . . I don't even hear insects chirping. There are no night sounds at all!"

"Lenc has worked well," said the *trilla* bird. "All bugs gone. Hungry times. I enjoy a good, juicy bug now and again." Zolkan clacked his strong beak shut.

"Lenc drives the people indoors, too?"

"He kidnaps unwary travelers. When you hold unchecked power, you must use it. Otherwise, what good is it? Lenc abuses his."

Even the insects had been destroyed? Kesira's stride lengthened until she almost ran into the darkness. The sight of a dozen small campfires blazing and valiantly holding back the emptiness of night made her heart skip a beat. She paused for a moment to collect her thoughts and regain her breath. It wouldn't do to confront Protaro acting as if she'd run all the way from Kolya—even though she had come very close to doing so.

"Mistake," said Zolkan. "Let me talk with captain."

"You're always urging me to hurry. Now is the time. Let's go." She straightened her tattered but clean robe and leaned on her staff. The baby still slept, snugly cradled in the knapsack she'd slung on her back.

She'd gone only a dozen paces when a guard challenged her.

"I have come to see Captain Protaro," she responded.

"Your name and business?"

"Kesira Minette, Sister of the Mission for the Order of Gelya. The business is—"

A sharp command cut off her explanation. Striding out of the shadows and standing with his back to a nearby fire was a commanding figure of a man. Even though the shadows hid his features, Kesira knew him.

"Captain, I want to apologize for all that happened at our last meeting."

"You disobeyed the Emperor Kwasian's command," Protaro said without preamble. No mention was made of Sergeant Tuwallan's death. Kesira thought that he might have accepted his friend's death as a battle casualty; in this way he might be able to remember without undue mourning.

"Ayondela is dead. That was more important than an audience with the Emperor." Even as she spoke, Kesira knew how hollow the words sounded. Everyone knew his place within society. Even something as vital as destruction of one of the jade demons ought to rank second to a direct order from the Emperor. Duty to family and Emperor took precedence over all other things.

The baby stirred in her backpack, rubbing tiny eyes with equally tiny fists.

Kesira gripped her staff. She had to explain quickly. "We need your help. Lenc is—"

"Sentry?" snapped Protaro.

"Sir! There is a small child in the knapsack." Kesira looked to her left where the guard still stood, sword drawn. Silvery glints shone off the long blade, showing where nicks hadn't been properly honed, giving the deep blood gutter an ominous appearance of fingers reaching from its shallow depths.

"Kill the child!"

Kesira's attention jerked back to the guard captain. Protaro drew his sword and advanced. Already, the camp had awakened. No matter where she looked, Kesira saw only naked steel and determined soldiers advancing on her.

"Kill the child!" The shout went up through the soldiers'

ranks. Kesira swung her staff and batted away the sentry's sword, but there were too many for her to fight.

But she could do nothing else. Kesira Minette stood her ground grimly, ready to die defending the baby's life.

Chapter Six

KESIRA MINETTE'S staff swung just above knee level. The snap when it connected with the guardsman's leg echoed through the night until his scream drowned it out. He clutched his knee and sank to the ground. Kesira finished him off with a thrust of the butt end of her staff to his temple. He jerked once, then lay still on the ground, the campfire light showing that his open eyes already clouded with death.

"Back," ordered Protaro. He stood, sword leveled, studying her. "We want the baby. It is evil."

"How can such a small child be evil?" she countered. But Kesira's thoughts turned to an old saying Dominie Tredlo had been fond of repeating: Evil events come from evil causes.

The baby had been spawned by Lenc. Nothing in Kesira's world touched evil more. The Emperor's demon Lalasa had spoken against the baby, Zolkan wanted him dead, all Kolya thought the baby evil, and now Protaro would kill the child unless she acted.

"You will have to kill me to get the infant."

"You think that deters me?" snapped Protaro. She read the hurt and need for vengeance in his eyes. The way his entire body settled down completed the picture. He would strike like a snake with that well-used sword and she would die.

Kesira parried the first thrust and landed the tip of her staff in his belly. The shudder ran the length of the staff. For an instant Kesira thought she'd smashed the wooden rod against a stone wall, but Protaro grunted and danced back. Her eyes widened. The man's stomach must be protected by steel bands!

Kesira began retreating, thinking to run even though she was bone-tired from her trip from Kolya. The others in Protaro's company circled her, cutting off her escape. Then they began moving inward to restrict her movements. She swung the staff in wide circles now, holding them at bay. But it was only a matter of time before she tired. They numbered more than fifty. Like a pack of dogs worrying its prey, they would have her soon enough.

But not without a fight!

Protaro's quick sword engaged her staff and knocked it from her hands when she became careless.

"Surrender now," the captain said, "and I will let you live."

She saw the immense concession he made; he wanted her death to atone for the loss of his friend and comrade in arms. Kesira heard no hint of duplicity in the words, either. Protaro was a man of honor and would defend his promise to the death.

"For that I thank you, Captain," she said, "but I cannot allow you to slaughter an innocent baby. You'd be no better than the one we both fight."

"Lalasa says the child is Lenc's son. We have been ordered to kill it!"

Kesira wondered why Lalasa hadn't simply taken the child when the female demon had visited her at the inn. Every indication of physical presence had shown Lalasa to be in the room. The cot had sagged. A faint hint of unidentifiable perfume had lingered for hours. And there could be no question of a demon's being unable to overpower a mortal.

Or was there? The idea shook Kesira. Had she somehow grown so powerful that even the demon advising the Emperor Kwasian feared her? Kesira pushed this idea from her mind as absurd. A more likely reason was Lalasa's fear that, if the baby awakened, it might use its loud cry on her.

Even this rang hollow and untrue in Kesira's mind. Lalasa was not of jade; she would not shatter as Ayondela had done. The baby's wail brought down palaces, but it affected only jade.

Kesira yelped when Protaro's blade nicked her arm. The

The White Fire

guard captain advanced, step-slide, step-slide, as if she were still armed.

The tusk taken from Ayondela's mouth came into her hand more from desperation than considered thoughtfulness. The tusk gleamed dully in the firelight. Whatever power dwelt inside had long since gone out. All Kesira had was a hard, round, sharp-tipped tooth of little value in a real fight.

"Back! She has jade!" cried one of the men. Even Protaro took two quick steps back. The captain eyed her with real hatred now. Kesira brandished the tusk, hoping no one noticed it was capable of inflicting only the most superficial of injuries.

"The witch tool will avail you naught," Protaro said. "Give us the child and you can still go unmolested."

Kesira said nothing. She edged to her left, swinging the jade tusk in a wide arc. The men fell back in an orderly fashion, not allowing her even the smallest gap to escape through.

Wait. Hold them off for a few minutes more.

Kesira jerked as if someone had touched her with a burning coal. The words had seared across her mind, but no sound reached her ears. She desperately searched for the source and found no clue.

"Zolkan!" she cried out. The *trilla* bird had taken to wing when Protaro advanced on them. "Help me, Zolkan!"

"She calls down her evil patron's wrath," muttered one of the men facing her. Kesira stabbed in his direction with the jade tusk, but succeeded only in tiring herself just a little more. From the corner of her eye, she saw Protaro motioning for the ring to again tighten around her. Without her staff, she couldn't keep them far enough away to prevent an occasional lunge from touching her flesh. They would attack and attack again until she bled from a thousand cuts.

Crystal clouds, soldiers' swords—what was the difference? The pain burned her soul in the same way.

"She calls for the *trilla* bird," said Protaro. "No demon, no evil patron. Get her!"

The world about me,
There are no eyes.

*Freedom of the air and sky,
I fade into nothingness.*

Kesira heard the spell within her skull. Once before she'd caught snippets of this, but what it meant she had no idea.

Just as the ring constricted to the point where any of the soldiers might impale her on spear or sword tip, she felt a stirring at her elbow. She blinked, trying to focus her eyes. It was as if her vision slipped to one side or the other off— Molimo.

Her momentary lapse signaled the soldiers to attack.

Run. Now, run and find Zolkan. He will guide you back to Kolya.

She fought to see Molimo. With extreme concentration, she saw his sinews rippling in the firelight, casting deep valleys of shadow and revealing broad plains of muscles tightening in combat. His sword flew like a silver bird, slashing, singing, fluttering on to knock away thrusts meant to kill her. He fought—and Protaro's men couldn't see him.

"She's ensorcelled us!"

"She doesn't touch us but we die!" another shouted in fear. Even Captain Protaro appeared confused. Kesira stood and watched while the guard captain's men were driven back.

Flee now. Hurry!

The source of that potent command had to be Molimo. But how? This wasn't speech as she knew it. The words came with too much clarity and force—and they boomed inside her skull. Molimo hadn't grown a new tongue in the few days he had been absent, but he seemed to have found a better method of communication.

Kesira fought the niggling sensation that she'd experienced this before. From Molimo? In Ayondela's palace she had felt something similar, but she hadn't recognized it as coming from Molimo. Now, there could be no one else originating the word-thoughts.

Still having trouble focusing her eyes on the man cloaked with the demon's spell of nonnoticeability, Kesira ducked through the break in the circle around her. She hadn't run fifty feet when she heard Protaro yell, and a dozen men start racing after her.

One by one, they screamed, and she heard their heavy footfalls no more.

Kesira gasped in pain when a heavy body crashed into her left shoulder. She stumbled and almost fell face-forward into the soft, yielding dirt. The nun managed to keep her feet, and continued at a slower pace.

"I could run faster if I didn't have to carry you, too," she told Zolkan. The *trilla* bird sat complacently on her shoulder again, flexing his talons into her fleshy shoulder. Dampness soaked her robe under Zolkan's feet. She hazarded a quick touch: blood.

"I am uninjured," the bird assured her. "Many of good captain's men lack an ear or an eye now, though."

"They wanted to kill the baby."

"Don't know why Molimo insisted on rescuing you," answered Zolkan. "Let them have bratling. Be for best. Nobody but Lenc wants the baby alive."

"He didn't take the child when he had the chance back at Ayondela's palace."

"Why bother? You provide better transportation. Also, how would Lenc feed bratling?"

Kesira swallowed and tasted ashes. All the *trilla* bird said was true. Until the baby grew and could be weaned, she provided his only reliable source of nourishment. Wemilat's kiss had turned into a curse burning like a brand into her breast. She wanted to claw out the mark and heave the baby into the night.

She could do neither.

"I don't understand," she gasped out, her strength beginning to fade. In the distance she heard the thunder of horses' hooves. Protaro had mounted and come after her. Not even Molimo, using his spell, could protect her now. She looked around for a hiding place.

Zolkan held out one long wing and pointed to a small ravine. Silently, Kesira turned toward it. When the bank caved in beneath her feet and sent her tumbling, Kesira twisted so that she scooted down the dirt on her belly, instinctively protecting the baby strapped to her back. The whole while, the infant didn't let out even a tiny murmur.

That action on her part, done totally without thinking,

convinced Kesira that she'd never allow anybody to kill the boy. She reached behind and pulled the tiny bundle around to where she could hold it. Rocking slowly, she soothed the infant. Those damnable pale, laughing eyes stared up at her, as if thanking her—and mocking her for her gullibility.

"Why don't I name you?" she said aloud. "A good name would save you from being forever called 'it' by Zolkan."

"Impossible to give name to it," said Zolkan. "What can be right?"

Kesira's head ached horribly. She cooed to the baby, as if it needed comforting, and tried to think this through. The *trilla* bird was right. No name she came up with fit the boy. Try as she might, names slipped off the infant like gentle spring rains off a tiled roof. The name formed, built, then vanished, leaving behind only the reality.

"All right, no name," she said, chagrined. "But you'll not end up spitted on any guardsman's sword."

The baby graced her with a soft chuckle. He reached up and tugged at her robe, then began nursing when he found a convenient tear.

"Protaro will ride past. Darkness hides your track," said Zolkan. "Molimo will join us soon."

"Good. I want to talk to him. I had the most unusual experience back in Protaro's camp. It was as if Molimo spoke directly to my mind. I'd had similar feelings on the way up to Ayondela's palace—and even before that. But these were stark, clear words."

"Quiet!" squawked the bird.

Hooves clumped along down the road at a pace slower than a gallop but faster than any walk. The voices mingled and became indistinct, but one rang out over the others.

"Lose her, and I'll have you walking sentry for a year!" Protaro's anger burned in his every word. Kesira caught her breath and barely dared to breathe as the guardsmen trotted by on the road. For a long time after the last sounds of their horses' hooves had faded to silence, Kesira maintained her strained, expectant pose.

"They are gone," said Zolkan. The bird jumped from her shoulder and waddled about, pecking and hunting through the debris caused by her fall down the ravine bank. "No good food anywhere in this miserable place. Want to go back to where pigeons don't get everything first."

Kesira tended to the baby while Zolkan continued to look for some small tidbit for his supper. The baby turned against her, and she felt a warmth beginning at her sash. Kesira put the baby aside and looked at the jade tusk.

It glowed with its inner light again. The baby had touched the jade tooth, and it recovered whatever power had been drained. Kesira turned cold inside. She dared not let the power of the jade overwhelm her or seduce the infant. The woman tried to grasp the tusk and throw it away.

It sailed through the night like a green comet, only to return as if it were on a string. Repeatedly, Kesira threw the jade tusk, and it always came back. She fell to her knees, sobbing with frustration.

"This can't be happening. I don't want it, I don't want it."

"Baby is sign of Time of Chaos," said Zolkan. "Evil. Change is evil."

"I know," sobbed Kesira. Her entire world had been structured so that each person knew his or her duty and performed it. Alter the world, and the roles changed. She didn't want the disruption the jade demons had brought, and she didn't want what the baby promised.

"If only it could all go back to the way it was."

"Change has started," Zolkan said glumly. "No turning back now. We must forge ahead. But kill bratling. That will help stop flood of changes."

Kesira held the glowing jade tooth in one hand and reached out hesitantly with her other hand. She touched the baby's head. He smiled. All she had to do was lift the jade dagger and bring it slashing down to the tender body. The tooth would penetrate and kill instantly. Kesira's hand quaked with indecision.

"I can't do it," she said finally, the tears drying on her cheeks. "Gelya taught us never to squander precious life. I can't murder an innocent."

Zolkan sniffed. "Some innocent. Pigeon shit! It forces Time of Chaos upon us. All we know will vanish. Do you want that?"

"No." Kesira tucked the jade tusk into her sash. "And I can't kill him, either."

Zolkan made a rude noise.

Before Kesira could reply, she heard the crunch of boots on the dried soil near the ravine bank. Kesira scooped up the infant and spun so that the overhang shielded her from sight. Zolkan stifled a squawk and waddled beside her. The way the *trilla* bird held himself, a quick leap would have him airborne and away from danger.

"Trail's already cold," came a voice. "She must be back in Kolya by now."

"Protaro's going to have our balls if she got away from us. You're supposed to be the best tracker in the outfit, Tamun. What do you read?"

Another voice piped up, shrill and almost feminine. "Not far. I don't read the trail, I sense it. I *feel* her nearby, and the baby's with her."

Kesira stilled her racing heart and kept her mind ready to respond to any attack. She pushed the baby from her when he reached out and touched the jade tusk once again. The brilliance from it now cast a faint shadow out into the dried riverbed.

Even as Kesira started to worry about the ghostly light being seen, she saw the two dark figures falling through the air. They landed in crouches not five feet away. Both had their daggers drawn.

"You'll win a promotion for this, Tamun," said the shadowy figure on the right as they moved forward with practiced ease.

But neither expected the loud complaint and the burst of feathers and beak when Zolkan launched himself into the fray. Kesira sat for a few seconds, stunned by the soldiers' sudden appearance, but when she heard a meaty fist strike Zolkan, she sprang into action.

The tusk came lightly to hand. Jade met steel—and shattered the tempered blade. Kesira never hesitated. She kicked out, found a vulnerable kneecap and broke it. Spinning, she caught Tamun's blade. Again, steel proved no match for the delicately veined jade dagger. As the two touched, the steel exploded into a million fragments like one of the Emperor's artillery bombs.

Tamun shrieked as his knife turned molten in his face. Kesira pressed the advantage and drove the jade tusk straight for an exposed throat. The tooth entered easily. As blood frothed around the wound, it stained the tusk and began to sizzle. Steam rose, causing Kesira to jerk back.

She stared at the jade stupidly, as if doubting any of this could have happened. But the two men on the ground gave mute testimony to the power of the blade—the jade weapon that had been activated by the baby's feeble touch.

Kesira stared at the infant. What might Lenc's son do when he became full-grown?

"Help me," came the low plea for assistance. Kesira hurried to a bramble bush where Zolkan had become entangled. She pulled the bird out gingerly, trying not to damage his precious, well-groomed feathers too much. He had told her once that he needed as much wing surface as possible for flight; his heavy body nearly overtaxed his wingspan even at the best of times.

"Pigeon lovers," grumbled Zolkan. "Why do they skulk about like that?"

"You're all right," Kesira said, checking out pinions and tail feathers. "Just a little dignity missing."

"Bruised. Hurt inside." Zolkan stretched, and used one wing to point off into the darkness. "Hurry off. They find us soon."

When Kesira bent to pick up the baby, the one whose knee she'd broken tried to grab her. Zolkan flapped over, ripped with his talons and produced a fountain of blood that quickly vanished into the thirsty sand.

"Doesn't make me feel better," the bird confided. "Might, though, if I get enough of them."

"They are the Emperor Kwasian's personal guard," she said. "They aren't our enemy. Lenc is. We ought to try to make our peace with them."

"Easy for you to say. You killed one, crippled another. What peace is Protaro likely to offer?"

Kesira shut up. She hated it when the *trilla* bird came this close to pointing out how wrong she could be. Baby safely tucked away in the backpack, she trudged through the darkened countryside, intent on the faint necklace of gaslights showing the entry portals to Kolya.

"Where's Molimo?" she asked. Zolkan sat in the corner of the room and sulked. He hadn't said a dozen words all the way back from their encounter with Protaro's guardsmen on the road.

Kesira began pacing the small room, then stopped, heart leaping to her throat when she heard a hard banging on the inn door. The innkeeper grumbled and shuffled his way across. Kesira heard the portly man mumble something, but the response froze her.

"Emperor's Guard. We seek a woman with a small child." Protaro was searching Kolya door by door, seeking her out. She clutched at the jade tusk, for once glad that Gelya had forbidden the use of steel weapons. If she'd relied on a sword against the guardsmen, she'd've been dead. As it was, the magicks inherent in the jade had saved her.

But at what cost? She felt no different from using the evil jade, but then she wasn't a demon. The demons were easily—quickly—perverted by the jade. How long would it take before a mortal succumbed?

Kesira didn't want to consider that.

The jade tusk rested cool and reassuring in her hand as she listened to the innkeeper arguing with the guardsman.

"You can't search my place. Damn fool shame to disturb any of my customers. Too few, now that Lenc's come into Kolya. Why don't you concern yourselves with the likes of him, why don't you, eh?" The innkeeper jabbed a stubby finger into the soldier's chest. Kesira sucked in her breath in surprise. To touch one of the Emperor's troops was an act tantamount to treason.

The guardsman said nothing. He spun and left without demanding a thorough search—or the innkeeper's head for his action. Kesira relaxed.

"Protaro looks everywhere," Zolkan said. "He won't find us. He looks as if you leave a trail in forest. Must look for trail in city. Different. Pigeon-shit bratling."

The sudden change in topic confused Kesira for a moment, then she realized he spoke of the baby sleeping peacefully on the cot. Kesira ran a gentle hand over the baby's wrinkled, almost hairless head, then gusted a deep sigh.

Her life had become too confused, too far from the norm that society demanded. She no longer knew her duty—and, from the innkeeper's actions, neither did anyone else. The soldier, in turn, had acted wrongly in not slaying the man instantly. And all people were slaves to Lenc.

Where would it end?

Without even noticing what she did, Kesira pulled out the bone box and tossed the rune sticks. She disliked doing this too often for fear of "wearing out" whatever talent she had. But she needed guidance to know the proper path to follow.

Her eyes widened as she read the runes. Lenc—that one she knew all too well. But this time it showed strength followed by abrupt weakness. Protaro—he wove through the pattern. Nehan-dir and even Molimo.

"Molimo is everywhere in the new patterns," she muttered.

"What of demons?" asked Zolkan, peering over her shoulder, trying to find a comfortable perch on her arm.

"Only Lenc and Molimo. Some of Lalasa, but little, very little."

"Those?" Zolkan asked, pointing out a strange pairing of sticks.

"Victory. I read a monumental battle with Lenc—and *I* win." She sat on the floor, astonished. There was no equivocation in these runes. No vagueness. No ambiguous runes to be misread.

She would fight Lenc—and win.

Kesira experienced an inner glow of triumph at this—but the runes left out some crucial information.

They didn't tell her where to battle Lenc, when, or most important of all, how.

She would triumph ultimately. But how?

Chapter Seven

THE SMALL, scrawny man with the pink spiderweb of scars across his face pointed off to a cloud of dust indicating a troop of soldiers hard a'ride toward Kolya.

"There," Nehan-dir said. "That must be the damned guard captain and his sycophants."

Nehan-dir's lieutenant wiped a dripping nose on her sleeve, then stifled a yawn. To those of the Steel Crescent, it mattered little whether they fought the Emperor Kwasian's guard or some ragtag band of other-beast hunters out on the plains. A battle brought out the best in a warrior, gave definition to life, set bounds and presented opportunity to display courage and talent. Under Nehan-dir, there had been many fine battles for the order, even if their accursed bad fate decreed continual loss of patronage.

"So?" asked Famii Bren-ko, wiping her nose on her other sleeve. "Their blood spills just like any other."

Nehan-dir half turned in the saddle and glared at her. "Lenc wants his son returned to him unharmed. What will an enraged demon do to us if we allow Protaro to kill the child? A demon's blood *doesn't* spill like any other."

Bren-ko grinned wickedly, showing yellowed, broken teeth. "In such a case, our loving patron might not take out his wrath on all the order. Just our leader." She rocked back in her saddle and hefted a sturdy leg up and around the pommel. "Might be a good opportunity for a strong second-in-command to move up, eh?"

"You'll be smiling from a second mouth before that happens," Nehan-dir said, moving his index finger along the woman's throat to indicate where his dagger would go before Lenc could slay him.

Famii Bren-ko jerked away and stared at the vanishing dust cloud.

Nehan-dir's attention turned inward, to plans, to schemes, to ways of entering Kolya without arousing much ire or creating a stir. Even though Lenc controlled the city with the power of jade, the populace still rebelled at odd times. Nehan-dir chuckled at this. Even in rebellion, Lenc ruled. But that was another concern, one beyond the scope of Nehan-dir's orders.

Even the battle-hardened mercenary shivered at the thought of his meeting with Lenc. The demon had appeared in a cloud of choking vapor. The thunderclap accompanying his arrival had deafened the Steel Crescent leader and had driven him to his knees with pain. Only then had Lenc spoken to him.

"Worm!" the jade demon had roared. "You disgust me. You are a pathetic nothing. Why do I tolerate your continued existence?"

"I seek only to obey, Master!" Nehan-dir had shouted, his words louder than he'd expected because of the ringing still hindering his hearing.

"Then know this, low one. I have allowed Gelya's whore to keep my son by the mortal Parvey Yera. She suckles my heir when no one else can. But the time for this charity on my part draws to an end. I want my son beside me in my hour of total triumph. You will go to Kolya and retrieve my son from Kesira Minette."

"Why Kolya?"

Lenc had strode back and forth in front of the kneeling mercenary; the demon's eyes flared a brilliant green and tiny sparks danced off his arms and legs. When the demon clenched his fists, Nehan-dir had thought he would die for asking an impertinent question. To have come so far, to have endured Tolek's bartering of his worshipers, to sorrow over the loss of Howenthal and Ayondela, only to die at an angered patron's hand!

Lenc's rage subsided. "Why not Kolya? For my purposes, it is ideal. Emperor Kwasian still commands the populace in Limaden. Lalasa is no threat, but she manages to annoy me."

The White Fire

Nehan-dir sucked in his breath as the thought occurred to him that Lenc might actually fear what the Emperor's demon might be capable of accomplishing with only mortals at her command.

"Further," Lenc had gone on, "I have decided my main temple will be constructed in a city untainted by other demons. Kolya is my choice. To have throngs come and pay me homage. To hear their voices uplifted in prayers beseeching me not to destroy them. To know that I of all the demons rule supreme!"

"The Order of the Steel Crescent will not fail you, Master!"

The demon had snorted and pointed a green-blazing finger at him. "Fail and die, worm. Succeed and you will be my vicar to the people of this world. Of all mortals, you, Nehan-dir, will be elevated above even the Emperor."

Nehan-dir had bowed deeply, hardly daring to believe such grandiose promises. Tolek had promised; he had lied. The other patrons sought out by the Steel Crescent had proven weak and had perished before delivering their payments. The thunderclap had repeated itself, and the noxious odors vanished with the jade demon. Nehan-dir had risen on weak legs and staggered away to mount and ride hard for Kolya.

Nehan-dir decided that the soldiers under Protaro's command numbered fewer than a hundred. Perhaps even less. The mercenary leader worried over ambushes, attacks, the proper method of attack. Those following his banner had grown in the past weeks to over seventy. Power drew power. With the structure of society weakening, the Emperor Kwasian unable to provide the services of defense and leadership, many drifted, unsure of their places.

Nehan-dir told them their places, and they rejoiced to again know their duties.

If only he could find another to replace Famii Bren-ko. Her allegiance was plain to any who even dared ask: she fought for herself. Nehan-dir didn't understand this or her need for personal power. He sought only to serve his order and give them the best he could. When another came along able to give the Steel Crescent more, Nehan-dir would step aside.

This would not come willingly, true. He would be dead, the other having triumphed in individual combat. But it would be an honorable death, and Nehan-dir could find his rest knowing that a stronger leader rode at the front of the Steel Crescent's battle column.

Service to his order came first, always. But what of Famii Bren-ko? He mistrusted her motives.

"We ride south, then into Kolya."

"Why ignore the guard?" the woman demanded. "Let's engage them now, while they are still worn out from their long ride across the plains. We won't have any of those accursed Kolyans getting in our way. Waste of time, hacking through a crowd of peasants armed with nothing more than daggers and spit."

"We are tired, also," Nehan-dir said. "The battle might go against us since Protaro holds higher ground. We enter Kolya. We rest. We pick our target well, *then* strike."

The woman shrugged as if it were a matter of total indifference to her and pulled a filthy cloak tighter around her well-fleshed body. Nehan-dir started to reprimand her for such disobedience, then stopped. Bren-ko had a small but loyal cadre among the order's newer members. This was neither the time nor the place to challenge her for complete control.

But Nehan-dir knew it had to come soon, if the order was to survive.

"We find Lenc's son, then we fight," he promised.

"Bastard," came the faint, derisive word. Nehan-dir didn't know if Famii Bren-ko meant Lenc's son or him, though the epithet was true in both cases. The small leader spurred his horse toward the distant city, glad once more to feel wind whipping against his face, robbing his ears of the words of those behind him. No other feeling rivaled the sensation of galloping at the head of a column of mercenaries intent on battle.

None.

The newly promoted sergeant failed to replace Tuwallen, in either friendship or ability, but he was the best of the surviving guards. Protaro listened to the report with only

The White Fire

half an ear, more intent on considering the ramifications of those who'd been following them for almost a week.

"Thank you," Protaro said, breaking off the scouting report. "I am convinced that only the Steel Crescent could mount a troop the size of those to the south."

"Should we prepare for battle, Captain?"

Protaro snorted. The silvery lace of his breath hung in the cold night air until a slight breeze grabbed hold and carried it away, a captive of approaching winter. He slapped himself on the upper arms and restored what circulation he could. Ayondela's curse had laid a snowy blanket across the land for most of the summer. What brief respite there'd been counted more as autumn. Again, for the second time in less than three months, winter's frosty grip squeezed and shook the land.

The only consolation lay in that this winter came naturally and not at the beck of a jade demon.

"Nehan-dir wants the boy sheltered by the nun," Protaro said, more to himself than to the newly promoted sergeant.

"Why should the Steel Crescent fetch the infant for Lenc? Why doesn't the demon simply take the boy himself? He has the power of jade to enforce any whim."

"Perhaps it is nothing more than that—a whim. Or it might be more." Protaro kept thinking along those lines, and came to the unsettling conclusion that Lenc might be afraid of Kesira. What power did Gelya's nun command that a jade demon feared? The woman had claimed to have slain the other three demons, but Protaro discounted this as wild ravings. Lenc had eliminated competition for sole rule. Kesira had not mattered.

But many things about the nun struck Protaro as odd. The *trilla* bird with her, for instance. Such birds were often the messengers of the demons—or had been, when a significant number of demons had existed. And the tongueless youth. Molimo, the woman had called him. He seemed familiar to Protaro, and the soldier didn't know why. The youth was too young to have been a soldier serving along the lines when the barbarians had launched their final attack. Protaro knew few others outside the Emperor's service.

Where lay Kesira Minette's power? Protaro found it hard

to swallow the notion that Lenc feared her. She commanded no powerful magicks, or she would have unleashed them against him and his men when she'd blundered into their camp the night before. Kesira had fought her way free, the *trilla* bird aiding her in some mysterious fashion. Protaro thought it had been as if another battled on the nun's side, one unseen by even the keenest-eyed of his sentries.

The guard captain shrugged this off. He had been given a mission to accomplish, the orders signed by the Emperor's own hand. Protaro touched the now almost disintegrated paper hidden inside his tunic. Emperor Kwasian's own chop made it official: the boy with Kesira Minette must be returned to Limaden. Barring this, the child must die.

Protaro didn't like the idea of being executioner to such a small one, but his duty shone bright and clear through the murk cast by Lenc's ambitions. The Emperor desired the boy's death. Protaro was a good soldier. He would obey even if he did have a grudging admiration for the nun's courage. Still, the vision of his good friend and comrade Tuwallen lying dead back in the rocky Sarn Mountains returned to haunt him. Kesira had caused that sudden death.

Now she taunted him by dangling the boy in front of him while they camped outside Kolya.

"Lenc fears something," Protaro told his sergeant. "Even with his immense power, he is fearful. Why pick a city like Kolya for his capital?"

"It is untainted by other demons," suggested the sergeant. The man shuffled uncomfortably. These matters lay beyond the realm of his thoughts. Such considerations, however, obviously engaged much of his commander's time.

"A better symbol would be crushing Emperor Kwasian, humiliating Lalasa, then assuming the throne in Limaden. Lenc comes here for a reason—Kesira Minette is still some weeks distant from Limaden. Does Lenc fear her joining forces with the Emperor?" This made no sense to the captain. Lenc ought to be able to stop any single traveler along the empire's roads. Only the capital remained in Emperor Kwasian's power. Even more to the point, Kwasian wanted the boy dead, something Kesira fought bitterly against. Seldom had Protaro seen one of any religious order more adamant and in violation of the Emperor's direct command.

The sergeant shrugged, it being a matter of no real import. He cared more about a full belly and a good night's sleep, both of which had been in short supply. He told his captain this.

"We'll enter Kolya by the west gate. The nun can't have gone far. We will track her through the streets, if necessary, but the baby will be ours before the sun reaches zenith today. Prepare to ride."

This the sergeant understood. He spun and began barking orders, getting the men into formation, checking gear, readying them for what had to be a battle.

Protaro watched in silence, his brain churning with the infinity of possibilities generated by Emperor Kwasian and the demons. He gave up finally, convinced it was a fool's game. He would obey his orders, and Lenc take the reasons behind it.

"The guardsman has left," Kesira said, peering out into the moonlit street. One moon hung just above the rooftops and cast a pewter glow over Kolya. Nobody but the Emperor's Guard strayed this night, making it easier for her to determine her own safety. "They won't be back soon. There are too few of them and too many places to search."

"Some search. Pigeon-brained soldiers didn't even poke around inside," said Zolkan.

"Whose side are you on?" she demanded angrily. "If they'd found us, they would have killed the baby."

"No loss. Need bratling dead. Bad, very bad."

"He's too young to be bad," she said, her confidence eroding as she watched the baby stir. Those penetrating pale eyes opened to affix firmly on her. Intelligence unlike any she'd known blazed within those cool eyes. Kesira saw now that this was no mortal baby but the true offspring of a demon.

Why did he have to be Lenc's son? She cursed her weakness in not giving in to Protaro—Emperor Kwasian!—and Lalasa and Zolkan and even the citizens of Kolya who wanted the baby dead. Stubbornness had always plagued her. Sister Fenelia had cautioned her repeatedly about obstinance, but Kesira had chosen her own path over that dictated by her superiors. This made her a misfit, a social outcast in many ways. As much as she tried to obey, to know her place in society, the more it rankled.

"I will *not* give up the child."

Zolkan made a rude noise and an even ruder gesture.

"And if I catch you trying to harm him, you'll end up in a stewpot."

"No need to get nasty," Zolkan said with ill grace. "I cannot harm baby. But bratling must die. Too dangerous."

Kesira settled down on her cot, the door into the public room open slightly to allow her a view of the large window in the outer room. Shadows fluttered across the window, often nothing more than clouds obscuring the rising moon; but now and again she saw the harsher shadows of soldiers.

"Zolkan," she whispered. "Protaro's men are outside. They've tracked us down!"

The bird fluttered around the small room, then smashed into the door, knocking it open. Like a nocturnal bird of prey, he darted out into the public room and sailed directly for the window. Perched there, he pressed one beady eye against the dirty pane. For long minutes, he did not stir. Then he returned.

"Not guardsmen. Steel Crescent mercenaries. I saw Nehan-dir at end of street. Somehow, he senses your presence. He follows *that*." Zolkan indicated the baby with the tip of his long wing.

"Can we flee?"

"Where? All seek you, all want bratling dead. Protaro, Nehan-dir, even people of Kolya, if they find you harbor Lenc's son."

"Where's Molimo? If we can only..." Kesira's words died when she heard the click of steel against steel.

"Outside. Many soldiers. Hurry, flee, flee!" urged the *trilla* bird.

Kesira's mind raced, awash with the paths of escape open to her. They all amounted to little more than hope. The only one giving her even a modicum of a chance was Kene Zoheret and his rebel underground. If Zoheret could smuggle her to the outskirts of Kolya, she might be able to steal a horse and ride.

But to where? Molimo and Zolkan had urged her to go to Limaden. She doubted her own safety there—and she knew what the baby might expect at Kwasian's hand. Even Lalasa sought the infant's death.

"Can we get out across the roof?" she asked Zolkan. The bird flapped away to scout. Kesira edged out of the room, her few belongings already gathered. For a weapon she had nothing more than the jade tusk taken from Ayondela's mouth. She longed for the firm, secure feel of a thick, well-seasoned stonewood staff in her hand. At least, having the wood—sacred to Gelya—nearby would have allowed her to more easily calm herself.

". . . inside," came the thin, reedy voice of a woman. "I can slit the bitch's throat for you, if you've no stomach for it, Nehan-dir."

"I don't care what you do to her," came the Steel Crescent leader's voice. "Just leave the boy untouched. So much as scratch his precious hide and yours will be tanning in the sun."

The laugh that answered told Kesira that Nehan-dir had trouble on his hands. The woman with him fought for the joy of killing, not for the joy of serving.

The door exploded inward as a heavily booted foot kicked against it. Standing silhouetted was the woman.

"Get her, Bren-ko. Don't block the way for the rest of us," came Nehan-dir's impatient command.

The woman—Bren-ko—laughed, and charged forward, swinging her sword. Kesira crouched, ready to react to whatever form Bren-ko's attack took. Before the warrior woman reached Kesira, however, a flash of green from above exploded in a mass of feathers and slashing talons. Zolkan's claws embedded firmly in Famii Bren-ko's right wrist and caused a fountain of blood to spray outward.

Bren-ko swore as she jerked back, swinging sword and arm and Zolkan hard into a wall. The *trilla* bird let out an almost human squeal before sliding to the floor, unconscious. Famii Bren-ko had lost her sword, and her right hand hung, limp, at her side, but the feral glow in her eyes told Kesira that the woman had just begun to fight. She would attack and attack and attack until the last breath was driven from her lungs by death's cold grasp.

Kesira helped Bren-ko along that path. Two quick steps, a feint, a lunge. Bren-ko almost parried the lunge, but her injured hand betrayed her. The tip of Ayondela's tusk entered the warrior woman's leather armor and plunged into flesh beneath. As it traveled, it sizzled and popped, like grease dropped into a hot skillet.

Bren-ko opened her mouth in a silent scream of pain. She clutched at the tusk's point of entry, her fingers charring when she touched the tusk. Famii Bren-ko stepped back a half-pace, pulling herself free of the jade weapon. Then she fell face-forward onto the floor. Kesira knew that her opponent had died in terrible agony.

"Thank you," came the soft, menacing words. Nehan-dir stood in the doorway, sword drawn. "You saved me the trouble of dealing with poor, ambitious Famii. Now, give me the boy."

Kesira said nothing. She held the tusk in front of her, point up and dancing lazily in wide circles, as if she held a real knife. The baby had been securely strapped down in her backpack, and Kesira thought she could get by Nehan-dir. The mercenary twisted to his right, then swung his sword in an arc aimed at her knees—a maiming stroke.

Kesira lightly jumped the edged weapon and confounded Nehan-dir when she didn't come back down to the floor. He had jerked hard on the sword and brought it back in a move designed to cut her off at the ankles. To his surprise, Kesira swung in midair, hands gripping an overhead beam. She kicked out and caught him on the shoulder. The leader of the Steel Crescent stumbled and gave her the chance to dart for the stairs leading to the second floor.

Kesira took the steps in long strides, whirled quickly at the top and kicked. She again caught Nehan-dir by surprise and sent him tumbling back down into the common room. Kesira looked about frantically. Zolkan had seen a way out. She had to find it in the next few heartbeats before Nehan-dir summoned the others of his order.

Already, heavy footsteps below warned her of the dangers of lingering.

Through a door, lock it, through another and out a window. Kesira felt as if she had sprouted wings and was flying. Onto the roof she tumbled. Kesira tried to keep from rolling over onto the baby and barely succeeded. The baby's tiny fists grabbed at her robe and tugged. She ignored him. There wasn't time.

Frantically, she looked for an escape route. Not finding it, she dashed across the sloping roof and leaped to the next building without breaking stride. Kesira's footing proved too tenuous; she slipped on her belly all the way down the tiled roof and crashed into the street not fifteen paces from where a tight knot of the mercenaries stood, hands on weapons and muttering among themselves about what transpired inside the inn.

"There she is! And the baby!" The cry went up before Kesira regained her feet.

She rolled over and came to hands and knees, but the feel of a dozen blades poking into her body halted any further attempts at escaping.

"Get Nehan-dir. Bring him here. He'll want to see the bitch brought to her knees like this!"

Sword points prodded her back to her knees when she tried to stand. Panting, angry at herself, Kesira Minette crouched on hands and knees and waited for Nehan-dir to come.

She expected a slow, lingering death at his hands. And for the baby? She didn't even allow herself the slightest thought of the child's being given over to Lenc.

Chapter Eight

KESIRA MINETTE winced as a sword pinked her upper arm. A slow trickle of blood ran down her bicep, across her forearm and dripped onto the cobblestone paving. Worse than the pain was the humiliation the mercenaries forced upon her. Gathering her strength, she tried to stand, only to be driven back to the pavement with the flats of their swords and their derisive laughter.

"Good work," came the all-too-familiar sound of Nehan-dir's voice. The small man strutted around and planted his feet wide apart. With a flourish he drew his blade and rested the point on the ground just inches from Kesira's face. Nehan-dir leaned on the blade, bending slightly at the waist so that he could whisper to her.

Kesira roared in rage at the man's words. She flushed when he straightened, laughed and pointed at her. She had done nothing but feed the man's reputation for toughness among his followers. Kesira had forgotten one of Gelya's prime tenets: pride and weakness are twin sisters. She allowed her own pride to betray all she stood for. Not only were those of the Steel Crescent seeing her humiliated, they saw weakness, too.

No more.

Kesira stood, ignoring the pain and the solid blows descending on her from all sides. She looked Nehan-dir directly in the eye, with courage now, secure in the feeling that he had done all he might to her. She would permit nothing else.

"Back, stay your swords," he ordered sharply. "She is vanquished."

Before Kesira could say a word, the clatter of horses'

hooves echoed down the night-darkened street. Moonlight caught on the flashing war spurs worn by the horses and sent messages of death to those of the Steel Crescent.

Screaming, they scattered when the Emperor's Guard crashed through the sentry lines in the small street. Protaro's men reined in their animals, caused them to rear and kick out with their hooves. Each spiked hoof struck one of the Steel Crescent mercenaries, to rip open a bloody wound— or worse.

Kesira whipped around and backed into a doorway, making sure the infant had the protection of her body against the fight raging now. She saw one man, mounted and swinging a longsword, and knew Captain Protaro had once again found her. Kesira's mouth turned to gummy cotton. If the Emperor's order carried and Protaro won this skirmish, the baby would lose his life. If Nehan-dir won, the baby would be raised as heir to the evil generated by Lenc and his abominable jade.

Either way, Kesira saw little future for herself.

Nehan-dir brought his sword up and around in a wide arc, blade meeting one guardsman's horse just above the leg. The sword edge slashed open the horse's shoulder, spilling blood, innards and rider to the ground. The hideous death sounds from the horse filled the cold night air. And not a single citizen of Kolya ventured even a frightened glance outside to see what disturbed the silence of the night. Lenc had prowled the streets too long, perpetrating his horrors, for any to be unduly curious.

Kesira held down her rising gorge only through extreme effort of will. Nehan-dir had been bathed in blood, both animal and human. His scars gleamed pinkly as he fought, standing out through the gore besmirching him. The small man stood with legs spread far apart, swinging his sword with a power that belied his stature. Guardsman after guardsman fell to the mercenary's blade—and Kesira saw this scene repeated everywhere she looked.

The initial attack by Kwasian's guard had caught the Steel Crescent by surprise. The flailing horses' hooves had gouged and cut and destroyed at will. But then the tide turned when Nehan-dir wrested control of the battle by sheer effort.

The White Fire

Whether he did it out of fear of Lenc's retribution if he failed or because he was the superior fighter, Kesira couldn't say.

More and more of the guard fell.

"Kesira!" came a cry. "To me!" She peered out of the doorway and saw Protaro waving to her. For a moment, the nun almost ran across the blood-slickened street to join him. Then she paused. Finally, she ducked back into the relative safety of the portal. Protaro would kill the infant. She couldn't allow herself—and the baby—to so easily fall into the man's hands.

The cry had alerted Nehan-dir to his adversary. The small man grinned. The effect of blood over his face—the white teeth shining, the pink network of scars glistening—all turned Nehan-dir into something less than human. Even when Molimo became a wolf and ravaged the countryside, he seemed more human than this swearing, fighting juggernaut.

Nehan-dir slashed his way through the few remaining guardsmen until he reached Captain Protaro.

"Again we meet," Nehan-dir said, and without any further words he launched a vicious attack. Protaro countered easily, but then lost ground when Nehan-dir pressed in savagely, ignoring the risk of personal injury. Protaro fell into a more stolid defensive stance and battled head-to-head with Nehan-dir. Kesira saw that the pair was well matched. What Nehan-dir lacked in skill he more than made up for with intensity—and she also saw that Protaro was exhausted. His long days on her trail had taken their toll.

She darted away from the doorway and into the inn as the tide of battle moved down the street. Kesira squinted in the dark room, then dropped to hands and knees and began searching. She bumped her head into the wall in her excitement when she found the huddled mass on the floor.

"Zolkan!" she shouted. The ringing of steel from Protaro and Nehan-dir's battle filled her ears. "Are you all right?" She tenderly touched the limp bird. He didn't stir. She pressed her fingertips into his side and felt the rapid beating of the *trilla* bird's heart, the slow rise and fall of his chest. Stroking, cuddling, she held the heavy bird close. "Be all right, please," she sobbed. "I need you so. You're the only friend I have left."

The bundle of feathers stirred, then one wing brushed across her cheek. "Molimo is your friend, too," Zolkan said weakly. She clutched him tightly to her breast and received an outraged squawk for her trouble. "You smother me. You mash me. Isn't it enough I crash into pigeon-shit wall helping you?"

Kesira placed the bird on her shoulder. She noticed right away that Zolkan's claws didn't grip her shoulder as strongly as in the past. She'd have to be careful not to unseat the battered creature.

"Nehan-dir fights Protaro."

"And?" the bird asked.

"Nehan-dir is winning."

"That ought to make you happy. This way the bratling lives."

"I don't want want him raised by his father." Even mouthing the word *father* in connection with Lenc and the boy struck Kesira as vile. "I want him to live a normal life, free of threats from the Emperor, free of Lenc's jade influence."

She expected Zolkan to protest as before. It was a mark of his injury that he said nothing. But his claws tightened on her shoulder, reassuring her that his strength was slowly returning. Kesira rushed to the door and peered out. The two soldiers fought, but the outcome was apparent from the onlookers.

All were Nehan-dir's followers. Every last guardsman had been killed or routed. Only Protaro fought on. Even granting the valiant man the strength and cunning of a demon, Kesira saw no way Protaro could survive.

Unless she helped him. Kesira worried over this decision. Protaro wanted the boy dead. He was an honorable man and his Emperor had ordered the deed done. In spite of this, Kesira dared not let Nehan-dir capture the infant and turn him over to Lenc.

"Run," urged Zolkan. "Find back door and run. We can find Molimo. He is somewhere in city. We can find him."

"I can't leave Protaro out there. He'll die."

"Always help the foundlings, is that it?" said Zolkan.

"I helped you when you flew into our sacristy more dead than alive. You'd nearly frozen to death. In spite of Sister Fenelia's complaints, I kept you and nursed you back to your cantankerous self. And Molimo. What of him? Didn't I help him after he got caught in the shower of jade fragments? Where would he be without my help? And the boy. He is an innocent."

"Point made. Do what you must. But don't expect me to like it." The bird burrowed down and found what remained of her cowl. He burrowed deeper and completely hid himself in the folds of her robe until she looked like a hunchback. But no hunchback's hump ever quivered and squawked to itself like this one.

Decision made, Kesira faced the problem of actually rescuing Protaro from the Steel Crescent. Too many mercenaries ringed Protaro and Nehan-dir for any easy escape. She didn't think any simple diversion would work against the battle-trained order, either, but she carried one weapon which might prevail.

If only she could use it.

Kesira swung the baby around and saw the pale gray eyes looking up at her. "I need your help," she said simply. "Nehan-dir would take you away from me. Protaro would kill you, but Protaro is a good man. I cannot let him die. If you won't aid me, I'll have to try to save him on my own. I will in all probability die if I do that."

The tiny boy pulled a wet thumb from his mouth. Kesira saw that white ridges of teeth formed; he had the look of a child teething for some time, yet she had felt no teeth when last she'd breast-fed him. Growth came in giddy spurts—giddy for Kesira Minette.

"Help me," she repeated.

The baby opened his mouth. A tiny gurgle came out. The gurgle turned to a chuckle. The chuckle rose in pitch and power until window glass broke in all nearby buildings. The fighters paused, and all attention turned to Kesira and the boy.

The cry rose until Kesira wanted to clap her hands over her ears and never listen to it again. When it began to undulate, she heard a new, more resonant snapping sound.

All the steel weapons borne by the mercenaries became brittle and broke, just as the jade in Ayondela's palace had, just as Ayondela herself had. The shattered weapons fell to the street in shards. As soon as the last dagger had been reduced to metallic dust, the baby stopped his shattering scream.

Kesira stood stunned by the cry's intensity, but so did the Steel Crescent. Their weapons had been stripped from their hands in the span of a dozen heartbeats. Nehan-dir stood covered with blood and gore, a confused look on his face. Whatever Lenc had told him about the baby, this had not been mentioned.

Protaro seized upon the chance to push Nehan-dir aside, cuff another behind the ear and kick a third in the groin to get free of the imprisoning circle. He spun out of the grasp of a fourth to join Kesira.

"To the rear of the inn. Run!" he ordered. Protaro slammed the door and saw that the bar had been broken earlier. He grabbed a low bench and braced it against the door to make a crude barricade. Even as he ran to the back of the inn, the Steel Crescent mercenaries crashed through the remains of the window, bypassing the door.

"Where now?" panted Kesira, waiting for Protaro in the alleyway.

"They'll be around in seconds. Down there. Through that warehouse and out onto the street beyond."

They ran in silence, the only sounds their own pulses hammering in their temples and the harsh grating of gasping lungs pushed beyond all reasonable limits. Protaro provided the muscle to smash through locked doors, and Kesira's quickness through tightly stacked rows of crates got them to the far side of the warehouse long before the pursuers even found the building.

"Almost sunrise," Protaro said. "This hasn't been a good day. I have let Emperor Kwasian down."

"Not your fault," Kesira said, trying to catch her breath. "There were too many of Nehan-dir's soldiers. Too well armed, trained. Rested." She put the infant into the backpack, then leaned forward, her hands on her knees. Air

The White Fire

came into her lungs more easily now, even as sweat dripped onto the paving from her forehead.

"What happened?"

Kesira looked up, not sure of the question's intent.

"My sword. Theirs. Even my dagger." Protaro touched his empty leather sheath. Faint metallic sprinkles remained.

"Gelya warned against the use of steel weapons," Kesira said. "I'd never understood why before. Now I know." She had said this in a flip tone, intending to divert Protaro's attention from the baby and his incredible power, but her own mind turned down different roads. Had Gelya known the future, that such would happen? She touched the jade tooth thrust through her sash. It had escaped undamaged. Kesira pushed this from her mind. The boy had destroyed Ayondela and her jade palace with his cries; jade was not immune to his power.

But wood? It must be impervious to the baby's sonic attacks. Stonewood in particular. Kesira vowed to replace her trusty staff at the earliest opportunity. Items wrought by man might fail, but natural implements couldn't. All things fit together into a harmonious whole. It was up to her—using Gelya's teachings—to find how the infant met some need.

"It was no dead demon's warning that reduced my sword to powder," Protaro said. He eyed her curiously, then changed the subject. "We need to find refuge. Any ideas?"

Kesira had one or two, but she didn't know if Protaro would agree to them. "I know of one group, a rebel group, that might give us shelter. They seek Lenc's downfall, but their efforts have been pitiful so far."

"They set fire to the temple? We passed it on our way through the center of Kolya."

Kesira nodded. She remembered all too well how that destruction had brought Lenc's personal attention to the city. The jade demon had strode along the streets, killing, maiming, raping at will. If anything, it seemed better to keep activities against the demon to a low point until the killing stroke could be administered.

"Sounds as if they need someone to do their planning for them," Protaro said. "Since I have failed Emperor

Kwasian so grievously, do you think these rebels would accept me into their ranks?"

Kesira looked sharply at the guard captain. His tone indicated he sought absolution for his failure—the absolution of death. Kesira didn't know the man at all well, but this hunched, dejected figure squinting into the rising sun was not the confident warrior she had met previously.

"I've even lost my sword." His hand fluttered like a dying butterfly over his empty scabbard.

"You still live. In that lies hope."

"But I don't live by my own hand. Another saved me." He frowned, as if returning to a difficult topic. Kesira cut him off before he again asked how she had reduced all the weapons to dust.

"We must find Kene Zoheret soon," she said. "Nehandir will be searching the streets for us. He might even appeal to Lenc to seek us out."

"Lenc comes," Zolkan moaned. "Find Molimo. We need help. Lenc is coming!"

Protaro stiffened at the disembodied voice.

"Be calm," Kesira said, resting her hand lightly on his shoulder. "Zolkan is a friend. Come on out. It must be stuffy in that cowl." The green-feathered *trilla* bird shook himself free and returned to his usual perch on her left shoulder. "See?" she asked of Protaro. "Only a *trilla* bird."

"Only!" exclaimed Zolkan. "Is that all you think of me? Only?"

Kesira stroked gently over the brilliant blue-and-green feathered crest, soothing her friend's injured feelings. "You are more. Always."

Zolkan snorted and settled down, his feathers sadly in need of preening. The bird tucked his head under one wing and slipped off to sleep as Kesira hastened through the slowly awakening city streets.

"They are the messengers of the demons. Does he spy on us, or for us?" asked Protaro.

"I nursed him back to health. He and Molimo are my only true allies."

Protaro nodded, remembering the fracas in the mountains. "I know of this Molimo. No tongue. You say you trust him, but what of this Zoheret we seek out?"

"He is prone to rashness. He is harmless otherwise." Even as she spoke, Kesira wondered if she believed this. For all his apparent impracticality, Kene Zoheret struck her as something more. But how much more? And Protaro's words needled her. Did she truly consider Zoheret a friend to trust with her life? While she had no choice, it seemed to her that Zoheret would sell her out to Nehan-dir for a few bent coins.

"Zoheret mentioned coming to an inn when he left the one where I worked."

"You *worked* at that public house?" Shock rolled over Protaro's features. It had never occurred to him that Kesira might seek employment. "As a means of hiding out?"

"As a way to earn my keep. I have no money. The Emperor Kwasian does not pay me a regular fee for my services." Kesira grew impatient.

"The Emperor doesn't pay me now, either. Not after I have so severely disgraced his service."

"You failed," Kesira said brutally. "That doesn't make you worthless."

"I should have prepared better. We had the advantage. We timed the attack poorly. We failed. I may be the only survivor."

"Battles against overwhelming numbers shouldn't be anything new for you. I've heard the tales of fighting during the barbarian invasions."

"Thousands were reduced to tens," he said. "But we triumphed, even at such a great cost."

He fell into a moody silence that suited Kesira. She worked along the slowly filling streets, not daring to inquire after Zoheret. By sheer chance, the nun sighted a battered wooden sign dangling above the entrance to an inn.

"The Falling Leaf," she said. "This is the place." Cautiously Kesira looked up and down the street. They had moved quickly enough to stay ahead of Nehan-dir's methodical house-to-house search; but with the Steel Crescent's power ascendant in Kolya, it could be only a matter of hours before Nehan-dir located them.

Inside the dimly lit inn they found a mug-ringed table in the dank back corner. The place smelled of spilled ale, and the innkeeper took no pride in maintaining a high standard of cleanliness. Kesira's nose curled at the odors and she repressed an urge to take up a rag and start tidying.

"What'll it be?" the innkeeper called out from his position near the fireplace. "Got some breakfast cooking." He prodded the contents of a stewpot on the fire and peered inside. From his expression, Kesira wasn't sure if she even dared ask what he prepared.

"We're looking for a friend," she said.

The innkeeper turned and faced them, studying them more closely. "In Kolya, no one's got a friend anymore."

"Zoheret," Kesira said softly. "We need his help."

The innkeeper turned back to his pot, gave it a few tentative stirs, then ambled over to the grimy window and peered into the street. He stood watching for several minutes, assuring himself that the shabby nun and the bloody man weren't out to trap him. Finally sure than no one dangerous lingered in the street, he came over and perched one fat buttock on the edge of their table.

"Zoheret's not here. Why not come back later and see if he's made it here? Ofttimes he won't put in an appearance for days, even weeks." The innkeeper rocked to and fro on the table. Kesira started to comment that there were better ways of cleaning a tabletop, but she held her tongue.

"We're fleeing Nehan-dir," Protaro said, taking the initiative. "The Order of the Steel Crescent," he added when he saw noncomprehension in the man's face. This produced a tiny spark of fear. "Lenc's mercenaries," Protaro added, finally fueling a definite response.

"Zoheret's not here. Hasn't been in weeks."

Even before the innkeeper's words faded in the room, Kene Zoheret entered, trailing three of his lieutenants. Seeing Kesira and Protaro, Zoheret motioned the three to posts.

"Good work, Sandor," Zoheret said loudly, slapping the suspicious innkeeper on the back. "We've been out hunting these two. Just the ones we need!"

The innkeeper smiled weakly and went back to his cooking, glad to be free of such intrigues. Noxious green vapors rose from the stewpot and the odor of burning garbage filled the room.

"They're hunting everywhere for you!" cried Zoheret. Protaro and Kesira exchanged glances. To this man, it was all a game.

"Then you know the guard company has been wiped out. The Emperor doesn't have another to send," Protaro said honestly. "Whatever response to Nehan-dir and Lenc will have to come from the citizens."

"From *my* underground!" gloated Zoheret.

"Yes." The way Protaro said it told Kesira that the man sought an honorable death to ease the humiliation of his lost command and failure to carry out Emperor Kwasian's orders.

"A captain, oh, good, very good," crowed Zoheret. "We need a tactician for what I have in mind. We will strike at Lenc's jade heart this time, when the demon comes to secure his rule over Kolya."

"It's already in his control," Kesira said. "We must wrest it from Lenc."

"Not his," contradicted Zoheret. "He must make a public appearance and openly destroy all the other patrons."

"No great problem. Kolya has never been famous for its piety," said Protaro. "Even Lalasa has found no great acceptance in Kolya."

"Here's our plan," Zoheret said, reaching into his jerkin and pulling out a tattered piece of paper. With nimble fingers he pressed out the wrinkles. To Kesira, the squiggles on the paper were meaningless. She saw that they meant little more to Protaro, even when Zoheret explained their significance.

"So," said Zoheret, "we gather in front of Lenc's temple. His new one hasn't been completed yet, so he still appears in the one on the Street of Colored Paper. That's where we attack."

"With your bare hands? Against a demon relying on the power of jade?"

Zoheret ignored Kesira, turning his full attention to Protaro, who seemed more interested and less skeptical. "Even demons can die. Lenc can be killed, if we attack him when he least expects it. He can only direct those fireballs in one direction at a time. He is tricked into releasing one—we attack. Simple!"

Kesira's head threatened to split with the inconsistencies and outright mistakes Zoheret proposed. But she kept silent.

"I agree that Lenc can be destroyed," she heard Protaro saying. "The jade weakens him, even as it gives him power. His immortality was forfeit when he first used the jade. A sword thrust through the midriff will dispatch him."

"Yes, right!"

"But I need a sword. We all need weapons. Can we get them before Lenc appears to proclaim his complete power over Kolya?"

Zoheret frowned. "The only remaining source of weapons is the Steel Crescent; Lenc destroyed the city guard. Few others have even a dagger, much less a sword. Yes, definitely, we must steal arms from the Steel Crescent."

Kesira stroked Zolkan's greasy, broken feathers. The *trilla* bird cooed like a dove, stirring in her hand without waking. She shifted about on the bench, keeping the knapsack out of Zoheret's sight. Protaro had mentioned nothing about turning the infant over to Emperor Kwasian since she had rescued him, but the thought might intrude at any time if she reminded the captain of the baby's presence. Protaro might see this as a way to regain lost honor.

And Zoheret? She didn't want the overzealous underground leader thinking the baby was an easy road to even greater power over Kolya's populace. Publicly execute Lenc's son and be proclaimed a hero. No, she didn't want him thinking along those lines.

Mostly, Kesira felt an incredible lassitude settling over her. Too much had happened. Now she listened to crack-brained schemes that had no chance of succeeding. Without casting her rune sticks, she knew these plans would fail. Lenc might be demented due to the jade, but he hadn't lost his analytical powers. The demon had to know any meaningful resistance against him had to come when he proclaimed his regency over Kolya.

Crush all civil disobedience in plain view of the city, and he had achieved what he wanted most: power. Anyone who secretly considered rebellion would then forget it.

Kesira agreed on the need to raid the Steel Crescent's armory for weapons, but afterward? What must happen then? Only magicks could match Lenc's magicks. The burning white fire that was his sigil had to be dealt with, using—what?

She didn't know.

Chapter Nine

"WHAT IF their headquarters is protected by magic?" Kesira Minette asked. She crouched next to Protaro and Kene Zoheret. Both men peered at a map spread on the ground, corners held by small rocks. Zoheret held a sputtering torch overhead so that they might be able to interpret the map's wondrous information.

Kesira sighed. They had memorized this worthless map back at the Falling Leaf. Now they mistrusted their memories to the point they endangered the entire mission by lighting the torch and revealing their position, should any of Nehan-dir's patrols be close enough to wonder what cast such horrid illumination. If they couldn't mount a successful assault on a human-manned base, what would they face going against Lenc?

She preferred not to consider that horror at the moment.

"Do you sense magicks?" asked Zoheret, not looking up from the map. He and Protaro made arcane notations on the margins.

"I'm no witch, no sorcerer able to command vast spells and create a demon's magicks. Peering occasionally into the future with the rune sticks is the best I can do."

"You foresee disaster?" Zoheret quickly focused his full attention on her. Whatever he feared in the future, she had never seen it. In fact, she had never cast the rune sticks specifically aimed at finding out a modicum of Zoheret's future.

"No," she said, "but this is obviously a poor plan. You just walk up and knock? Is that it? You expect Nehan-dir to meekly offer you all the swords and spears you can carry off?"

"Nehan-dir is away patrolling the city," said Protaro. "His lieutenants are in disarray. Apparently, his second in command was killed in the foray this morning."

Kesira started to tell of Famii Bren-ko's death, then bit back the words. Protaro wouldn't believe her, and why should he? He didn't even believe she'd had anything to do with Howenthal, Eznofadil and Ayondela's deaths.

Kesira closed her eyes and turned all her training on devising a workable plan of attack. After all, she *had* been responsible for the death of three jade demons. Mounting a raid against the Steel Crescent's armory ought to be simpler than fighting her way across the Quaking Lands or enduring the agonies meted out by Ayondela's crystal clouds.

The more she considered their position, the more it seemed that the two men plotted with the sole purpose of losing their lives. Protaro she understood. He had been a captain in Kwasian's fabled guard and had failed to live up to his high office. The dishonor that went along with losing so ignominiously to Nehan-dir had to make him think in terms of death. But Zoheret was another matter. Was the man merely stupid? Protaro certainly played to that idiocy with this wild scheme for breaking into the Steel Crescent's headquarters.

"We number a full twenty," Zoheret said. "More than enough."

"Stick against sword. A good match," Kesira said sarcastically. She didn't try to keep the contempt from her voice. Even a handful of the Steel Crescent mercenaries ought to be able to repel any attempt to breach their walls.

The men continued to ignore her. Kesira moved away, reached over and pulled Zolkan from his perch on her shoulder. "Can you fly?" she asked.

"Poorly. Wings hurt."

"Go scout. Return with a count of the mercenaries inside the building."

"You don't want much, do you? It's not enough I am battered in your defense. Now you ask me to kill myself on *trilla* bird eaters' sword tips."

"It'd be an easier trip for Molimo," she said, "but you

seem to have lost him." Kesira baited Zolkan, but he ignored it. "Go. We need the information."

Zolkan protested with a wordless squawk, then launched into the air. The force of his takeoff staggered Kesira. She watched worriedly as Zolkan wobbled and dipped through the air separating them from the mercenaries. He hadn't been pretending when he claimed to be injured sorely.

Kesira waited. In less time than it takes to cross the square to the armory, Zolkan returned.

"Bad," he said. "Twelve inside. Two more with bow and arrow on roof. All alert. No sign of disarray. Need to make strong attack to overcome opposition."

"I was afraid of this." She smoothed Zolkan's head feathers and let him crawl back into the safety of her cowl. Kesira rushed back to talk with Protaro.

"Not now. We are almost ready for the attack."

"You'll go against a dozen inside, two sentries with bows and arrows on the roof. How do you plan to escape them?"

Protaro blinked. "We didn't know of those on the roof. How did you find out?"

If he'd thought on the matter for even a fraction of a second, he'd have known of Zolkan's abilities. That he didn't showed Kesira how suicidal this attack would become. Whether Protaro still reacted to his loss or had lost permanently any tactical ability he once possessed, she declined to say.

"You'll have to infiltrate, sneak up close and take out the rooftop patrol before continuing. If you don't, they'll fill you with arrows before you get halfway." Kesira took a long breath, then hunkered down by the crude map. "Here. Buildings. They'll shield you most of the way. The risk in crossing this space is great, but men dressed in dark clothing might blend with the shadows, if they don't hurry. Slow movement, coupled with vagrant breezes, might lull the bowmen into thinking they see nothing. Those reaching the base of the armory must climb here and here. With skill they can remove the bowmen and open the way for the rest."

"Might work," Protaro said.

"We have to use our original plan. It's too late to switch. We'll get confused!" Zoheret almost screamed in agitation.

"We'll do it her way," Protaro said, the snap of command in his voice. "Look. See? A careless sentry on the roof."

A dark outline occluded the stars, then slowly disappeared behind a low wall.

"Get me the men you claimed were hunters."

"We dare not change now. We have no time to change plans. Nehan-dir will return before we can—"

"Do it."

Kesira saw that Protaro wanted a decisive victory. No longer would he agree to anything Zoheret said. Now Protaro wanted the coppery smell of blood in his nostrils and the sweet taste of winning on his tongue.

The men arrived, received their new orders, then went on their way. Kesira peered out from her hiding place, straining to see in the shadows between the two buildings. To her, the rebels' progress was as obvious as if they'd banged gongs and shouted praises of the Emperor, but to the sentries they were virtually invisible. Kesira wished she knew the spell Molimo used to make him so hard to detect.

As the men reached the armory wall and began their painful ascent Kesira's thoughts strayed to Molimo. Where had he gone? Once in Kolya, the man had vanished. She hoped fervently that he restrained his shape changes. The other-beast hunters on the plains had been vicious; what would city crowds be like? She had visions of Kolyan citizens taking out their wrath on Molimo, skinning him alive, the wolf fur changing to human skin even as they stripped it from his body. She shuddered.

Molino had helped her escape Protaro when they were on the road, but where he had gone afterward remained a mystery. If only Zolkan weren't so close-beaked about what the pair of them did. Not for the first time, Kesira felt like an outsider. Molimo and Zolkan could communicate in ways she did not understand. A minute of the shrill singsongy words used by Zolkan conveyed more to Molimo than an hour's talking. And in some fashion beyond her ken, Molimo spoke to Zolkan without uttering a word.

But she loved Molimo, in spite of everything.

"One is at the top. Another... now the third!" whispered Protaro. "There—they attack."

The sounds of muffled combat drifted across the square. Kesira worried that those inside the armory had overheard, but the men of the Steel Crescent weren't straining to hear the smallest of sounds. They joked and argued boisterously, thinking themselves safely guarded by rooftop archers.

"Now," said Protaro, waving his arm. The small band made more noise than a Spring Fair celebration, but they reached the door to the Steel Crescent's headquarters without being filled with sharp-pointed arrows.

Zoheret knocked on the door, nervously shifting weight from one foot to the other. When one of the mercenaries opened the door a crack, Protaro smashed into Zoheret and sent the man reeling into the mercenary, who toppled; and the rabble burst into the main room.

Kesira hardly believed that the Steel Crescent's sentries could be surprised so easily. The fighting turned fierce, but only for a few minutes. Then Protaro grabbed a fallen sword and slashed and thrust like an invincible fighting machine. Half of Zoheret's rebels perished, but Protaro made sure all the Steel Crescent mercenaries died, steel ripping through their guts or across their throats.

Kesira walked through the carnage, placing her feet carefully. She finally stopped trying to keep from getting blood on her boots or robe. It had sprayed everywhere in the battle. She had seen so much killing, but it still sickened her. The Order of the Steel Crescent sought only what others had found in a patron. Guidance, a sure knowledge of their place and duty in society, occasional encouragement. That their original patron had been Tolek and that he'd exchanged his worshipers for a gambling debt was unfortunate. Since then the Steel Crescent's search for its place in society had been pathetic, but not truly evil in the way Lenc was. Kesira wished she could talk with Nehan-dir and see if they couldn't come to terms with the small mercenary's need for power.

If only Gelya hadn't died. If only Lenc hadn't killed off most of the demons.

Kesira smiled humorlessly. If only she had Zolkan's wings she could fly. She didn't, she never would, and she had to live with her own limitations. Kesira had worked to overcome her faults; but Nehan-dir had come to look on his as virtues.

"Such fertile fields for your philosophy, Gelya," Kesira said softly.

The nun took no part in the raid. The steel weapons sought by the others were prohibited by her dead patron, and with good reason, as she had learned. But a stout staff—not of the stonewood sacred to Gelya—leaned against the far wall. Kesira took it and poked through the debris, trying not to touch the cooling corpses on the floor.

"What do you seek?" Protaro asked.

"There must be some hint as to their purpose in coming to Kolya. They want the . . . baby." She hardly got the words out. Protaro's eyes showed no desire to fulfill that order to kill the child. Perhaps it was his earlier failure or maybe just a symptom of the Time of Chaos, but somehow Protaro had decided that he need no longer serve the Emperor as he once had. His duty had changed.

"You think there's more?"

"Lenc chose Kolya for some reason. It might be merely a desire not to confront the Emperor in his stronghold. Lenc could establish Kolya as his, then march on Limaden later."

"Forever is a long time," Protaro said. "With no opposition anywhere in the empire, Lenc might get bored. Leaving the Emperor's capital intact and heavily defended might give the accursed demon years of pleasure."

Kesira nodded. She'd considered this. Even though Lenc had forfeited his longevity for the power of the jade, he could still outlive any mortal now walking the empire's land. Forever was a long time, indeed.

"Look," she said, thrusting with the tip of the staff. The body of a woman who'd been sitting at a broad table toppled to the floor. Bloodsoaked papers littered the table. "Organizational plans. I'm not familiar enough with Kolya to know the locations."

"Lenc's new temple," Zoheret said, pointing. "There. That'll be the new center of Kolya where Lenc's temple is being constructed."

Kesira's quick eyes worked over the columns of numbers. "A date only six days hence."

"The work must be nearing completion," said Protaro. "These are troop placements. They have ordered in a full company and more to be scattered around the square. To keep the crowds in close, from the look of it. Many minor governors do the same when they make speeches. It wouldn't do having a bored populace wander off."

"Lenc wants all the populace present," mused Kesira. "He must be planning to appear on the steps of his new temple. Why else arrange such a show of force?"

"Lenc returns in six days." Protaro's eyes lit with excitement. "This is our chance. We can attack then. We have the weapons from this raid. We can recruit the soldiers we need before then. One swift, sure thrust, and Lenc dies!"

Kesira hardly believed Protaro deluded himself in such a fashion.

"The demon throws fireballs," she pointed out. "Any massive attack must deal with Lenc's magicks. None of us can even construct a defensive shield."

"Is that possible?" asked Zoheret.

Kesira started to tell of the mysterious force that had protected her, Zolkan and Molimo in Ayondela's palace, then stopped. Something in the way Zoheret asked the question kept the truth from her lips.

"I've heard stories—but they might have been rumors or tall tales meant to amuse the children on cold nights."

"We can't waste time searching for spells when no one can use them," said Protaro. "We must practice, plan, get every detail worked out. There's so little time. If we don't stop Lenc at what he considers the moment of his triumph, we may never be strong enough to fight him effectively."

Kesira left the room, the others hurriedly looting whatever else they could find. She walked into the night, colder than ever before. In her backpack the baby stirred.

Kolya bustled with activity as its citizens prepared for the ceremony, but Kesira Minette saw no gaiety. The people seemed grim. Children didn't play their usual games but listlessly sat and watched their elders, absorbing the gloom.

Commerce continued, but not with its usual boisterousness. Street vendors didn't seem to care if they sold their wares; merchants in stalls sat and stared into space, their vegetables spoiling from lack of attention; friends passing in the street hardly acknowledged each other.

And everywhere stood the mercenaries of the Steel Crescent. Nehan-dir had been recruiting heavily over the past week since the raid on his armory. The hirelings annoyed the citizens and occasionally killed one, just to keep in practice. Nobody objected openly. The muttering done behind closed doors amounted to little.

"The people are ready to rise in revolt to aid us," said Zoheret. He peered out the dirty window of the Falling Leaf. "Give them back the leadership that has been taken from them and they'll follow. This will be memorable, oh, yes, very memorable." He rubbed his hands together as if they were cold.

Kesira wondered at Zoheret's motivations in this. He seemed an unlikely sort to play the rebel. If he thought to supplant the Emperor in anyone's heart or mind, he knew very little of the empire and the bonds that held it together. No one blamed Emperor Kwasian for Lenc's victories. Whoever defeated Lenc might earn the Emperor's gratitude; but that mattered little to Kesira. It was merely her responsibility as a loyal servant.

Loyal servant? Hardly—not now that she'd openly flouted Kwasian's command to give the baby to Protaro. Kesira twisted about on the hard wooden bench and saw the soldier standing in the corner, eyes focused on distant memories. She had been responsible for his defeat. If she had obeyed the valid command and turned over the boy, Protaro wouldn't have followed her to Kolya and run afoul of the Steel Crescent. Still, she couldn't part with the boy. While he wasn't family in a blood sense, she considered him as precious as her own son.

If only the boy hadn't been born to a mortal mother, with Lenc his father.

"My scouts report that the Square of All Temples has been decorated according to Nehan-dir's order. Nehan-dir claims that Lenc will appear at sunset." Zoheret continued

The White Fire

to rub his hands together and peer outside, as if he might spot Lenc a few minutes earlier than anyone else.

Kesira checked the shadows marching slowly across the room: a few minutes past zenith. Almost six hours before Lenc would come to bless Kolya with his jade presence.

She rose silently and slipped out the back way. Even though Nehan-dir's hirelings patrolled constantly, Kesira had found a safe route through the streets. No handful of armed soldiers might hope to check all byways, especially those leading into treacherously turning dead ends where ambushers might lurk. Kesira walked quickly to the inn where she still maintained a room. As she entered the deserted public room, the innkeeper looked up. His smile at seeing her was genuine.

"You've come for a spot of ale?" he asked.

"I've come to ask a favor." She settled down at the table near him. "Will you look after the boy for me?"

The portly innkeeper nodded.

"I know it is a great deal to ask, but keeping him out of the crowds tonight is of great importance to me."

"You're going to see Lenc's arrival?" the innkeeper asked.

"I must. And that's why I don't want the boy hindering me. I . . . I fear Lenc might be able to sense the boy's presence. Here, you'll both be safe."

"Give him over to me now. There," the innkeeper said, holding the baby. Pale eyes stared up emotionlessly. "Such a big one he is now."

"He eats solid food." Kesira almost choked as she said it; her hand went to the spot on her breast where Wemilat had kissed her. The baby no longer suckled. Like Molimo, he grew older even as she watched. In a short week, the boy had taken a few hesitant steps. While he still preferred to be carried, Kesira thought he might be able to walk on his own. What changes would another week bring?

"We'll be fine here. I have no urge to see Lenc lord it over us. He seeks only our humiliation."

Kesira had nothing to say. The innkeeper was right. Lenc came only to show his true power. He had no reason to formalize his rule because everyone obeyed without question—or they died.

"I haven't cast the rune sticks," Kesira said. "I fear the outcome, yet one casting shows..." She looked at the innkeeper. It wouldn't do to burden him with the details of what she'd read. She would emerge victorious over Lenc; the rune sticks told her this. Kesira had pondered the question regarding Lenc's possible influence over the runes. While he might have sent her false visions in the past, this one carried the ring of truth.

She *would* defeat the jade demon, just as she'd vanquished the other three. But how? And when? Life might prove very long under Lenc's rule, waiting for the proper instant to destroy him.

"Keep him safe, and I'll return when I can. Perhaps by midnight." She bent down and lightly kissed the baby on the forehead. Pale gray eyes watched her, almost pityingly. She pushed such thoughts away. The baby couldn't know what lay ahead. Even the rune sticks remained clouded on that at times.

"Be...until you return," the innkeeper said. Kesira smiled. He had almost told her to "be careful," a whimsical order in this dangerous city.

Kesira ducked into a storefront doorway just in time to avoid a mounted Steel Crescent patrol. She bent double and hid behind a low row of baskets to keep Nehan-dir from spotting her. The small, scarred leader rode proudly at the head of the column, banner fluttering in the sluggish afternoon breeze. Kesira let the column turn and pass down a side street before she emerged.

While more than four hours still remained before Lenc's promised arrival, she found herself walking toward the Square of All Temples. A huge fountain in the center of the square had been torn out and paved over to make room for the throngs that would begin crowding in a few hours later. At one time the square had been the focal point for most of Kolya's orders. No longer. Most of the temples and altars to the other patrons had been razed; some remained as burned-out husks. Nor did Kesira see anybody venturing close to worship or even meditate.

She closed her eyes and sank down into her churning inner thoughts. Meditation brought relaxation, and with the relaxation the opportunity to consider what might happen here a few hours in the future.

Lenc had ordered the other temples destroyed. Only the one built of ugly black volcanic stone remained—Lenc's. She did not for an instant consider entering it. Sitting on the edge of the square was enough for the moment. Kesira saw nothing but trouble ahead, but she knew she would triumph. The rune sticks said so.

People passed through the square, not speaking, not joking, shooing away small children. It was as if this was a monument to war. Kesira sighed. In a way, it was. The war had been fought, and the losers were the patrons of the empty temples.

Those demons had already perished. Now it was time for the souls of every person in Kolya to die, also.

As the afternoon wore on, shadows grew long over the buildings. Gaslights popped on and cooking fires flared, only to be quickly extinguished when the Steel Crescent's mercenaries came through, rousting everyone they could find from their homes and crowding them into the streets. They herded the people like cattle toward the Square of All Temples.

Kesira sat and watched, grieving. She tried to find where Protaro and Zoheret would stage their attack, and failed. Somehow, the square didn't seem the same as the one on Zoheret's maps. What she'd thought to be the rebel assembly point lay too distant for the quick attack they had planned.

"All hearken!" came a crier's ringing voice. "All hearken, the mighty lord of all demons demands your presence. All hearken!"

Kesira levered herself to her feet using the staff. With back to a stone wall, she watched as the square became crowded, then overcrowded. People jammed together shoulder to shoulder. If anyone should faint for lack of air, it would be impossible to ever fall to the ground.

A cold, wintry wind blew through the assembly now, making Kesira even more aware of how Lenc had planned all this. The jade demon had left nothing to chance. His appearance would be dramatic, memorable.

The mercenaries blocked off the streets leading into the

square. Long minutes dragged by. The crowd began to mutter. Twilight turned into night, and the evening stars gleamed like twin beacons just above the horizon. Even more stars above popped into existence. Kesira began to wonder if Lenc had misjudged the crowd's acceptance.

He hadn't.

The clap of thunder drove the thousands huddled together to their knees. It was as if they had a single mind, a single body.

Kesira edged along the wall and dropped to her own knees to avoid unwanted attention.

Another thunderclap, then a bolt of lightning crashed into the hulk of a temple on the west side of the square. Fragments of stone rained down; nothing but a smoldering crater remained of the building that had once been consecrated to Toyaga. Another bolt: more destruction. The air filled with a garlic stench. The actinic glare of the lightning forced Kesira to squint and shield her eyes.

Then, silence so absolute she thought she'd lost her hearing.

She clutched her staff until her knuckles turned white. Even though she told herself Lenc was manipulating her emotions, she felt a surge of fear and anticipation. She stared at the black temple, the only one still intact.

The force of the words hurled her against the wall.

"People of Kolya," boomed the voice Kesira Minette knew and loathed. "From this day forward, you will worship only me.

"I am Lenc!"

Dazzling jade-green light bathed Lenc as he strode forward, arms raised.

"Worship me!"

Chapter Ten

LENC'S WORDS reverberated off walls and buildings, down streets, into alleys. Kesira almost fainted from the impact of his cry, "Worship me!"

A nimbus of green swirled around Lenc's head, bathing the planes of his face in a harsh jade light. Tiny bolts of lightning jumped from his arms and shoulders to the cloud, to be swallowed there by the miniature storm brewing.

"You are my subjects. You will worship me!"

The people kneeling closest to the bottom steps of Lenc's temple withered and died like autumn leaves caught by an early frost as the flesh burned off their bones. They screamed as they died.

The demon pointed and the next rank of people died also.

"You will cast aside all other patrons. No other demon will be allowed within the bounds of Kolya!" Lenc gestured.

Another group of people died.

"Any who insist on opposing me by continued belief in other patrons will receive no mercy."

"All praise mighty Lenc!" the cry went up. Kesira watched the Steel Crescent mercenaries raise their weapons high. They began to push through the crowd, shouting, inciting others to join in the calls of approbation for the new lord of Kolya.

Never had a demon meddled in mortal affairs to this extent. They might be petty, venal, malicious, but Kesira knew of none who ordered worship on pain of death.

Gelya had never wanted to be worshiped. He dispensed his wisdom because he was good. His goodness carried over into his order, and his disciples ventured forth to carry on other works needed in society. Kesira's dead patron had helped them define their places in society, then gave them the training and inspiration to fulfill the roles.

Lenc wanted only power. And anyone who refused his whim received only death.

Kesira craned her neck to try to find where Protaro and Zoheret were assembling their men. According to the battle map she had memorized, the rebels ought to be in sight now. She shifted and peered in the other direction. Coldness seized her belly and twisted, threatening to nauseate her.

"No!" Kesira tried to warn Protaro. "Don't attack from there!" But the crowd's roar swallowed her words. If the guard captain tried to rush directly down to where Lenc stood basking in the cheers from the captive crowd, Nehan-dir's men would slice the rebels to bloody ribbons. It was almost as if the mercenaries had deliberately opened a corridor for the rebels, to make the tube through which Zoheret and the others would run.

Kesira toyed with the idea of defectors in the Steel Crescent's rank. She pushed that aside when she saw Nehan-dir using the flat of his sword to drive back some of the crowd.

Nehan-dir had set up a trap—and Protaro was going to run headlong into it.

Kesira grabbed her cowl and shook hard. Zolkan protested, then tumbled heavily to the ground. The fall stunned the *trilla* bird, but he quickly recovered.

"Haven't I suffered enough at your hand?" the bird complained.

"Zolkan, be quiet. Listen carefully. The rebels are heading into a trap. Nehan-dir *wants* them to attack Lenc. See?" She grabbed the heavy bird and lifted him above the heads of the crowd around her, making sure he saw what she meant. "If they don't retreat immediately, Lenc will seize them all."

She tossed the bird into the air and yelled after him, "Stop Protaro!"

Green feathers flashed and vanished into the darkness just as Zoheret's voice carried clear and strong across the square.

"Death to traitors!"

Kesira stared in disbelief as she saw Protaro rushing

forward, sword in hand. He and several dozen rebels met no resistance as they dashed down the strip cleared for them. Only Kene Zoheret hung back, a strange exultation in his expression.

Kesira didn't have to read her rune sticks to know that Zoheret had betrayed the underground to Lenc.

The crush of the crowd prevented her from charging forward to aid Protaro in his futile attack on Lenc. She saw the captain reach the slagged lava steps and start up them. Lenc turned, an amused look on his hard jade face. The cloud whirling about the demon's ears took on more substance, flowed, formed an arrow. The green mist solidified and sailed straight for Protaro.

Kesira watched in horrified silence as the jade shaft impaled him. It moved in slow motion, entering his body an agonizing inch every dozen seconds. Protaro twitched and jerked, dropping his sword. Some acoustical quirk allowed Kesira to hear the metallic click-click-click as the fallen sword clattered down the temple steps.

No sound in the world could have drowned out Protaro's shriek of pain. At first Kesira thought the baby had been brought to the square and had begun crying. Then she realized it was Protaro. The jade shaft passed halfway through his body, then stopped. The soldier stood, trying to pull the misty arrow free and failing.

"See, loyal worshipers?" bellowed Lenc. "See how I punish those who dare offend me!"

Protaro's body levitated and spun in midair, the jade arrow still embedded in his chest. Poised above the spot where the old fountain had been, the man rotated slowly on the spoke of magic. Whatever spell held him had to be one of the greatest potency. His pain seemed to grow instant by instant—and death was denied Captain Protaro.

"He will live forever, a captive of jade," bragged Lenc. "See how he suffers. Know you that I can grant anyone within my hearing even worse agony if they oppose me."

Lenc spun, his stubby finger pointing to the edge of the crowd. "You. You are a Senior Brother in the Order of Toyaga. No more!"

A pillar of cold white fire enveloped the man. His screams

mingled with those Protaro still mouthed. Then the flame consumed him and black ash descended on the crowd. But the pillar of white fire still burned, turning the volcanic rock molten beneath it, yet giving off no steam, no heat. That white flame burned with the fury of a polar hell.

Kesira's ears shut out Protaro's cries for mercy; her eyes became blind to the mass of people. She saw only the dancing flames on the temple steps. Similar white fire had consumed Gelya's altar—and still desecrated the nunnery hidden away in the Yearn Mountains.

With a shout, Lenc gestured at the other rebels. Tiny bits of jade spewed forth from the demon's hands. Each shard flew directly for the left eye of a rebel. No matter how the men ducked, no matter how they tried to protect themselves, a splinter of jade buried itself in each brain. Those poor wights kicked and moaned in agony long after ordinary men would have ceased struggling. It took them long minutes to die.

"That is how I treat rebels," said Lenc. "And this is how I reward those loyal to me. Behold Kene Zoheret, the one who betrayed his friends." Lenc's tone carried extreme scorn for Zoheret, but the traitor seemed not to notice. Proudly, the man strode down the cleared corridor toward the temple. He fell face-forward and gave himself willingly to Lenc.

Kesira didn't know how any man could barter his soul so cheaply, yet Kene Zoheret had. She clenched her staff firmly in her hand and used it to beat her way through the milling crowd. She had not been with Protaro when he had begun his abortive attack, but she could bring Zoheret to some measure of the justice he deserved.

"Back," squawked Zolkan. "Lenc awaits you. Go back!"

Kesira hazarded a quick look above her head. Zolkan fluttered about like a crippled bug, green feathers raining down from body and wing. She impatiently motioned him away. Nothing seemed left to her but revenge on Zoheret for his betrayal.

Her order was dead. Lenc had consolidated his power in Kolya—and throughout the realm, except for Limaden. And nothing awaited her in Limaden save the Emperor's

The White Fire

wrath for disobeying his direct command to hand over the baby.

For a moment the thought of the boy slowed her, then she pushed it away. He no longer needed her. The innkeeper could find a foster home for him. She had finally decided the only mission worthy of her meager talent lay in killing Zoheret.

Gelya wouldn't have approved, but Gelya was dead, too.

Kesira got through the crowd, passing not a dozen paces from Nehan-dir. The leader of the Steel Crescent didn't see her in the sea of faces. She came close to the spot where Zoheret stood so proudly, relishing the attention he got from Lenc.

Kesira took her staff and swung it with all her might. Never had her aim been more precise, her arm so strong. The impact shattered the stout wooden staff, sending splinters flying. Shock numbed Kesira's hands and arms and drove her to her knees.

She blinked, expecting to see Zoheret's bloody, ruined head in front of her. Instead, he stood there, a startled expression in his face. A column of white fire had formed between the man and Kesira's staff. She had dashed her staff against the pale, dancing tongues of flame and not the traitor's skull.

"I wondered where the little nun was," mocked Lenc. "You joined the rebels, I see. A mistake. You have suckled my son. For that I owe you a debt of thanks."

Kesira stayed on her knees, too shaken to move or speak. Lenc fashioned another spear from the jade cloud encircling his head. The shaft hardened and then drove directly for her breast. She tried to scream, but the words jumbled in her throat. Only tiny trapped animal noises escaped.

"I will now repay that debt. I will *not* leave you as I have Captain Protaro." Lenc laughed at her. "Am I not the most generous patron who ever sullied his hands with you silly mortals?"

"Master, allow me to kill her!"

"Silence, worm," Lenc snapped at Zoheret. "Compared to her you are a nothing, a failure, a mistake of nature. Look upon her courage and learn—if you can."

"Wh-what are you going to do?" Kesira's voice firmed, but inside she was quaking.

"I shall continue doing as I please: toy with the Emperor. Lalasa provides another diversion, but she is too weak to give me much opposition or pleasure. Ruling the empire will give me another instant of delight. I will find others."

"What of me?"

"You, my little whore of Gelya? You shall be forced to watch my son mature and grow into my successor!"

Kesira used all her training and forced her way to her feet. Tottering, she advanced. The expression on Lenc's jade face spurred her on. He stared at her in complete amazement that she could do more than twitch. Kesira's fingers tensed in anticipation of closing on Lenc's throat. She had no idea if a demon could be strangled to death; since her hands were the only weapon left to her, she'd use them.

"You disobey my command!" Lenc roared. "For that you will die!"

The misty green spear formed once more from the clouds circling Lenc's head like a crown. But again the spear didn't find her body. She heard a strange clicking behind her.

Kesira gasped when a gray form flashed past her, intent on Lenc's throat.

"Molimo!" she cried. "Don't!"

The man-wolf's fangs snapped against Lenc's hard jade arm. Sparks of blue and white danced off into the night as Molimo swiveled and jerked about, trying to find a vulnerable spot on the demon's throat.

With a pass of his hand, Lenc tossed Molimo away. The wolf tumbled down the black lava steps and lay snarling at the bottom. Kesira saw eyes greener than the jade of Lenc's body fill with hatred. The shape change altered Molimo in so many ways she didn't dare think about it—but those eyes! They rivaled Lenc's in cruelty.

"Don't Molimo, please. You can't harm him."

"She's right, boy. I am invincible!" Lenc sent his fireball searing toward Molimo. To the demon's obvious surprise, the fireball exploded at the tip of the wolf's nose, leaving the sleek gray body unscathed. Molimo launched himself once more, attacking an exposed leg, pawing hard at a jade belly, seeking out the throat again.

Once more, Lenc used his magicks to toss the wolf away. They stared at each other like adversaries who knew each other. A curious expression crossed Lenc's face, then vanished.

"I ought to know you, wolf. You are so familiar."

Before Molimo tried another time to destroy the demon, Lenc erected a barrier of white flame between them. Molimo dodged, but column after column of cold, soul-burning flame rose to block his path.

"There, wolf, see how you enjoy my hospitality." Lenc clapped his hands. The circle of fire began to shrink, to move in on Molimo. The wolf howled piteously. Then the cries turned more human as Molimo transformed himself back into man form.

"You are a versatile one, other-beast. Cease your crying. I have a reward in store for you. For you and the nun."

Kesira paid little attention to the jade demon; she was staring openmouthed at the way Molimo cried out in a most human fashion."

"Your tongue," she said.

"'Row bath," Molimo said. It took Kesira an instant to realize he was trying to say, "Grow back."

Strong hands lifted her and hurried her forward. Kesira saw Nehan-dir's scarred face off to the right. He motioned to the soldiers of the Steel Crescent to put her inside the white fire circle with Molimo. As she passed through the barrier, Kesira thought she'd go mad with pain. Deep within her soul the burning refused to stop. It gnawed and ripped and ate until she wanted only to die.

The sensation passed as abruptly as it had begun. She clung to Molimo.

"How did you endure it?" she asked. "It felt as if every inch of my body, inside and out, had been roasted."

It affects me differently.

Kesira looked up sharply, knowing Molimo hadn't spoken. Deep in his black eyes burned tiny flecks of green. She saw the heavy worry lines, the aging, the burdens Molimo carried written on his once-youthful body. The Molimo she had first nursed back to health had been hardly past seventeen. This man had seen forty summers—more.

"What's happening to you? How is it you can speak?"

"No worrs," he said, slurring heavily.

"You don't want me to talk?" He nodded. Kesira obeyed, feeling secure in the circle of Molimo's strong arm as she turned to face Lenc. The jade demon continued to harangue from his position at the top of the lava steps.

"... all will worship in my temple once a week. Those failing to do so will *die!*"

To punctuate his command, Lenc fell silent and let the crowd listen to Protaro's unceasing misery.

"You might die," the demon continued, "or worse." He pointed needlessly to the spot where Protaro twisted slowly in midair, the magical spear turning him over and over to increase his agony.

What tore at Kesira the most was the lack of obvious physical damage done to Protaro. No blood dripped from the entry or exit points. No wound gaped. Only pain etched the man's face.

"You think you have thwarted me," Lenc said, directing his awful gaze at Kesira. "Try to hide my son from me. Try to destroy me. Try—and fail!"

Lenc signaled. The crowd split apart as mounted Steel Crescent mercenaries trotted forward. Immediately behind them stumbled the portly innkeeper, tightly clutching the baby. Tears rolled down the man's cheeks. Kesira knew he did not enter the square willingly. Lenc's coercion obviously tore at the man's heart.

"All behold! My son!"

As one, the crowd dropped to their faces. The closeness caused many to fall on top of others. Kesira wondered what Kolya—and the rest of the empire—would be like in a year. Ten? Lenc misused his power constantly; Kesira couldn't see the empire surviving past that. Lenc, in his boredom, would have killed off everyone by then.

"See how I punish those who oppose me."

"No!" Kesira strained forward. Molimo held her back. The innkeeper's entire body came awash in Lenc's white fire. The innkeeper sputtered and burned, producing a greasy black smoke that rose and found wintry upper air currents. The sickening stench of human flesh afire vanished mercifully as a result. But the sight of the man's imploring gesture, not blaming, turned Kesira dead inside.

Was life to come to this? A slave for a demon and nothing more? That wasn't what Gelya taught. And what of the rune sticks? They'd told her she would triumph over Lenc. Kesira saw no way to destroy the demon from the interior of this magical prison.

"My son," cooed Lenc, holding the baby awkwardly. Even in her present straits, Kesira marveled at how the baby had grown. She had left him only a few hours earlier, and already he was toddler size. Guiltily, she looked up at Molimo. His lined face showed the same aging. Whether this rapid growth was the product of the unleashed jade or something more, Kesira couldn't say. It affected those around her in ways she didn't like.

She wondered if she was as young, and young appearing, as she had been.

"Worrs come," Molimo said. She had to agree. There had to be even worse times ahead. The only bright spot Kesira saw lay in Zolkan's continued freedom. The *trilla* bird had tried to alert her to the trap, then had taken to wing. Where he might be, she didn't know, but as long as he had escaped Lenc's wrath, Kesira would rest easier.

"You will worship my son as you do me!" roared Lenc. The ripple passed through the crowd. They rose up, then flung themselves prone once more in abject obeisance.

"Take these two away. To my *special* prison." Lenc spun and stormed back into his dark temple. As he went, he made casting motions. Everywhere he pointed, tiny white fire sputtered and grew to a soul-burning foot-thick column. Lenc vanished within the temple, and a huge sigh of relief rose from the crowd.

For the moment, their ordeal was over.

Nehan-dir trotted up next to the pen where Molimo and Kesira stood. He saluted his departed demon patron.

"Take them to the prison," Nehan-dir ordered.

A full score of mounted soldiers came forward, lances lowered. Kesira again felt the tearing fear and pain as they forced her through the barrier of white fire. Molimo came through more stoically, but even though he did not cry out, he sagged to his knees. Kesira had to help him to his feet.

Like animals they were herded through the streets of Kolya.

Kesira felt rather than saw the citizens watching from behind closed shutters and partially opened doors. She didn't blame them for not attempting a rescue. They had just witnessed Lenc's wrath. Not to want to draw it down on their families by a precipitous act like rescuing failed rebels seemed only right to the nun.

She still wished someone would have tried.

The lancers forced them into a cold stone building sitting in the center of a large field. On the grounds camped hundreds of Steel Crescent mercenaries who all curiously watched as Nehan-dir rushed Kesira and Molimo to the building.

"This isn't the same building you used before," she said.

"Lenc demolished the other, on my suggestion. It doesn't pay to allow reminders of failure to exist." He stared down at her. "In a way, I am sorry you will die. You've shown extreme bravery. No sense, but bravery. For that I salute you."

"There's still a chance," she began. Molimo's grip on her arm bruised her flesh. She subsided. Kesira had thought to sway Nehan-dir, but she knew how impossible that was. The man sought and had finally found his position in society. That it meant the destruction of her society was secondary to the Order of the Steel Crescent.

"Inside," Nehan-dir ordered.

They entered the low stone building, then spiraled down ramp after ramp into the bowels of the planet. Kesira lost track of how far they went, but she guessed it had to be a hundred feet or more. Escape from this prison would be impossible if they had to fight their way back to the surface.

It was impossible on all scores when she saw the prison-cell doors. They burned with bright green light similar to that encircling Lenc's head. He held his prisoners securely with magic, as well as with force of arms.

Nehan-dir held the door. Both Molimo and Kesira entered. The iron clang as Nehan-dir closed the door might have been a judge dealing out an execution order.

"Molimo," she began. He pulled away and sank to the cold, rocky floor, head on curled-up knees.

Kesira shared his despair. She dropped into another corner of the cell and stared at the green glow barring their exit without really seeing it. Gelya had taught that defeat was nothing but a new lesson to be learned, that the defeated might emerge stronger and wiser.

Kesira felt no wiser.

Her mind tumbled and roiled about until one snippet from what Lalasa had said came to her: Merrisen lived. Had the Emperor's demon meant that literally or figuratively, in the same way that Gelya still lived because he and his teachings had not been forgotten?

"Merrisen," she said softly. "If you live, hearken to my words. The world cannot long endure Lenc. We need your strength, your wisdom. You, who are called the greatest of demons, aid us!"

Merrisen didn't respond. Kesira soon fell into a troubled sleep populated by leering demons and Lenc's cruel tortures.

Chapter Eleven

KESIRA MINETTE cast her thoughts back through the years, to her parents dying at the hands of brigands, to Sister Fenelia and Sister Dana and Kai and Dominie Tredlo and her years in the nunnery. Bad times, but good ones, also. Kesira refined verse after verse of her death song, honing it, making it lyrically say the exact things she desired. Without doubt, she would die soon.

Kesira touched the box containing her rune sticks. The casting showing her unconditionally triumphant over Lenc had been a lie. Perhaps Lenc had sent the vision so that her defeat would be even more intense. She thought any cruelty possible for the demon. He had used his friends and seduced them into the awful power of the jade so that they would do chores he shied away from.

Ayondela, most of all, had been lured to evil by her need for vengeance. Kesira sighed at the sad memory of the female demon. All Ayondela had wanted was revenge for the death of her half-demon, half-human son.

Kesira had watched Molimo rip out the throat of Ayondela's son and had been unable to prevent it. Cold-numbed fingers touched the warmth of Wemilat's kiss on her breast. Through the death of Ayondela's son, Wemilat had been freed; he had subsequently given his life to slay Howenthal. But Ayondela saw only the fact of her mortal son's death.

Kesira had come far to have her life end in a small prison cell a hundred feet below the surface. Humming her death song to herself, she repeatedly went over every lyric, every word. When the verses satisfied her, she wrote a new verse dealing with all that had occurred in Kolya.

The saddest lines were those relating Protaro's fate.

"Molimo?" she called out softly. "Are you awake?"

"Wake," he mumbled.

"Tell me how your tongue regenerated. I've never heard of anyone growing a new one. This is as fantastic as sprouting a new arm or leg." While Kesira was interested, she sought only to pass the time.

In the dank, windowless cell time had ceased to have meaning. The only illumination came from the green-glowing doorway that Kesira could barely force herself to look at. It reminded her too much of Lenc and how the demon now held the baby she had carried for so long.

"Magic. Demon magic."

"Which demon? Lalasa?" Molimo nodded. "I met with Lalasa," Kesira said, almost dreamily. "She came to me while I hid at the inn. She wanted the baby killed, too. She was the one who had suggested this to Emperor Kwasian. I refused her this, but she must have strong principles if she helped you with your tongue."

"Good demon. But die soon," Molimo said.

"What? Why?" Kesira sagged. "Oh, you mean Lenc will kill her soon. I suppose so. A shame. I liked her, even if she was a demon."

"You haf strong powers." Molimo obviously strained to form the unfamiliar words. As he did so, Kesira watched the man age. White streaks shot through his ebony hair and turned him even older. While Kesira saw no hint of physical weakening, it had to come soon. Molimo would die of old age soon, very soon.

"Are you this way because of the jade?" she asked. Molimo nodded. She had seen the way Ayondela's jade palace had affected him. The man had turned infirm and required help to retreat down the road away from the jade. Not for the first time, Kesira wondered that she wasn't similarly affected. The more she thought about it, the more puzzling it became. No human she had seen reacted only to the jade.

"You spoke to me in the square, but not with words. How did you do that?"

At times, it is easier, came the thought inside her skull.

"You've spoken to me this way before. I caught only

fragments then. But now I can understand more, perhaps all."

Some, Molimo corrected.

"Is this how you 'talked' to Zolkan?"

"Yisss," Molimo said. "Zolkan speech birdlike, mine in head."

"Don't tire yourself. Why not speak inside my head all the time? I...I like it." Kesira found herself saying this almost shyly, as if such admission had to be perverted. The intimacy it gave, fleetingly, aroused her in many ways. Molimo had stayed distant from her because of his otherbeast affliction, but Kesira found herself wishing for more from the man.

Much more.

"Tiring. Har-hard talk this way."

Kesira settled back. Talking with Molimo helped her pass the time, and kept her mind off their predicament. She didn't want to consider how long it would be before Lenc decided on their fate. Since he could have left her spinning in the square as he had done to Protaro, she decided the demon had something more in store for her. Something even worse than the magical impalement.

"Why does jade give such power to the demons?" she asked, almost to herself rather than to Molimo.

Vibration enhancement, came the thought. *Jade increases vitality of a demon, even as it robs life. Insidious.*

Kesira rose and stood facing the barrier. Reaching out, she brushed her fingertips along the periphery of the green glow. She bit back her cry as agony arrowed up her arm and into her shoulder. The lightest touch had set off more pain than she could endure.

"Not like the cell we occupied in the Quaking Lands, is it?" she asked. "There I managed to—well, I don't know what I did. I managed to hold the magicks at bay long enough for you to slip through. Should I try it again?"

Molimo shook his head.

"I thought not. This spell *feels* different. More deadly." The woman walked back and forth until she realized she was acting like an animal in a cage. Then the nun settled back down on the floor, concentrating on escape.

"What bothers me the most," she said, "is Kene Zoheret. You don't know him—he's the one Lenc rewarded with whatever it was. I never thought he'd betray us all to Lenc the way he did."

Zoheret is Lenc's high priest now, Molimo supplied.

"Zoheret prospers, we die. The man only sought to unite opposition to Lenc so that he could remove it all with one quick cut." Kesira snorted in derision. "And we believed him. There's probably not a single man or woman in Kolya willing to oppose Lenc now. Even if there are, they'd be hesitant about revealing their intentions to anyone else for fear of betrayal."

Lenc comes.

Kesira sat up straight. She heard nothing, but began to sense what Molimo already had: a tension building in the air, making her edgy. When the flickering green barrier winked out of existence, she had no chance to rush out of the cell. Lenc's huge green form barred her exit.

"Stay on your knees, slime," Lenc roared. Kesira winced but tried not to make any show of her raging fear. "You have angered me, but I am merciful."

"You are a tyrant. Insane and a tyrant," Kesira said without rancor. She was too exhausted to work up a good hate toward Lenc.

"A lesser demon might have slain you out of hand for such words. Not I. Rather, I intend that you will live for some time. For exactly a year and a day."

"Why so long? You don't give me the chance to prepare my death song."

Lenc laughed. Kesira tried to told back the involuntary shudder and failed. Against such power she was little more than a pawn. Lenc could do with her as he pleased.

"It will take you that long to die. Slowly, a bit more each day, you will suffer. That much more of your life force will vanish. Pain will haunt you. All hope will flee. You will beg for death—but I will not grant it."

"What have you done with the boy?"

"My son? You ask after my son when your life is being bartered away?"

"I barter nothing. You can kill me whenever you choose.

The White Fire

I cannot stop that. But I will never beg you for my life. Nothing you do can demean me."

"Oh?"

Kesira rolled on the floor, screaming, whining, choking to keep from pleading for mercy. As suddenly as the pain began, it stopped.

Trembling, she pulled herself to her feet; managed to remain upright by leaning against one wall. "Do it a thousand times and I will still not give you the satisfaction of breaking my spirit."

"You make this claim today. There will be a full year more. Of this, and *this,* and even *this!*"

Kesira lost consciousness from the brutalities Lenc heaped upon her. Somewhere in the muzzy fog swirling through her brain she heard Molimo calling to her. She struggled for that sound, the tiny point of light that his voice promised.

"Passed out, didn't I?" she asked. He cradled her head in his lap. He nodded. "The pain was almost more than I could bear. I . . . I don't know if I can endure a full year of this. Lenc will get more and more diabolical as the days go by." Again Molimo agreed.

She tried to push herself into a sitting position, but Molimo held her down. Kesira decided she liked it.

We must escape now. No more hesitation. Within you is the power. We can break through the barrier.

Kesira studied the glowing mist where the door was. She had no idea how to penetrate that jade fog. Even with another piece of jade.

This time she sat bolt upright, her hand going to the jade tusk tucked away in the folds of her robe. She ran clumsy fingers along the tooth that had once belonged to Ayondela.

"This way?" she asked.

"Yesss," Molimo said. "Cannot touch it. You can. Use it. Must escape soon or Lenc will wear us down."

"He didn't torture you, did he?"

"Lenc unsure of me. He knows I have been touched by the jade but doesn't know how."

"Can you use this?" She held out the tusk for Molimo to take. He recoiled.

"No! I would perish if I tried. You must. The jade gave

me other-beast change, took away power. I regain my strength slowly, but the cost is dear."

Kesira saw the lined, aging face and knew the cost. Molimo had grown old in the span of a few months. He would be dead from infirmity within another few months. The touch of the jade had done this to him.

For Molimo, death would come relatively soon. For the rest of the world, Lenc's cruelty might linger for decades as he destroyed the very fabric of society.

"Why didn't Lenc sense this jade?" she said, taking the tusk firmly in her hand and holding it like a short dagger.

He is too far into the mind-warping power of the jade to sense other fragments. This piece is too minute. Use it!

Kesira approached the curtain of shimmery magicks and tentatively thrust out the jade tusk. She jerked away when the brilliance flared at the tip of the tusk. Nothing had happened. Bolder, she again thrust with the tusk. As if she had pulled the plug from a drain, the tusk sucked in the power of the barrier.

"Molimo, hurry. Get through the door. I don't know how long this will last." Kesira watched in fascination as green mist flowed *into* the tusk. She shivered and knew that the tooth alone did not perform this miracle. Something within her commanded the tusk to rob the barrier of its energy. Kesira tried to isolate that portion of herself and failed. Too many responses had become instinctual with her. The teachings of Gelya had been drilled into her over a lifetime. Now she responded without knowing how.

Molimo pushed past her, went to the iron door. Weakly he banged against this physical barricade. Kesira's heart crept up until she thought it had lodged firmly in her throat; she feared Lenc had barred the door as well as placed this spell upon it.

Molimo shoved the door open, using his weight more than his strength, then tumbled out into the corridor and fell heavily to the rocky floor.

Carefully Kesira held the tusk stationary while she moved around and got out of the cell. With incredible caution, she pulled the tusk out of the green mist. The barrier snapped back into place with a blinding surge that left her eyes watering and seeing blue and yellow dancing spots.

"We're out!" she exulted.

"Still underground," Molimo said.

"You're worse than Zolkan. Always looking at the bleak side. Now I know why you two get along so well."

But Kesira's enthusiasm died when she realized that Molimo spoke the truth. To regain their freedom, they'd have to fight their way up the spiral ramp—and they dared not set off any alarm. Hundreds of Steel Crescent mercenaries were camped overhead.

"We may not make it, but we can try—and we can make certain that a few of them won't live to aid Lenc."

Almost crawling, Molimo began the ascent. Kesira followed warily, fearing detection with every step. She tried to help Molimo, but the man shook off her assistance.

Need to concentrate. Need to locate him.

"Him? Who? Lenc?"

The answer became obvious a few minutes later when the powerful flapping of wings sent currents of air down against Kesira's face. The nun looked up, ready to fight, until she recognized Zolkan.

"Pretty sight," grumbled the *trilla* bird. "Hurry now. You can still reach fifth level."

"What's there?"

Both Zolkan and Molimo said as one, "Zoheret."

It took Kesira a few seconds to realize what they meant. Escape to the surface wasn't possible, but wreaking vengeance on the traitor might be.

"He has personal office on fifth level," Zolkan said. "Not well guarded. Lenc dislikes traitors as much as any human. Doesn't trust Zoheret."

"He'll die by my hand," Kesira said, thrusting the jade tusk into her tattered yellow sash. She unfastened the knotted blue cord that told of her selfless devotion to Gelya. It seemed fitting that this would be the instrument for Zoheret's death. The symbol of faith used against the faithless.

"Quiet," said Zolkan. "Guards on next level. Sentries everywhere. Nehan-dir takes no chances."

"We can get up to Zoheret's level," Molimo managed to say. "Must escape, though. Must stop Lenc."

Kesira focused all her attention on the one task: killing Kene Zoheret. The man's treachery had removed any chance for effective resistance to Lenc in Kolya. That alone made him a target for her wrath—but it went deeper. Zoheret had violated the precepts of society, had betrayed all Kesira held as dear by embracing Lenc and the ways of the jade.

She and Molimo started up the spiral ramp, only to halt when the scrape of boots sounded above them. Pressing themselves flat against the wall did little to hide them. Anyone who looked over the railing would spy them instantly. Realizing this, Kesira continued her climb, forcing tired legs into action. Molimo followed at a slower pace, obviously worn from his exertions.

"Sentry, take me to Nehan-dir," she called out when she came within a few feet of the guard. The man turned, started to salute and then saw who commanded him.

Caught midway between salute and sword hilt, the guard couldn't effectively stop Kesira's short, hard punch to his throat. He staggered back, gagging. Zolkan fluttered down and fastened hard talons into the man's jugular. In less than a minute the guard lay dead.

Kesira started to pick up the dead man's sword, then hesitated. She still carried Ayondela's tusk. That seemed a more potent weapon, and didn't violate Gelya's edict against steel. Molimo scooped up the sword and pulled it free, checking its razor edge. He smiled wickedly.

"Better. My strength returns, but too slowly. This helps." He made a few whirling cuts through the air.

"More guards come. Hurry, hurry!" squawked Zolkan.

The *trilla* bird's warning alerted the sentries. Four rushed forward while a fifth held back. Brawny arms grabbed Kesira, intent on flinging her to the floor. She twisted, found her center and upended the Steel Crescent mercenary, sending him over her hip. He crashed to the floor and lay there, the wind knocked out of his lungs. Kesira could see the crescent scar on his chest where the man had accepted his order's cruel sigil. Kesira used it as a target for the jade tusk.

The White Fire

The mercenary twitched once, then died.

And Kesira found herself knocked away by the flat of another's sword. Had it not been for Zolkan's claws closing on the tall, stringy-haired woman's sword wrist, the blade would have sliced through Kesira's hamstrings.

"Fight!" bellowed Zolkan. "Can't do it all by myself!"

Kesira needed no such urging. She regained her balance and swung around, inside the sword's arc. She closed with the woman and hammered a hard fist into an exposed temple. The mercenary jerked away, stunned. Kesira and Zolkan both followed quickly with kicks and raking talons until the woman lay dead on the floor. Panting, Kesira bent double to regain her breath.

"Two dead," Molimo said.

Then, inside her head, she heard Molimo tell her, *Another escaped. We have only a few minutes before all of Nehandir's order floods into these levels. Do we try to flee or do we seek out Zoheret?*

For Kesira there was no question.

"Zoheret!"

Up two more levels, they ran. Zolkan wobbled in midair and indicated a side passageway leading away from the spiral ramp. "He is down there."

Even as the *trilla* bird said the words, Kene Zoheret appeared, rubbing sleep from his eyes and mumbling to himself.

"What's going on?" he demanded, irritable at having been awakened by the noise of combat. Zoheret's eyes grew wider when he saw Kesira and Molimo. For an instant he seemed frozen to the spot, then he turned and bolted back into the room.

Zolkan prevented the traitor from barring the door behind him. Then Molimo's powerful kick sent the heavy iron door slamming open against the wall.

"Wait, I can explain all this. It . . . it's a trick. I'm finding out what I can about Lenc to use that knowledge against him."

"You betrayed your comrades. You told Lenc where to find the baby. You are responsible for Protaro's fate, the death of the innkeeper, the subjugation of all Kolya. Worst of all, you have not lived up to your responsibilities as citizen of the empire. You have failed your city and your Emperor."

Zoheret spun to the side and pulled forth a short sword. Molimo started to engage him, but Kesira's grip on his upper arm stayed him. His dark eyes, now flecked with green, bored hard into her brown ones. No longer were Kesira's eyes softer. She had purpose. Zoheret had betrayed much of what she had struggled for over the past months since the reign of jade terror had begun.

Zoheret was solely responsible for Lenc's regaining his son.

Molimo stepped to one side.

This action, more than anything else, drained the color from Zoheret's face. He looked at the small nun in the tattered robe and read his death in her eyes.

"Give yourselves up," Zoheret said, his voice cracking with strain. "You can't hope to escape. The alarm's been sounded."

Kesira moved with deliberate steps toward the traitor. Zoheret lifted his sword, then made a clumsy lunge. Kesira let it go past, between her arm and body, then trapped it and lifted. She caught Zoheret's elbow in a lock that raised him to his toes and forced him to drop the sword.

"You'll break my arm. Stop! I submit!"

With a deft twist, Kesira released the arm and stepped behind Zoheret. The knotted blue cord around her waist came free. She whipped it into a quick loop and dropped it around Zoheret's neck. For a brief instant, Kesira thought he might have thwarted her. He succeeded in getting two fingers of his left hand between cord and throat.

She jerked hard on the cord; the action severed Zoheret's fingers. The doomed man let out a tiny cry, then sagged as the knotted cord cut deeper into his flesh, shutting off air and blood. His tongue protruded and swelled and his eyes bulged.

He is dead, Molimo communicated. Kesira hung onto the cord grimly. *Release him. You can do no more.*

Only when Zolkan landed on her shoulder and nipped at her cheek did she let Zoheret's body fall to the floor.

"It doesn't regain the baby, does it?" she said, staring at the corpse. "Gelya had always said that revenge is thought sweet by fools." She released the cord and refastened it around her waist. "I'm not so sure."

"He deserved his fate," Zolkan said. "But we must hurry, or share it."

Molimo stood silently by the door, listening intently. Kesira heard nothing, but as she went into the corridor she saw the rush of guards down the spiral ramp. Ducking back out of sight, she waited.

"They have gone back to level where we killed other guards," said Molimo. "Let's go before they return."

Kesira hardly believed their good luck. Foolishly, the Steel Crescent mercenaries had all hastened down to where their comrades had been killed. She started up the ramp, and knew instantly that escape was not possible.

Lenc stood in front of her, mighty arms crossed on his bare chest. The jade demon's tiny nimbus flickered and crackled with lighting. If the demon's looming presence hadn't blocked their path, the bolts of lightning blasting from the cloud would have.

Kesira turned to retreat, only to find that the mercenaries had already started back up. She and Molimo were trapped between a score of armed guards and their patron.

Even worse than the sinking sensation of failure was Lenc's mocking laughter.

Chapter Twelve

LENC'S LAUGHTER first robbed Kesira of courage, then filled her with the need to confront the demon. He stood so complacent, so assured, so all-powerful, that she wanted to scream.

"You allowed me to kill Zoheret," she accused.

"Of course I did, little one," Lenc said. When he smiled, he revealed twin rows of jade-green teeth. Kesira fingered the jade tusk hidden in her robe and discarded the notion of using it. The time would come for an attack on Lenc. But not at this instant.

"You grow bored already?"

Don't goad him, came Molimo's thought. The man appeared to have aged another ten years. White streaks ran through his once black hair, turning him into one of advanced middle age. Kesira would have guessed him to be fifty if she hadn't known otherwise. *He is dangerous. To you, to me, to the world.*

Kesira smiled wanly to reassure Molimo that she knew the full extent of the danger in dealing with the demon. His capriciousness walked hand in hand with insanity caused by the jade. While Kesira had not known Lenc before he'd partaken of the awful green magic, she guessed that he hadn't changed—he'd just acquired more power. Now he could do as he pleased with no one to check him.

"What a burden it is, being so powerful. Is there nothing else but death and wanton destruction to keep you occupied?"

"Perhaps... when I tire of seeing insects such as you killing other insects." Lenc gestured, and a fireball raced from his fingertips. White flame burned through the rock walls and exposed the chamber where Kene Zoheret lay. Already the corpse provided a feast for scavenger beetles. "Fascinating, the way they clip and saw their way through flesh, don't you agree?"

Lenc clapped his hands. The ringing sound reminded Kesira more of stone against stone than flesh on flesh.

"You are becoming a statue," she said. "The jade is transforming you."

"It alters my flesh. A minor price to pay for the power I get."

"All your functions now depend on the jade," she guessed. "Do you enjoy another's gentle caress? Can you even feel it?"

Take care, came Molimo's warning. *This is dangerous ground. He is insane.*

Lenc laughed. "What are those to me? I enjoy the sensation of complete power. Mere animal functions are secondary now. I transcend such concerns."

"And what are your concerns?" she demanded. Kesira glanced back toward the Steel Crescent soldiers. They stood fingering their sword hilts, ready to attack the instant their patron ordered it. Kesira wondered how far she could goad Lenc before he ordered that—or if it was possible to go that far under any circumstances. He obviously enjoyed keeping her captive—for the amusement value, if nothing else.

"You transcend such functions? Yet you are the worst predator in all of the empire."

"All the world," the demon corrected with some gusto. "I take pride in this accomplishment. My fellow demons proved too cowardly to take the step to greatness. I shall be remembered for all time. Every human who ever walks the face of the planet, from this day forward, will quake at the mere mention of my name. No one will ever forget me." Lenc's laugh shook the foundations of the prison around them.

"Why is it so important to be cruel? Use your power for good!"

The jade perverts him. Stop this!

Kesira shook her head, not bothering to look at Molimo. Her brown eyes fixed on Lenc.

"Good, evil—what are those but meaningless noises," scoffed Lenc. "I do as I see fit. There is nothing evil or good in that—it is merely my will."

Before Kesira could answer, Lenc thrust out his hands and then spread them slowly in front of his ponderous body. For a moment the woman thought Lenc had turned entirely to jade and had started to topple, but it proved only an illusion caused by the rippling air around him. The magicks he commanded confused her senses and brought home exactly how powerful the jade demon was.

"Witness!" he cried.

Kesira no longer stood on the spiral ramp. She floated a thousand feet above the ground. The brief instant of vertigo passed. This was similar to the illusory tricks Lalasa had shown her when the female demon had spirited her to the Plains of Roggen and the defeat of Emperor Kwasian's most valiant general.

"How like bugs they are. Less than the beetles feasting on Zoheret's flesh," said Lenc. "Look at them and tell me you can't feel the same contempt for them I do."

Kesira swallowed hard. She saw what it meant for Lenc to be in absolute control of the empire. Outside of Limaden, in plain view of Emperor Kwasian and those huddled fearfully within the capital, Lenc had ordered thousands of men and women to begin construction of a towering monument—to the jade demon. The gleaming sides had been covered with sheets of jade, and the lofty central spire rose up to impudently challenge the sun for supremacy. Even as Kesira watched, hundreds died from their exertions.

"You haven't fed them!" she cried. "They need water, food, rest. Why do you drive them like this?"

"Insects deserve nothing more. When they have finished this tribute, perhaps then I shall allow them respite. Or perhaps I will require them to build a second monument, one even larger and grander."

"To what purpose? You kill them for no reason!"

"For every good purpose. I *desire* the monument. It pleases me. What else ought there to be? I have the power. I must use it. Otherwise it is pointless for me to have risked all to obtain it."

"You mock Emperor Kwasian with this monument."

"He can't do anything to prevent it from being built. Yes, it is a thorn in his side. That also amuses me."

"There's more," Kesira said, suddenly suspicious. Lenc shifted her in the air, causing cold winter winds to bite into her flesh and rob her of breath.

"There's more," Lenc confirmed. "Lalasa still opposes me. I will draw her into battle with this outrage. I can then enjoy the exquisite feel of slaying her as I have so many other demons."

Kesira said nothing. While Lalasa had hardly proven herself a worthy ally, Kesira bore the demon no malice. What she witnessed, what Lenc showed her so gleefully, was nothing less than genocide. Lenc had killed off most of his own kind, singly and in small groups, ever since the jade demons had fought for ascendancy. Now that Kesira had helped destroy Ayondela and his two other cohorts, Lenc sought to be the sole demonic survivor.

"She'll be lured out soon," Lenc predicted. "If I destroy enough of her precious pets, she will come to oppose me. Then I'll slay her as I have all the others!"

"Why show me? What am I to you? You claim to be all-powerful. Why try to impress me with your brutality?" Kesira's anger mounted with every passing instant. The workers on this pointless monument tumbled and fell to their deaths even as she watched. To Lenc this was nothing more than an experiment in torture.

Torture. Kesira's mind seized upon that. He had shown her everything to evoke this very response. He wanted her angry, confused, aroused at the indignity and horror. The demon fed on this. The more emotion he stirred within her breast, the headier his experience.

"You are different," Lenc said unexpectedly. "Somehow you managed to nurture my son. No other human female could have done that, save the weak thing I chose as Dymek's mother."

"Dymek? You call the boy this?"

"A strong name for one who will succeed me."

"You know the jade destroys you, and yet you continue to embrace it?"

"I'll last a thousand years, a million! To you that is inconceivable, but I must plan ahead. After that million years when I am no more, Dymek will reign in my place. The dynasty I establish will rule through all eternity."

"The jade kills you daily. You won't even live a hundred years." Even to Kesira her words sounded spiteful and petty.

Lenc was amused. "Ha! Look. Lalasa can take no more. She agrees to do battle with me. You deserve to see her fate."

Kesira had the sinking feeling that Lalasa might have been right. Perhaps the baby Dymek — the name tasted bitter on her tongue — ought to have been killed. The nun knew it might be considered weakness on her part that she couldn't do such a foul deed, but Gelya's teachings did not permit it under any circumstances. Dymek had not proven himself evil. The infant hadn't partaken of the jade and become a menace to demon and human alike.

What he might become depended more on the upbringing his father gave than on what he was at this instant.

Kesira whirled downward so fast she screwed shut her eyes in fear. The cessation of the fall caused her to peer out fearfully. She had alighted with the softness of a floating feather. A dozen paces away stood Lenc, green skin gleaming in the sunlight. The perpetual storm cloud above his head crackled and boomed with lighting, making him into a miniature mountain peak. Lalasa had appeared and stood nearby.

"The monument is pointless, Lenc," Lalasa said. The homely female demon appeared drawn, haggard. She shuffled forward and pointed accusingly at the jade demon. "Your soul will wither for this offense."

"I have no soul but the jade," snapped Lenc. "And what do *you* care for these pitiful humans? Weren't you the one who advised Kwasian and his generals in their battles against the barbarians? You oversaw the deaths of hundreds of thousands over the span of twenty years. Compared to your record for destruction, I am a piker."

"Count them as insignificant if you will," said Lalasa, "but they have not wiped out most of their own kind."

"No thanks to you."

"Sometimes it is necessary to prune a branch so that the tree may live—however distasteful the action. What *you* have done is destroy the whole tree. How many demons remain? How many, Lenc?"

"Only those I have permitted to live. Baram muddles about, roaring his unintelligible nothings against mountains and listening to the echoes. Tolek cowers on a distant island. You remain, darling Lalasa."

Lalasa frowned. "Noissa? What of him?"

Lenc laughed. "I killed him as he lay with his human slut. No demon ought to couple with lower life forms."

"As you did with the peasant woman?"

Kesira saw that Lalasa's swift retort stung. Lenc roared in anger. "Who among the demons would have me? You and those like you forced me into that perversion. Now suffer my vengeance for making me an outcast among my own kind!" Insanity flared and caused the small lightnings to sing and crackle in the cloud above the demon's head.

Kesira settled her emotions and began going over her death song, line by line. She doubted it would be much longer before she composed the final verse.

"My powers are no match for yours. Even when there were many of us to oppose you, there could be no real contest between us, Lenc."

"Yes, darling Lalasa, roll over, play dead. Let me have my way with you."

"Never! I know where my duty lies. You shall never . . . oh!"

The female demon sagged with the pain of Lenc's mighty attack, her face rippling and flowing into something not even vaguely human. For the first time Kesira realized how different the demons were.

Lalasa showed a truly alien aspect as Lenc increased the suffering he visited upon her.

"You will perish before your time, Lenc," moaned Lalasa.

"Not by your hand, weakling."

The White Fire 143

Lalasa made a small, almost unnoticed gesture. The air around Lenc began to swirl, a new storm forming to rob the one above his head of its virulence. At first Lenc ignored this, then fought against the swirling winds of the vortex. Kesira saw Lalasa gesture again; ice formed around Lenc's body. Green arms froze into a solid block of polar ice. When his halo of cloud winked from sight, the slow encapsulation sped up.

More and more of the jade demon's body vanished in the encasing ice.

Lalasa sank to her knees, expression drawn and complexion gray from the exertion. "Die as you have permitted so many others to die, Lenc. Die, curse you, die!"

The transparent block of ice began to turn frosty. The demon hidden within vanished. Lalasa fell face-forward to the ground, arms and legs twitching feebly. Kesira rushed to her.

"You did it," Kesira cried. "You stopped him. I never knew you had such power. You were magnificent. No wonder Emperor Kwasian listens so closely when you advise him. You—"

"Stop babbling," Lalasa said, letting Kesira help her sit upright. The nun had to prop the frail demon against her knee. The physical weakness appalled her even as the spiritual strength buoyed her.

"You succeeded when all others failed."

"Merrisen," said Lalasa, eyelids drooping. "So great. The greatest of us all."

"And he failed," came Lenc's voice, "just as you have failed."

Kesira jerked around and stared in disbelief at the giant block of ice. Already Lenc's face had melted free of the cold prison. Inch by inch, more of his jade body escaped until he stood in a puddle of cold water, totally free of the icy bonds.

"Do it again, Lalasa. You stopped him once. Do it again!"

"She did nothing, weak one." Lenc sneered. "Do you not see the exquisite torture I give her? She thinks me impotent, no longer a threat. Thereby she dares to hope.

Then I snatch away her hope. This makes her defeat all the more bitter."

"Lenc," Lalasa sobbed.

"Let my name be the last word to cross your lips." Lenc thrust his hands in front of him. Cold white fire leaped forth to engulf Lalasa. She gave one convulsive shudder, then fell from Kesira's grasp. The flames danced with polar delight, dining on demon flesh. In a minute only a skeleton remained. Then even these bones vanished. A few charred spots and myriad tiny white fires marked the ground where Lalasa had lain.

"No," Kesira whispered—so softly the word was almost drowned out by the beating of her heart.

"Baram!" screamed Lenc. The very sky quivered with the intensity of the demon's summons. "You are next to die!"

A roar like an enraged bull pulled Kesira's attention away from the spot where Lalasa had fallen. A giant demon had materialized: arms thicker than Kesira's waist, taller and heavier than any mortal she'd ever known, Baram bellowed forth an inchoate cry of rage and pain and frustration.

Lenc stood his ground, waiting.

"You are evil. You must die," said Baram. Kesira knew the outcome of this battle. Baram might be physically strong but lacked the required cunning and intelligence to defeat Lenc.

Baram and Lenc smashed together, arms around each other. Baram roared again and held the jade demon in a bone-crushing grip around the small of the back. Kesira dared hope for an instant when she heard Lenc's bones snapping and crackling loudly. She prayed that Baram would crush Lenc's spine.

Then Lenc reached out and took Baram's head in his hands. With a grin on his face, the jade demon started to twist. Baram finally had to release his grip on Lenc to avoid the excruciating pain in jaw and neck.

Baram kicked free, one massively thewed leg tensing so much that his leather trousers split. Lenc smashed a jade fist into Baram's face. The other demon took no notice of the thin trickle of blood coming from his crushed nose.

Kesira hoped that Baram was beyond pain; she feared that he hadn't sense enough to feel pain.

The powerful demon reached out and seized Lenc's arm, trying to break it. Lenc pulled free. They continued to wrestle, each giving as much as he received until Kesira saw the subtle change in Lenc's face. The jade demon tired of this new amusement.

With a twist both agile and adroit, Lenc got behind his adversary. A thick forearm circled Baram's throat and a heavy hand pushed down on the top of the struggling demon's head.

"Die now, Baram, you stupid oaf." Lenc applied more pressure, and the giant demon's neck snapped like a dried twig. Head canted at a sickening angle, Baram lay unmoving on the ground. Lenc's breath came in deep, gusty drafts, and perspiration shone on his green skin.

Kesira felt only numbness when Lenc pointed, and his white fire danced across Baram's body. In seconds only those flames remained.

"What now?" the nun asked. "Do I suffer the same fate? Twist my head off? Let your flames devour my body?"

Lenc's laughter told her that more subtle tortures lay in store for her.

"You still have a year of exquisite agony," Lenc told her. "FIrst we begin with breaking your will. Then we proceed to . . . more imaginative torture."

Kesira gasped as blackness swirled around her. She clutched her robe tightly around her spare body and tried to keep her teeth from chattering. As quickly as the darkness had swallowed her, it spat her out. She tumbled forward, skinning her knees and elbows on the rough floor of the prison cell.

Are you all right? came Molimo's comforting thought. His gentle hands helped her rise. She brushed off the dirt the best she could.

"Such a nice couple they make. The other-beast and the nun." Lenc barred the doorway with his massive frame, looking none the worse for his bouts with Lalasa and Baram. "I think you will make an even nicer pair when you do my bidding."

"Kill us and be done with it," Kesira said angrily. "We aren't toys."

"Ah, but you *are* interesting toys. For now. Outlive that, and you will die horribly."

Kesira bit her lower lip as pain drove into her body from all sides. One of Lenc's white fireballs had exploded in her gut, doubling her over. As the cold fire continued to burn, she knew she'd die then and there. But she didn't. The fire extinguished itself and left her physically unscathed.

"Obey and you will live—for at least one more day."

Do not anger him, Molimo sent to her.

Kesira still couldn't speak.

"Make love. I would watch you couple with an animal."

"You're more of an animal than he is, even when the change takes him."

Kesira's insult only amused the jade demon, who ordered, "Do it. Now!"

Kesira glared at Lenc. Then she heard a sound behind her—and it chilled her as much as anything ever had. Molimo's control had slipped again. Gray fur rubbed against her legs, moved up her body.

"No, please, this isn't . . ." The jade power controlled by Lenc flattened her on the floor and held her motionless.

"Go on," Lenc urged the wolf. "Mate with her."

The force holding Kesira in place eased somewhat and she escaped it, only to find this was what Lenc intended. She found herself on hands and knees, Molimo behind her. Savage teeth ripped at her robe to expose her flanks. Tears ran down her cheeks as she tried—and failed—to escape this degradation.

She gasped as the wolf jerked forward. Her emotions whirled: hatred, fear, shame, arousal.

Kesira hated herself for this blatant sexual arousal she experienced. Her passions mounted; the thrill of feeling the wolf enter her turned to something more. Ecstasy, yes, but more. She tensed and strained against the furry body.

All the while Lenc kept up a crude commentary.

Finally Kesira recognized the sensation underlying her

ecstasy. Power. Power flooded her arteries, blasted brightly into her brain. Power seared every nerve in her body.

And Kesira Minette knew that the rune sticks had not lied. She knew she could defeat Lenc. She now had the power.

Chapter Thirteen

KESIRA MINETTE collapsed onto the floor and felt the gray-furred wolf behind her change back into human form. She rolled over and touched Molimo's head. He flinched away.

"I understand. Lenc forced us to do this for his amusement. He *forced* us."

I wanted to. That was why it was so easy for him.

A tear formed in the corners of Kesira's eyes. "I wanted it, too," she whispered.

"How touching. A wolf mating with the last of Gelya's whores." Lenc laughed so hard he had to hold his sides. "This is rich. The finest I have arranged yet. Killing Lalasa provided me with much less pleasure than I'd thought it would. Removing Baram was more like stepping on an insect."

Kesira glared at the jade demon but said nothing. Any response she made would only amuse Lenc more. The horrifying thought occurred to her that the world was truly doomed if Lenc was already this bored with his existence. What would happen ten years hence, or fifty? Lenc would have tried every petty cruelty, every major perversion.

Kesira wondered that she wasn't more shamed by what Lenc had just forced her and Molimo to do. Instead of being degraded, she experienced an inner peace unlike any she'd known before. Even her deepest meditations had failed to achieve such a beatitude. Self-doubt and worry had assailed her before. No longer. Kesira had felt worn down and on the brink of exhaustion. Now exhilaration made her every nerve sing.

"Go on," Lenc urged. "Enjoy his furred body once again. Go on!"

Molimo let out a strangled cry and began the other-beast transformation into wolf. Kesira threw her arms around the thickening neck and hugged Molimo close. Lenc snorted in derision and left.

"Don't let the change take you over, Molimo. You can fight it. You can! I know it. I...I feel the power within me. Feel it within you."

Even as she spoke, the thick gray fur rippled and changed back to smooth skin. Molimo the human stayed within the circle of her arms.

"Wrong. I shouldn't have let him do that to us. So weak then. Still weak, but better."

"Don't talk," Kesira said. "Lenc still doesn't know you have regained your tongue. It might be better if he doesn't learn, unless he's spying on us."

"He's not. More I speak, the easier it becomes. Want to. So long. So much horror."

They kissed, and Kesira sank down against Molimo's strong body. He might have aged dramatically in the past few months, but this didn't stem the tide of her passion for him. If anything, Lenc had done them a favor. He had lowered barriers they had erected. She had tried to convince herself Molimo was nothing more than a poor, mute youth trapped by the jade rain. The strength of character, the kindness, the caring were still within him no matter what age the body. She loved him and had from the first time she'd spied his bloodied, battered body.

Afterward, Molimo asked, "Why did you hide your feelings for me all this time?"

"Why'd you hide yours for me?"

"Who wants a half-man? The shape change takes me too unexpectedly."

"I rather enjoyed you that way, also," she said.

The shock in Molimo's expression made her hug him close. "I love you for *you*, not just your shape."

"There's more."

"The jade ages you rapidly, that I can see. And you hide other details from me. No," she said, putting one finger across his lips to still the protest, "I've seen the way you

The White Fire   151

and Zolkan talk. There's a bond between the two of you that doesn't exist between us. But I love you."

"You didn't love Rouvin?"

"No." Kesira had fought long, emotional inner battles with this. Rouvin had been gallant, brave, a warrior second to none—and she had had strong bonds with him. But not love. Friendship, yes. When he had died—his throat ripped apart by Molimo's wolf fangs—she had grieved, but more for the psychic pain it caused Molimo than the passing of Rouvin.

"Others?"

"There have been others," she said. "Gelya preached moderation, not celibacy. All sisters of the order leave the nunnery for five years before returning as Senior Sisters. I had several more years to go before my journey into the world to find more of life than that taught by Gelya, but I had known others. In Blinn. Dominie Tredlo, our Senior Brother. Others in my order."

Molimo said nothing. Kesira wiggled as feathery caresses brushed over the surface of her mind. It seemed that Molimo's words ought to be forming as they had before, but no coherent message came. When she realized what he was doing, she jerked free from his arms and glared.

"You can see my thoughts. Stop it!"

You detected my prowlings?

"Yes!"

Unusual for one such as you to be able to know when I touch you.

"I see nothing odd in it," Kesira said. "In fact, since... since Lenc forced us to... to do what we did, I've been stronger. I got a great deal from you, just as I did from Wemilat." Kesira frowned. "Yes, that's it. I'm stronger now, just as I was after being with Wemilat. A vitality flowed into me."

And into me, said Molimo.

"I can almost believe the rune reading."

"Wh-what rune reading?" Molimo struggled to put his thoughts into speech.

"I didn't tell you. While you were off doing whatever it was you were doing in Kolya, I cast the rune sticks and asked about the future. Never have I seen a more positive reading. Each one indicated triumph over Lenc. Until now, I'd passed it off as another of his cruel tricks."

"Lenc s-sent you false castings?"

"That's what he claimed. But I don't think this one was his doing. Lalasa had just left me in the inn, and the casting went so easily. Nothing but victory indications over Lenc."

"I didn't send it, either."

Kesira looked at him. "Of course you didn't. But this power suffusing my every nerve... I don't know how to use it."

"Remember when we escaped from Howenthal's prison?" Molimo swallowed hard, then licked his lips. Speaking posed problems for him, but Kesira thought he remastered the skill well. "Your meditations opened the curtain. It was similar to this."

Molimo went to the green barrier and held out his hand. He jerked back as tiny green sparks arced over to bite him. Molimo silently inclined his head in the direction of the magical wall.

"You think my skill works against Lenc? I don't even know what it was that I did, Molimo. The demon is a master of his magicks. I can't even say I dabble. I don't know *anything!* What if I make a mistake?"

"Try. You are much stronger than you think."

"Molimo..."

"Do it for Gelya, for Emperor Kwasian, for yourself." In a lower voice, Molimo added, "Do it for the baby."

"Dymek," she said in a choked voice. "That's the name Lenc gave him. Dymek. An ugly name."

"Do it!"

Kesira took one hesitant step, then another, and a bolder third one. She closed her eyes and ran through the litanies taught her by her sisters. When she felt tiny pinpricks against her skin, she knew she approached the barrier and that her only reward would be excruciating pain. Kesira forgot the litanies and began humming her death song.

So many verses had been written in the past few months. How many to go before she gave voice to the song and let those at her deathbed hear her life's story?

"Molimo, it's not going to work. I—Molimo!"

Kesira Minette stood on the far side of the green barrier. Molimo stood beside her.

"I followed when you walked through. There is nothing you cannot do. Nothing. You have the power now, and it isn't the power of jade."

"Where does it come from, then?"

Molimo paled. "The Time of Chaos feeds your energies. The flux from the death of all the demons gives you power, just as the jade does Lenc."

"But all the demons aren't dead," she protested. "Lenc said Tolek still lived."

"No gain," Molimo said grimly.

"And Lalasa was sure that Merrisen had survived."

Molimo grabbed her arm and pointed up the spiral ramp again. "Guards. I can use the spell taught me by Toyaga so that they won't notice me, but you—I can't protect you with it."

"But when I walked through the magical barrier, you came along."

"My powers are different from yours. And being so near your jade dagger prevents me from full recovery."

"But why?"

Kesira had no chance for further questions. Two of the Steel Crescent guards overheard her and came to investigate. Kesira rushed forward, sidestepped one guard's clumsy sword thrust and jerked him around so that she could kick his foot from under him. He tumbled head over heels down the ramp to land in the midst of the green barrier still covering the cell door. He screamed once in stark agony, then died.

The other guard tried to run, but Molimo overtook him halfway to the next level. A hard fist to the side of the skull silenced the mercenary permanently. Molimo stripped the guard of his sword and dagger.

"Not much, but better than bare hands."

A wan ray of light caught Molimo and highlighted the white streaks in his hair. Kesira swallowed, trying to get rid of the tight knot in her throat. So handsome he was to be afflicted with the curse of accelerating age. First he had lost his tongue, had it regenerated mysteriously, still changed into an other-beast uncontrollably, and now this. Fate was unkind to the man.

"Fire tries gold, misery tries men," she said softly. The delicate touches over her mind told Kesira that Molimo had heard and understood.

Whether he communicated to her on an even more elemental level or she simply knew it, Kesira couldn't say; but the misery Molimo lived with only strengthened him.

"Four more levels to the surface," he said. "Few guards. They are in Kolya for ceremonies."

She didn't bother asking how he knew. Like Zolkan, he always managed to come up with needed facts.

They reached the top level of the underground prison before the heavy tramping of boots echoed down to them. Kesira stopped, knowing they couldn't possibly fight their way through so many soldiers. Above ground, they might be able to slip away; but in the prison area they'd be crowded back down, level after level. Fighting uphill was bad, but the designer had done even more. Any person wielding a weapon in the right hand found it pressed hard against a circular wall.

All the advantage lay with those above.

Even worse, Kesira knew the man they faced: Nehan-dir.

For the span of five heartbeats, Nehan-dir simply stood and stared at them. The disbelief flowed across his face, then turned into unbridled anger.

"Slay them!" he shouted to the dozen armed mercenaries behind. "Slay them both!"

"But Lenc wanted them for torture," a woman immediately behind Nehan-dir said. "To kill them means our own death. Lenc would see to it!"

"Fools! Don't let them past. I'll take care of them myself." The small, scarred mercenary drew forth his sword. Expression one of complete concentration, Nehan-dir came down the ramp toward Kesira. "How you got past the magical barrier, I can't say. But you'll never get by my cold steel."

He ripped open his tunic and showed the cruel half-moon brand on his chest signifying his membership in the Order

The White Fire

of the Steel Crescent. As if this were a shield, Nehan-dir rushed forward.

Kesira had learned not to act but to react. She did not initiate, but waited for her attacker, knowing that in every offense there is a weakness, a method of defense. While Nehan-dir was skillful and determined, Kesira instantly saw the vulnerable point of his attack.

Nehan-dir slashed down powerfully—and found only empty air. Kesira had stepped just enough to one side to let the deadly blade miss. She hopped forward, her arms encircling Nehan-dir's small body. She gasped at the power locked within such a tiny man, but she held on long enough to unbalance him. Turning to one side, she succeeded in getting one foot out from under him. When she released him, he had no choice but to curl up in a ball and roll down the ramp.

"Get Lenc," shouted the woman who seemed to be Nehan-dir's second-in-command. "Get him! We'll hold them here."

Kesira started forward empty-handed, but Molimo's touch on her shoulder stopped her. He handed her a long, stout spear he'd wrested from another mercenary before breaking the man's neck.

"No steel," Kesira said. She placed the razor-edged point against the wall and applied leverage. A loud *snap!* marked the breaking of the spear. "A staff is better."

Kesira proved that it was. The months of starvation and deprivation lay behind her. The power she had acquired by lying with Molimo now flooded her as soft spring rains cover a meadow. Every nerve responded fully. Each muscle screamed with power. Never had her mind been clearer, more settled, readier for the task ahead of her.

She fought. She won.

She and Molimo stumbled out into the crisp evening air. "The stars," she said, panting. "Never have they looked so good to me."

"Enjoy them, slut. You'll never see them again. After this, I will pluck out your eyes and force you to eat them!"

Kesira straightened and turned to face Lenc. The jade demon towered above her, thick biceps tensing. She had seen him kill the vastly more powerful Baram with little effort. He had worked his way out of Lalasa's most effective magicks. He had destroyed almost all of his fellow demons. Lenc ruled supreme in the land.

She faced him and felt no fear.

"You think I will rip out your eyes and then let you die?" he screamed. "Is that why you fail to quake in fright? I won't *kill* you, I'll torture you even more. I said I'd let you live for a year and a day. I'll stretch that into two years. Five! A decade!"

Kesira took two quick steps forward and swung her staff. The hard wood butt smashed into Lenc's leg just above the kneecap. The vibration traveling back along the wooden length told her the demon had become more jade than flesh, but the impact staggered him.

"You dare touch me? Worm!"

Kesira settled into a fighting pose. As Lenc came toward her, she estimated distances, then struck. The staff hit repeatedly, against head, on wrist, on knee, on ankle.

Lenc's bull roar told her she damaged not his body but his pride.

"Burn with my fire in your guts!"

Kesira kept her death song running through her mind, occupying her, forcing away fear. Everyone died eventually. Death was nothing to fear, unless death came by dishonor. She fought with a cold savagery she hadn't known she possessed. All that Lenc had done he would atone for. The tortures, the misery, the way he had taken Dymek away from her.

The staff crashed into the side of Lenc's head, sending him to his knees. For a brief instant, hope replaced the fighting calm that had taken over her senses.

"The runes spoke truly. You *are* vulnerable."

The expression on Lenc's face defied description. "I sent you no message of victory."

"You confused me before. No longer. I *can* read the rune sticks. I read your defeat."

Lenc laughed. "You think that I, killer of demons, cannot defeat a mortal? I play with you, nothing more."

Again he tried to send his fireballs to explode within her,

and again they failed to form properly. Kesira didn't question the source of her good fortune. That Lenc failed was enough to drive her forward. The nun slid both hands together on the staff and brought it up and then down in a vicious downward blow that ended on the top of Lenc's head. The sharp cracking noise told the tale.

His jade head had developed a small fissure. Like a man wounded and bleeding, Lenc reached up to touch the spot. He shook his head and got to his feet.

"You will die now, whore. No more toying with you."

Kesira measured her blow and landed it squarely on a jade kneecap. Lenc lurched to one side, off balance, but she didn't slow his advance. Massively powerful hands that had broken Baram's neck seized the end of her staff and wrested it away. Lenc held the stout quarterstaff so that one hand rested on each end of the rod. His chest expanded and he bent the ends downward, trying to force them together.

The staff exploded like lightning before he accomplished the feat. Lenc tossed aside the splinters.

"Come here. Let me kill you quickly. I will even be merciful and not let you suffer—long."

Curiously, Kesira kept calm. Fear was the killer, of mind and body and soul. She permitted it no entry into her thoughts. Lenc grabbed for her. She deftly ducked under his clumsy groping and slid her arm past. With a mighty heave, she threw the demon over her hip. He landed heavily, but unhurt.

"The rune sticks did not lie. I can best you."

Lenc's eyes blazed with the purest jade light. His lips curled back and ruined whatever handsome features he might have possessed. Kesira knew fear then. She could not hope to destroy the demon now that the full power of jade clouded his mind and robbed him of his soul. Lenc had succumbed to the lure of power untempered by wisdom.

He grabbed her by the arms and lifted. Feet free of the ground, Kesira could only feebly kick and twist. She tried to scratch and claw, but the power in the demon's grip proved too much for her to break.

"I'll pull you apart as I would a bug."

She gasped as he began pulling on her arms. Pain shot

into her shoulders. She knew that her arms would pop free of her joints at any instant.

"Merrisen, please, oh, Merrisen!" she cried. "Lalasa said you had survived. Help, Merrisen, help me!"

"Merrisen?" roared Lenc, sensing her pain and defeat. "I killed him. He was one of the first. I used a bolt of my white fire to sear him, then I turned him into the hardest of jade and shattered him. You might as well summon Gelya. I killed him with my fire, too!"

Kesira passed simple pain. Numbed, she stared directly into Lenc's face. The demon continued to apply the tension on her arms. Only seconds remained before he would rip them from her body.

The cessation of the pain took Kesira by surprise. Her pitiful kicks couldn't have caused Lenc to drop her as he did. She stared up into his contorted jade face and wondered at the confusion written in the planes and valleys.

"No," Lenc said, "it's not possible."

"You'll be defeated. The runes foretold it!" Kesira shouted. But Lenc looked not at her but past her. Kesira rolled over on the ground and saw Molimo standing quietly, arms dangling at his sides. In one hand he loosely held a sword. The expression on his face was unreadable.

Looking back at Lenc, Kesira saw the confusion replaced by sheer fright. All the panic and fear he had instilled in legions of others now boiled to the surface. The jade of his face turned noticeably whiter, showed more veining, actually began to chip away around the fissure she had started.

"It's not possible," Lenc muttered. "You're dead. You died by my hand, Merrisen!"

"No," said Molimo. "I did not die. But you will. You will die now!"

Lenc's scream of fear rattled Kesira's head and shook doors and windows in Kolya as Molimo advanced.

Chapter Fourteen

"Merrisen!"

Kesira couldn't decide whether to watch Lenc or Molimo. The stark terror now seizing Lenc fascinated her, but the transformation in Molimo was even more astounding.

He grew in stature as he advanced.

"You're dead!" the jade demon screamed. "I turned you into jade and you shattered into a million pieces. You rained down on the mountains. I saw you die!"

Molimo shook as if he had been caught in a high wind. Kesira saw gray fur popping out around the collar of his tunic, the legs tightening and the arms changing.

"No, don't, Molimo, don't let the transformation take you!" she cried. But it happened. Molimo changed into the sleek gray wolf she had come to love and hate.

The wolf launched himself directly for Lenc. The jade demon fell backward under the impact of the heavy body. Savage jaws closed on Lenc's throat. Sparks jumped and scattered into the night like giant red cockroaches. No matter how hard Lenc hammered with his heavy fists on the wolf's flanks, those ripping teeth continued to tear at the rock-hard throat.

Lenc succeeded in rolling over. With a mighty blow, he sent Molimo reeling. The wolf hunkered down, green eyes matching those of the towering demon in intensity and promised death.

To Kesira's surprise, everywhere Molimo—Merrisen?—had bitten, tiny fractures appeared. If he had kept at Lenc's throat for even another minute, he would have decapitated the demon.

"How did you survive? How, curse you, Merrisen, how?"

Lenc's fear couldn't be denied now. Kesira looked for an opportunity to join in the fight again but saw nothing. Molimo circled warily, steaming saliva dripping from his fangs. Lenc tried repeatedly to send forth his fireballs. Each died a sizzling death just inches from his fingertips. Even the storm cloud that had followed the demon with its forbidding lightnings had abandoned him.

"Don't let him escape," Kesira called. "Kill him!"

Even as she shouted encouragement to Molimo, she wondered. The rune sticks had shown her to be the victor over Lenc, not Molimo—not Merrisen. If Lenc had not sent the message to give her false hope and then snatch away even this shred from her, had Merrisen sent the prophecy?

That struck Kesira as wrong, also. Molimo had been startled when she told him in the cell of the rune casting. There could be no other possibility than that the reading had been accurate. She, rather than Merrisen, would destroy Lenc.

How?

Kesira looked around for a weapon, something to use against Lenc. The low stone building that provided shelter for the Steel Crescent beckoned to her. She left Merrisen and Lenc and rushed to the doorway and peered inside. Rude bunks lined the walls, and the weapons racks down the center of the room stood empty. All of the Steel Crescent had gone into Kolya for whatever ceremony Lenc had ordered. Those not at the ceremony walked sentry duty elsewhere and had taken their weapons. She started away from the empty room when a white flash caught her eye.

The nun raced into the deserted room and reached under one of the bunks.

"A staff. Of stonewood! Gelya be praised!" She hefted the quarterstaff of wood sacred to her dead patron. She had experienced a surge of power when she'd made love with Molimo . . . Merrisen. The staff of the sacred wood in her hands made Kesira think she floated inches off the ground.

Racing back to where Lenc and Merrisen still battled, she stood close, waiting for the proper opening. When Lenc turned sideways to her, she swung the stonewood staff with all her might. A tiny explosion marked the spot where she connected with the jade demon's rib cage. His screech of pain signaled the damage she'd done.

"You've committed enough foul deeds," she said, moving closer. "For what you've done, you will die, Lenc. Die!"

She attacked. And missed. Lenc quickly turned and got her between him and Merrisen. With a brilliant burst of light, Lenc vanished.

Kesira stood, openmouthed. She turned and faced the gray wolf. The other-beast transformation worked its magicks and the wolf form vanished, to be replaced by the aging figure of Molimo she knew and loved.

"You're all right?" she asked.

"You fool!" Merrisen shouted. "I held him here. If you hadn't gotten between us, I would have finished him!"

"I didn't know," she said weakly. The man slumped and took her in his arms.

"Yes, all this must be confusing for you."

"You're Molimo? Or Merrisen?"

"Both. You know me as Molimo. When Lenc and I fought the first time, I underestimated his power. I thought the jade had only barely augmented his abilities. I erred."

"He really did turn you into a statue of jade?"

"And shattered me, sending me raining down all over the Yearn Mountains. But he grossly underestimated *my* power. While he had stripped me of all but the most feeble of mortal abilities, I was able to recover slowly."

Kesira stared at the man—the demon—in silence.

"I had lost my tongue; it regenerated over the months. All my power had fled, but it has now returned."

"That's why the jade affected you so strongly. You're a ... demon."

"Yes," Merrisen said softly. The green light in his eyes had died down, but flecks still showed in the ebony. "Power gone, I was invisible to Lenc. He believed I had perished and had no reason to hunt me down."

"That's why so many of the demons thought they recognized you."

"Wemilat did know me. He was a wise demon, one of the finest. And at the end, my lover Ayondela also knew me. By then, much of my power had returned, but her jade kept me weak."

"Your lover?" Kesira said in a choked voice.

"Ayondela was, at one time." Merrisen smiled. "Among demons, time passes slowly, and amusing ourselves is of paramount importance. Our liaisons are everything you mortals rumor them to be—and more." Sadness filled him now. "I speak as if nothing had changed. All that is past. The Time of Change is upon us."

"I don't understand."

"Remember what Gelya taught you of the Time. Gelya and I had our differences, not the least of which was the nature of the Time of Chaos. He instructed his followers differently than I did the few of mine." Merrisen straightened, his stature growing. "I admit my error now. Gelya has been proven correct."

"The demons are all gone? But you're still here." Fear caught at Kesira. "You can't go. You can't!"

"Moment by moment, my power returns. Our coupling provided the trigger for its full return—or perhaps I tapped a reservoir deep within you, a power source unlike another in mortal or demon. It matters little the cause. I am again able to confront Lenc. I must."

"I felt the power, too. I thought it came from you."

"A mutual exchange. It is as it should be, neither taking from the other but each giving to the other."

"But you're still growing older." Kesira reached out and lightly brushed her fingers along the heavily graying streaks in Merrisen's hair. The texture felt coarser to her than what was left of his dark black strands.

"I must hurry." Merrisen chuckled. "I begin to sound like Zolkan. Always in a hurry. For one with such a short lifespan, hurry is necessary. I realize that now."

"Zolkan's life might be limited. So might mine. But you're a demon."

"Look at me and tell me you don't believe I will soon die. That's why I must find Lenc quickly. Age takes my body, not my spirit."

"I want to help. Let me. You can't leave me behind. Not after all we've been through together."

He looked at her, green dancing with midnight-black in his eyes. "I am touched by the jade. It's an insidious canker chewing away at me. You see it most when I change shape. Don't let yourself become contaminated, too."

"I'm going with you."

Merrisen smiled. "Determination always was your strong point. Very well, Kesira. But don't make the mistake of getting between Lenc and me again. I can bind him to one spot as long as no one breaks the magical bond."

Kesira shrieked as the ground vanished beneath her feet. But she didn't fall. Again she found herself transported through space. Higher and higher she and Merrisen went. Kesira clung to his strong arm and marveled at the lines in his face, the aging. All that mattered little to her. When they had given Lenc the end he deserved, she would find a remedy for the evil jade's touch on Molimo... *Merrisen*, she quickly corrected.

"Terrible," Merrisen said. "Look at what Lenc has accomplished in such a short time." They swooped down over the capital of Limaden. Those in the streets walked with a listless shuffle. No children played. Vendors sat silently beside stands filled with rotting foodstuffs. All commerce had ceased. Worst of all, many of the fine monuments and temples had been razed.

"Lenc destroyed any shrine belonging to another patron," she said. Virtually every street, every block of buildings suffered Lenc's cruelly burning fire.

"He is still here. I sense his presence."

Kesira gasped again as they rocketed down to Emperor Kwasian's palace. The usual contingent of guardsmen stood about in ragged ranks holding unpolished weapons. One or two pointed at the strangers but none of them reacted with the usual swift challenge. Merrisen and Kesira landed lightly and walked under the alabaster arch leading to the inner courtyard of the palace.

"All my life I've heard of this," Kesira said in a whisper. "Never did I think to see it."

"Lenc stalks these halls. He thinks to reduce our will by torturing the Emperor and the Empress. No matter what he does to them, remember that he must be stopped now or his reign will echo down through the corridors of time."

"I know." Kesira's quick eyes darted about, taking in the splendor of Emperor Kwasian's court. The paving beneath her feet gleamed with mother-of-pearl. The walls were hung with the finest of tapestries—or so Kesira thought until she neared them. Vines of surpassingly fine leaf had been trained to grow in intricate patterns to form murals. To her even greater surprise, the coloration was provided by different types of vine; no one had painted the lovely pictures. The living tapestries stretched over three of the high walls enclosing the courtyard. In the center rose a carved marble fountain spraying four different-colored fluids in a continual rainbow that confused sight and appealed to other senses as well. The liquids were perfumes, mixing in fragrance as well as color. The fourth wall of the courtyard glowed with enough inner light to illuminate the entire area.

"It's like Lenc's fire," she said, staring at the wall. "Cold light. Dare we go through the portal?"

"That is Lalasa's doing. Her magicks were benign, cosmetic. And we must go inside. Lenc awaits us."

Merrisen walked quickly to the portal and passed through, but Kesira thought a slight hesitation came to his step the instant he came even with the archway. She followed more slowly, more cautiously. Once inside the palace proper, she stopped and simply gawked at the richness like a country bumpkin.

"Never have I seen such majesty."

The hallway to the audience chamber sported more gems than Kesira had imagined to exist in the entire world.

"It's said that Emperor Kwasian can stand on this very spot and peer into the jewels and see any point in his realm, any suffering no matter how minor, and be able to correct it."

"No longer," said Kesira. She pointed to the thrones Emperor Kwasian and Empress Aglenella had once occupied. In their places burned tiny white fires.

Merrisen closed his eyes and slowly turned through a full rotation. He went through a small passageway hidden from sight by a screen hand-painted with intricate scenes of the empire's victory over the barbarians. Then Merrisen hurried down the corridor and to a room, where he kicked open the door.

Kesira had thought herself invulnerable to shock. Lenc's evil had touched her and everyone else: what more could the jade demon do? But now Kesira found out.

Empress Aglenella hung naked in delicate golden chains. Thousands of tiny cuts riddled her skin—not deeply but enough to produce a sluggish flow of blood. The pain had driven her insane. She drooled and chuckled to herself in spite of her condition.

"Molimo—Merrisen," Kesira said, "is there anything you can do? She's our Empress. All her charities, all the good she's done for the empire ... It's not right for her to end like this."

"I can do nothing. She has been damaged far beyond those wounds you see. Her skin is breached. So is her soul. Lenc has shown her atrocities beyond even my demonic understanding. There's only one gift we can give her."

For a moment Kesira didn't understand what he meant. When she did, lightheadedness assailed her. She had to support herself against one heavily jeweled wall.

"Do it, then. I have no heart for it." Tears streamed down Kesira's face as Merrisen stepped forward. The demon grasped Empress Aglenella's nose between thumb and forefinger. Tightening, he cut off her air. As she opened her mouth, he clamped his palm over it. She died quickly, relatively painlessly.

"She is beyond Lenc's control now."

"What else did he do to her?"

"He started with her sexual abuse by every guardsman." Merrisen held up his hand to forestall Kesira's protests. "The guardsmen might not even remember they did it. Probably not, or they would have killed themselves from the shame. Lenc probably found it amusing to be able to restore such memory at random and see the guards' reaction."

"He *started* her torture with rape by hundreds?" Kesira turned numb. "I don't want to know the rest. I just want Lenc dead."

Merrisen got a far-off look in his eyes. "He is near. With

Emperor Kwasian. In the rear of the palace. A makeshift dungeon, since the Emperor didn't have one of his own."

The demon walked off without even a glance at Kesira or Empress Aglenella. Kesira couldn't show such restraint. She had to take one last backward look at the Empress so adored by all in the empire. Her eyes refused to focus properly; all Kesira truly saw were the specks of blood staining the gold chains.

A bull-throated roar filled the palace. Merrisen hurried along toward it and burst into a room at the back of the throne room. A spiraling ramp downward had been crudely cut into the wood inlaid floor.

"Lenc's prison?" she asked.

Merrisen had already started down. "He won't escape this time. I drained him of a considerable portion of his power before. He hasn't had time to regenerate, even using more jade." Merrisen laughed without humor. "If he tries to use more jade, he'll cast himself into an immobile state. Our only problem then will be finding a sledgehammer to smash his head to powder."

"The Emperor," she gasped. What Lenc had done to Empress Aglenella was terrible. The horrors he continually applied to Emperor Kwasian were a thousandfold worse. Kesira took an involuntary step toward the man dangling upside down in the cruel chains before she realized Lenc was also in the room.

The jade demon tried to position her between himself and Merrisen. Kesira doubled up and rolled like a ball to one side.

"She knows my power, Lenc. And yours," said Merrisen. "You escaped by accident once. Not this time."

"I have recovered my strength. You are losing yours," accused Lenc. "Look at you. Already your hand shakes with age. Liver spots stain your flesh. Your hair turns white with the years."

"Such is the penalty of coming so close to the jade."

"That's the penalty of not embracing the jade! You could have ruled with me, Merrisen. The jade has made me invincible!"

"It's made you crazy." Merrisen sighed. "It might have

The White Fire

been inevitable. The Time of Chaos has been precipitated by your insane urge for power. Now all the demons are dead or dying."

"I still live. Tolek, also. But you, Merrisen, you will die!"

Kesira threw up her hand to shield her eyes from the brilliant flares as the two locked in combat. While they locked like a pair of mortal wrestlers, their battle became both physical and magical. Arms might break, but the real conflict came in the bursts of white fire, the flashes of intense jade green.

"They do go at it, don't they?" came a light, almost mocking voice. At first Kesira thought Emperor Kwasian had spoken, but the man still hung upside down and incapable of speech. The ruler's glazed eyes told of the tremendous psychic trauma he had endured.

Kesira pulled her eyes away from the battling demons and found the speaker. He sat cross-legged to one side of the crude torture chamber. It took several seconds for her to decide who this had to be.

"You're Tolek." The statement came out as an accusation.

"None other than. My, don't they make a majestic sight? Where are the sculptors when something truly dramatic happens? This ought to be captured for the mortals to ogle later."

"Help him, curse you!" Kesira cried. "Merrisen needs your help. Destroy Lenc!"

"Are you joking?" The demon appeared uneasy at the suggestion. "Lenc has allowed me to live. Granted, it gets lonely on that island where he exiled me, but I still live, which is more than I can say for the others." Tolek eyed her slyly. "Your Gelya, for instance."

"Do something. Help him! Fight your exile. Be brave!" She realized this was similar to begging the dirt to be water or the air to be stone. It wasn't in Tolek's nature. He had sold out his worshipers. Without his cowardice, Nehan-dir and the Order of the Steel Crescent would never have fallen into Lenc's power.

Kesira reached down to her blue knotted cord. She had used it on Kene Zoheret. It might work on Lenc, though she doubted it. She remembered how Merrisen had changed into wolf form and been unable to rip out Lenc's jade throat. But cracks had appeared. She had put them there herself with her staff. A chance still existed. Hope could not die so easily.

"If you won't help me, I'll try by myself."

If Kesira had thought to shame Tolek into aiding her, she failed. The tall, thin demon pointed and said, "Be my guest."

The tide of the battle ebbed and flowed, bringing the combatants back to where she stood. Kesira didn't understand the weapons used by either, but she knew Lenc could be stopped. The rune sticks had told her she could do it.

"Watch out!" Merrisen shouted. Kesira threw herself flat on the floor and avoided one of Lenc's cold, white fireballs. The screech from behind her, however, told that it had found a target.

Tolek burned in the center of a column of the pure white flame. He crumpled, leaving behind only dark, greasy ashes.

The two remaining demons continued their battle. Merrisen's arms locked around Lenc's body and held his arms at his side. This seemed to prevent the jade demon from launching his fireballs. But Merrisen took a brutal beating as Lenc smashed his head repeatedly into Merrisen's face. Bloodied, weakening—aging, to Kesira's horror—Merrisen could not survive long.

The knotted cord slipped from the nun's fingers when she remembered she had another weapon. From under the dirtied yellow sash proclaiming her to be Sister of Mission, she took the jade tusk. Lenc had been unable to see it, or perhaps he had discounted its danger. Kesira remembered how it slashed through steel and bone.

As she would lift a dagger for a downward stab, Kesira held Ayondela's jade tusk. Merrisen's eyes widened when he saw her. He grunted and whirled Lenc about in a tight circle so that the jade demon's back was exposed to Kesira. She lifted her jade weapon and brought it down on the base of Lenc's skull with all the power locked within her body.

The tip sparked when it touched jade flesh, and she realized mere physical strength wouldn't deliver the killing stroke. From inside, all of the goodness she possessed rushed

The White Fire

upward to stiffen her resolve, to give her the energy needed. Added to this came the full force of her wrath for all that had been done to her and her world. Her nunnery destroyed by Lenc; her life in shambles because of the demon; Howenthal and Wemilat's death; Rouvin and Molimo's otherbeast affliction; Eznofadil and the frozen waves on the Sea of Katad; Ayondela driven mad by Lenc and the jade; the horrors Lenc perpetrated once he had triumphed.

The Time of Chaos.

Jade dagger point entered jade flesh at the base of Lenc's neck. The demon stiffened, then screamed. A sound like an explosion replaced the jade demon's death agony. Green dust erupted like a blizzard and finally settled across the room.

Lenc was no more.

Shaken, Kesira staggered back and found a wall. She slid down it and doubled up, hugging her knees. She felt as if nothing remained inside. Like a water jug during a drought, she was empty and dry.

"He's dead," she said in a flat, emotionless voice. "Dead."

When Merrisen didn't answer, she snapped out of her shock. "What's wrong? Molimo, please, Molimo!"

"Merrisen," he said weakly. "Molimo was only a name to keep you from suspecting. I had to hide from Lenc and the others until I regained my power. Now, there's no need."

"I'll never call you Molimo again."

"No," the demon said. Even as Kesira watched, he aged. His skin turned to parchment and the blue veins beneath pulsed spasmodically. "The Time of Chaos is at hand. We demons have had our day. Now it's time for ... something more."

"Don't," Kesira cried, clutching his frail body as if she could prevent his death by force of will. "I love you."

"And I love you," Merrisen said. The green light in his eyes faded. "You have much to do. I see it now. You have so much to do. Zolkan will help you."

"Zolkan?"

"He was a messenger for many demons, and remained loyal to his ideals even when many demons did not. He will see your future clearly now that there are no more of us."

"Merrisen."

"My final gift. I will return you to Kolya. If you are truly the one I think—and you must be—you will know what must be done." His voice faded.

Their eyes locked and told more than simple words.

Do what you must, came the final words.

"No, Merrisen, no!"

Kesira grasped thin air. The aging body had vanished, replaced by the crisp cold of the field outside the Steel Crescent's headquarters. Alone, Kesira Minette sat in the field and cried for all that she had lost.

Chapter Fifteen

KESIRA MINETTE clutched herself tightly and sat in the field, crying. It hadn't been enough to have her sisters and order destroyed. The man she loved turned out to be a demon, and now he too was dead.

"Molimo," she sobbed. "Merrisen."

Kesira wiped the tears away and stared up into the cold darkness of night. Merrisen had returned her to Kolya for a reason. With Lenc dead, that could only mean one thing. She had to find what Lenc had done with Dymek. The bond between her and the boy strengthened even as she thought about it.

What else did she have left?

The world might be free of the evil posed by the jade demons, but everything else had turned to ash. Emperor Kwasian couldn't possibly survive his terrible wounds. Empress Aglenella hadn't. The empire lay in ruins.

"But demons are gone," came Zolkan's voice. The *trilla* bird waddled up to her and cocked his head to one side so he could study her. "You live. Bratling lives."

"Merrisen died," she said in a voice without emotion.

"I know. We were always closest. Of all demons, I loved Merrisen most."

"You could have told me."

"No," said Zolkan. "Merrisen did not want it that way. When Lenc first accepted jade, I carried message to others and was thrown into blizzard for my trouble."

"That's when you came into the sacristy? Even then you were allied with Merrisen?"

"Always," said Zolkan. "He watched me hatch and raised me from fledgling. I failed to warn him and found myself trapped in your order's nunnery. Merrisen fought Lenc and..."

"I know the rest," Kesira cut in. "The jade rain, him posing as Molimo. He died of old age. He just kept getting frailer and frailer until he died."

"Time of Chaos," agreed Zolkan.

Kesira started to rise, then doubled over with pain in her belly. She dropped to one knee, arm across stomach. Dizziness almost cast her back to the ground.

"I've been through too much, I guess," she said. "Never felt this strange before."

"It gets worse," Zolken said. "You will find out."

"What are you talking about?"

As he had so many times in the past, Zolkan changed the subject. "Nehan-dir knows his patron is destroyed. There seemed to be some thread binding him and Lenc."

"Is he aware that *all* the demons are gone?"

"Doesn't matter to Nehan-dir. Events have driven him insane. Or maybe he sees opportunity to consolidate all of empire under his rule. Emperor Kwasian is dead, after all."

"He is?" Kesira wondered how Zolkan might know this. It didn't surprise her.

"Yes," squawked Zolkan. "I felt him die. Awful pain. Awful. Be many weeks before new Emperor can be chosen. In that time Nehan-dir can do much to forge his own domain."

Kesira stood and tried to straighten. She again bent double. "I don't feel well. Nausea. Everything's spinning."

"It happens quickly," Zolkan said. "You will be fine. Must go and save bratling."

"You've changed your mind about Dymek." She shivered. The name still didn't seem right to her. It had been given by Lenc, and that alone tainted it with evil.

"Merrisen showed new future. Time of Chaos must be ridden through with minimum problem. Then..." The *trilla* bird shook all over, sending a feathery shower in all directions.

Kesira saw that chaos would reign in the empire. Emperor Kwasian dead, all the demons gone, society itself would need an anchor. Where to look for it? She had no idea on that score. The foundation of society had been duty to Emperor and family. Everyone has known his duty, his place, and had performed his duties to the best of his ability. Whether it was a simple farmer, a moneylender dealing in exotic currencies, the Emperor or a beggar, all knew what was expected of them—and they did it.

The demons aided with philosophy and occasional intervention, but always before the aid had been intended to maintain the stability of society. Now that the leaders were gone, everyone would have to find new ways of keeping the fabric of the country together.

"I feel a little better now. Such a burning deep inside me. It churned, almost as if someone had shot me with an arrow." Kesira rubbed her stomach. All pain had vanished and a peace settled over her. Without even knowing she did so, her hand went to the tattered robe and the left breast below it. Wemilat's kiss glowed warmly, a comfort to ease any discomfort she might experience.

"Nehan-dir has whipped his mercenaries into a killing frenzy. They must cow all citizens in city before taking over. Without Lenc to enforce his will using his magicks, Steel Crescent might otherwise be deposed by angry people."

"What can we do?" Kesira hardly considered herself to be in any condition to rescue all of Kolya's citizenry, yet Dymek needed help. She had no idea where Lenc had sequestered the boy, but wherever it was, she had to be the one to arrive before Nehan-dir. The Steel Crescent leader would see Lenc's son as a threat to his own supremacy—or would use the boy as a figurehead to ensure that the Kolyans would buckle under to his reign. When the infant grew older, Nehan-dir would from necessity have to kill him.

Either way, Dymek would die. Kesira refused to allow that. She had already lost too much. Like a sailor drowning, she clutched at the feeblest of twigs.

As she and Zolkan began the walk into the deserted streets of Kolya, she asked, "What of Lenc's magicks? Do they linger or have they vanished when he died?"

"You think of Protaro?"

"No one should endure the agony he went through. The sight of him turning on that jade-green shaft tore at me almost as much as it did him."

"Jade power is big unknown. Protaro might have died or he might have been freed. We must see for ourselves."

"I hope he's all right."

"He is in disgrace," pointed out Zolkan. "He failed Emperor Kwasian. He did not do his duty."

"Against the jade demons? Against *us?*" Kesira laughed harshly. "We, the ones who have killed four jade demons, could hardly be expected to obey meekly."

"Danger, wait, wait!" the *trilla* bird squawked. Zolkan took to wing and quickly disappeared into the murky shadow of nighttime Kolya, now that its gaslights had flickered out from lack of attention. Only wan starlight and the occasional window that held a lighted oil lamp illuminated street and square.

Kesira kept walking, stopping only when she reached the corner of the Square of All Temples. The sight before her did little to convince the woman that her course was the proper one. Protaro still turned slowly in midair, the green shaft penetrating his gut. On the black slagged lava steps of Lenc's temple stood Nehan-dir. The short leader of the Steel Crescent waved his sword about wildly.

His words came to her as insane snippets. In a way she had hoped Nehan-dir had not succumbed to the madness of the jade. A rational leader might form new alliances, forge new bonds, bring the empire back to the old ways. If he understood his duty, she would not have been averse to seeing Nehan-dir as Emperor.

The thought flickered and vanished, a feather in a flame. Nehan-dir could never perform the duty of Emperor satisfactorily, she saw. He hadn't the total selflessness to place citizens above his own needs. He had been too warped by the Steel Crescent's poor choices of patron to think properly. Nehan-dir still saw the various patrons' actions and deaths as betrayal.

Gelya had not betrayed Kesira or his order when he died. His teachings lived on. Their truth or falseness would be the proof of the demon's worth. She mourned her patron's passing, but did not grieve over it to the exclusion of all else. It didn't matter how long anyone lived, but how well. Gelya had been kind, and everything he'd given humanity was proof of that.

A rush of air across her face brought Kesira around. Zolkan landed heavily. In spite of steeling herself for his landing, she sagged. The woman realized how feeble she actually was. Too much had happened too quickly to accept. She needed a long rest and time to meditate. Lenc's death seemed remote, Merrisen's a vaguely remembered dream. Both ought to be more, she knew.

"Well? What of Nehan-dir?" she asked.

"Bad, very bad," the *trilla* bird reported. "He has rousted out most of citizens for this rally. He executes any who dare voice opposition. Many are already dead."

"He's scarcely different from Lenc in that respect," she said.

"Nehan-dir has opposition within rank of Steel Crescent. Many others see opportunity for power. He has killed several, but others think to unseat little man."

"Stature has nothing to do with his determination." Kesira remembered the first time she had confronted Nehan-dir. The diminutive frame had fooled her into thinking he lacked strength. Both physical and spiritual strength lay within his scarred body. That she didn't agree with the course his spirit had taken did not detract from its power.

"How do we rescue Protaro? If we can't do anything about Nehan-dir right now, we ought to free the guard captain."

"You are expert when dealing with magicks. I always bowed to Merrisen on such matters. I report and little more." The bird rubbed his crested head against her cheek. She stroked over it, soothing him. For the first time she heard the pain of Molimo's loss in Zolkan's tone.

"You are much more. Always, Zolkan, always. Now, let's see about Protaro."

She slipped into deeper shadow and moved around the periphery of the sullen crowd. Nehan-dir continued to harangue, occasionally pointing at Protaro. The agony visible on the captive's face tore at Kesira's heart. The misery had not lessened. If anything, it had increased.

"Nehan-dir must leave square before rescue of Protaro is possible. Cannot go and take him down in plain view."

"I hate leaving him even an instant longer." Kesira considered. "I think I know how to free him, if we can get close enough. Somehow, I can interrupt the flow of magicks for a few necessary seconds. Twice Molimo—Merrisen—and I escaped the jade demons' prison cells that way."

"You destroyed Lenc's flame, too," Zolkan said, reminding her of how she had broken Ayondela's powerful curse that had laid an eternal winter on the land. "How close must you be?"

"I don't know. What did you have in mind?"

"Create diversion on far side of square. Nehan-dir chases me. You pull down rotating hero."

It sounded farfetched, but Kesira saw nothing else to try. If they waited for Nehan-dir to clear the square, he might declare it off-limits for all citizens. This would give Kesira no chance at all of rescuing Protaro. And, she had to admit to herself, thinking of him in such pain for even one second longer bothered her. How long could the man endure it without permanent damage?

Kesira didn't even consider the possibility that Protaro might have been driven insane already.

"Go," she said. "I must prepare. By the time you decoy Nehan-dir away, I will be ready."

"Don't fail. We get no second chance," said Zolkan. "Now, hurry, hurry! I go to annoy those pigeon shits!"

"The *trilla* bird took to wing and circled. One or two of Nehan-dir's mercenaries saw and pointed. Nehan-dir ignored them—and Zolkan. Kesira closed her eyes and began the meditations that unleashed powers deep within her mind. She sank into the darkness of her soul and drew strength from Merrisen's memory. To her surprise, another hard, glowing point blazed inside. Unlike anything she'd detected in her meditations before, Kesira almost forgot about Protaro in an effort to probe this unexpected source of energy.

Zolkan's loud squawk pulled her back to her mission. The *trilla* bird dived down, then pivoted in midair, hind-

The White Fire

quarters pointed at Nehan-dir. The bird squawked as he deposited load after watery load on the top of the mercenary's head. Outraged at the soiling, Nehan-dir whipped out his sword and tried to impale the bird. Zolkan lightly flapped to one side, mouthing obscenities.

Nehan-dir's control was too tenuous for him to allow such open rebellion. He ordered his followers after Zolkan. The crowd squeezed into the square provided Zolkan the time needed for his escape. By the time the Steel Crescent soldiers forced their way toward the street taken by Zolkan, confusion reigned supreme.

Kesira silently walked into the square and stood where the old fountain had been. Above her slowly spun Protaro, the magical green shaft through his belly. His hands clung to the axle as he turned, but this did nothing to keep down the pain.

She looked up, her mind calm and ready. All the tricks she'd used before to rob the magical green barriers of their integrity came into play. And they failed. In frustration, Kesira summoned up the feelings when she had interrupted Lenc's column of white fire. It had been for only an instant, but it had released the world from the jade curse of perpetual winter.

"Almost," she sobbed, just missing it. The sensations within her defied description. Ineffable, they bordered on magic without actually entering that realm. "Again. Again!"

This time the brilliance blazing within her surged upward. She guided the seething power and focused it on the green shaft.

Protaro fell heavily to the square, freed of Lenc's magical punishment.

He rose to hands and knees. She had always thought the expression "sweating blood" had little basis in reality. Blood dotted the soldier's forehead. So extreme had been his pain that his insides oozed through his skin.

"Words can never say enough," Protaro gasped out. "My life is yours."

"I give it back—on one condition."

"Anything."

"Your life must be devoted to the teachings of Gelya."

Protaro stared at her as she helped him to his feet. "Even at this juncture you proselytize? You amaze me."

"Do you agree?"

"I'll need a teacher. I've been a soldier and know little of philosophies."

"I can instruct you. After all, I'm Sister of the Mission now."

"And we'll both be dead if Nehan-dir returns and sees I've been let down. If your patron's words show me how to perform such miracles, I'll happily learn anything you can teach me."

The people still milling in the square began to gather around Protaro and Kesira. The unwanted attention drew Nehan-dir's mercenaries back.

"Go away, go on!" Kesira shouted at the Kolyans, but it took the mercenaries' hard-swinging swords to clear a path.

"Up the steps to the temple," said Protaro. "Our only chance to get away before they reach us."

The pair raced up the black lava steps, only to find that Nehan-dir blocked their way. The Steel Crescent leader had wiped off the humiliations Zolkan had dropped on his head and stood with sword drawn.

"I wondered at the bird's timing. Where he goes, you have always trailed." Nehan-dir advanced on Kesira. "I felt it the instant Lenc died. While I do not know for certain, I feel you had a part in my patron's death."

"All the demons are dead," she said. Then, seeing this did nothing to placate Nehan-dir, she said, "Yes, I killed him. With my own hand I killed him. Lenc lies beneath the Emperor's palace, nothing more than powdered jade now."

"You killed him and Howenthal. Every patron of the Steel Crescent, you kill."

"Tolek died, also. Lenc turned him to ash with a single speck of white fire."

Nehan-dir spat. "So be it. Tolek sold us. We don't need them. Any of them. Good riddance to all demons! We have the chance now to take our own destiny in hand."

"You won't be the one guiding that destiny," said Protaro. "The Emperor won't permit it."

The White Fire

"The Emperor's dead," snapped Nehan-dir. "Oh, you didn't know that? But of course not. You were swirling around and around, letting your guts turn to mush."

"You'll never replace Emperor Kwasian. There are others," said Kesira, seeing the train of Nehan-dir's logic.

"I'll carve my own empire. Let those in Limaden do as they please. Let them rot! Here in Kolya I'll build the foundation for a kingdom of my own!"

Protaro rushed the small man, giving him no chance to use his drawn sword. Fists hammering, feet kicking, Protaro attacked with all his might. Although weakened by his ordeal, Protaro proved a worthy opponent. But Nehan-dir was rested, and stronger than his thin frame suggested. They locked together and rolled over and over on the rough lava, lacerating backs and arms, knees and hands.

Kesira had started to help Protaro but halted when a sharp pain lanced into her side. One of the mercenaries blocked her, dagger ready. "Let them fight," the man said past a harelip. "If the wrong one wins, well, then I'll have to kill Nehan-dir myself!" He laughed with his twisted mouth; but the look in his eyes stayed ice cold.

Nehan-dir got one leg between his body and Protaro's. A powerful kick sent the guardsman somersaulting through the air to land heavily at the foot of the lava steps. Protaro swung back, facing Nehan-dir's sharp sword.

Just as the mercenary lunged, a green streak plummeted to strike at his wrist. Zolkan's talons raked four long, bloody gashes along his forearm. Nehan-dir screeched, more in surprise than pain. He spun to engage Zolkan; Protaro dived and knocked Nehan-dir to the ground.

When the man holding his dagger at Kesira's side tried to kick Zolkan as he waddled back from the fray, Kesira acted. One slender-fingered hand gripped a brawny wrist. She pulled slightly. Placing her other hand on the wrist she jerked backward, using her entire weight against that arm. The mercenary yelped with pain as his arm popped from the shoulder socket. She finished him with a kick to the throat. He lay gasping for a few seconds until Zolkan ripped repeatedly at throat and face.

"That wasn't necessary," Kesira chided.

"He tried to kick me. Pigeon-shit mercenary."

Kesira waved back others coming up the steps. They stared at her, then at their leader locked in mortal combat with Protaro, and then they obeyed.

A shove from Protaro sent Nehan-dir stumbling back. When Zolkan plucked up the fallen dagger that had been aimed at Kesira's heart and tossed it to Protaro, the odds became more even.

Nehan-dir with his sword circled warily around Protaro and the dagger.

Kesira expected Protaro to be at a disadvantage, even with his longer reach. But she underestimated the man.

The nun blinked, and in that split second Protaro made his move. Kesira opened her eyes to see Nehan-dir stiffen, his face devoid of expression. The tiny webbing of pink scars on his face glowed, then faded. His sword clattered to the lava steps and down to the square. Nehan-dir toppled after it like a felled tree.

Bloody dagger in hand, Protaro stood on the steps. Long years of command came into play. He pitched his voice in the proper fashion to ensure swift obedience.

"Go home, citizens of Kolya. Go home and rest from your ordeal. It is over. And mercenaries of the Steel Crescent..." he said, pausing. Kesira saw dozens of them tense. "You are not responsible for leader or patron. I grant you amnesty. Take it or die."

"What are we to do?" demanded one of the Steel Crescent at the side of the steps.

"The empire needs rebuilding. Emperor Kwasian is dead. So are all our patrons, the demons. We are alone now, and much depends on the next few years, how they are spent, what steps we take to maintain order."

"We can become brigands," muttered one.

"Do, and we will hunt you down like animals," shouted Protaro, angry. "Be productive, not destructive. We have all suffered enough. Do not add to the confusion and misery still stalking our land. Now go!"

Those living in Kolya drifted away, silent. The Order of the Steel Crescent left at a slower pace, talking quietly

The White Fire

among themselves. Only when the square was entirely deserted did Protaro collapse.

Kesira ran to him and propped him up, head in her lap. For a heartrending moment, she thought he'd suffered a fatal wound at Nehan-dir's hand. A quick examination showed only superficial injuries from the fight. To her amazement, not even a red spot showed where Lenc's green shaft had penetrated the soldier's body and left him suspended in the air. The only evidence of that cruel torture Protaro carried within him as memory. Kesira was glad to see that the exhaustion that caused the weakness was due to all that had happened and not to weakness of spirit.

"They listened," he said in wonder.

"You are a potent leader."

"A leader of nothing. My troop is dead. I failed Emperor Kwasian."

"And you owe your life to Gelya. You've made a good start to restoring peace to a land twisted by suspicion and death."

Protaro said nothing for a few minutes, then, "You still seek the boy?"

Kesira nodded.

"He is within the temple. I heard Nehan-dir mention it."

"He may be Lenc's son, but I have been a mother to him. I cannot abandon him now. Without Lenc's evil, there is hope. Gelya can guide Dymek, with words if not presence."

Leaning on each other, Protaro and Kesira went up the last of the steps to the temple door. There Zolkan huddled, grumbling loudly to himself.

"Did you find Dymek?" she asked.

"Didn't look. Best to leave."

"That isn't what Merrisen wanted for the boy. It's not what I want, either. Get out of my way." Kesira pushed past the *trilla* bird.

She stopped, heart rising to clog her throat.

"I warned you," squawked Zolkan.

Dymek, Lenc's son, stood encased in a pillar of the jade

demon's white fire. Even from a distance of a hundred feet, Kesira felt the evil fire's power.

For all eternity the boy would be trapped inside that magically raging inferno.

Chapter Sixteen

"IT CAN'T BE. No!" Kesira screamed. She dropped to her knees and stared. The dancing pillar of flame totally engulfed the boy. What horrified Kesira even more was Dymek's size. He was no longer the infant to be carried in her arms and suckled at her breast. He might have been four or five years old, standing trapped in the center of the white flames.

"Lenc wanted his son safe. This is how the demon did it," said Zolkan. "No way to free bratling."

"There must be. We did it before."

"Merrisen was there before. He might not have possessed full power, but he did have some left after first battle with Lenc."

Kesira feared that the *trilla* bird spoke the truth. Why should she have any power? She was nothing but a nun from an order long since destroyed. Even if Gelya had lived and her order had survived, what made her think she held the reins of any power at all unusual?

"The rune sticks. I can cast them and read the future," she said, clutching at the thinnest of hopes. "Molimo—Merrisen—said that was a skill few had, even in the demons' ranks."

"True," said Zolkan, "but that is far from being able to free boy from Lenc's magicks."

Kesira stood and slowly advanced. The crackling sounded louder. Only cold radiated from the flames, but she felt a fire burning within her. Kesira had to squint a little to see Dymek standing unconcerned and even expectant.

"We have to get him out. Remember how I destroyed

Eznofadil's power? How I destroyed the white flame powering Ayondela's spell?"

"You didn't destroy it," said Zolkan. "You only interrupted flow of magicks. Much different."

"Can you do that again?" asked Protaro. "Interrupt the flow for a few seconds? I don't know what you're talking about, but if you can release the barrier around the boy for even five seconds, I can go in, grab him and get back out."

"No," Kesira said. "That's too dangerous. The times I've thwarted the demons' spells have been for very brief durations. Less than two or three seconds."

"Let's get closer." Protaro tried, but the force of the white fire drove him back.

"You can never reach boy in three seconds. Or five," said Zolkan.

"And you'd never be able to fly in, grab him in your claws and fly out, either," Kesira told him firmly.

"Not thinking about it." The bird looked hurt that she'd believe him possible of such an altruistic act. "Merrisen wanted boy to live, for some reason."

"Why not?" asked Protaro.

"Would you be willing to hasten your own death?" Zolkan squawked. "Boy is at front of Time of Chaos. Demons die, humans muddle along, gods arise. No one likes to become obsolete, even a demon."

Kesira didn't bother listening to Zolkan and Protaro discuss possible means of entry. She circled the column and found no weakness. The spell had been wrought perfectly. Closing her eyes, she settled herself for the effort. She'd done it before. Calmness. Find the proper spot, twist with that portion of her soul so well trained by Gelya.

She remembered the feelings when she had blanked out the magical cell door in Lenc's dungeon. She duplicated it. The power rushed through her, into the fire—and away.

"Brief flicker," said Zolkan. "Nothing more."

"Maybe I do need Merrisen," she said glumly. "But we can't just *leave* him there. We can't!"

"Tunnel in from below?" suggested Protaro. "I don't see any chance of dropping in from the temple roof. It's too high, and the flames come together in an arch."

The White Fire

Kesira didn't have to try it to know that tunneling beneath the column wouldn't work. The *feel* was wrong. She had matched wits with the jade demons for long months now, and such an easy solution would reveal traps carefully laid by Lenc.

"Is there no one else who can perform such spells?" she asked out loud, not wanting an answer. She quickly ran through a list of all who had even a passing hint of magic at their command.

Most were dead and buried. Not for the first time did she miss Molimo.

She turned when she heard Protaro dragging something across the stark black temple floor. He had several long wooden beams which he dropped at her feet.

"We build a barricade," he said. "The flame can't chew through these thick beams too fast. And if they do, then you just shove a bit more into the flame and force the fire to digest that, too. We make a tunnel from the beams and I crawl down the center. When the fire wall is breached, I go and get the boy."

Zolkan only snorted from his perch on Kesira's shoulder.

"The fire is different," she said, trying to explain to the guardsman. "It doesn't take time to burn the wood, even wood soaked with water. It'll come directly through."

"What have we to lose?"

Kesira watched in silence as Protaro sweated over the exact arrangement of the beams he lugged in from outside. The man constructed a tunnel hardly wide enough for his broad shoulders. When he'd finished, he began sliding it toward the fire.

"Tell me when I break through the fire. Maybe the boy can crawl out on his own and save me the trip."

Protaro kept shoving and Kesira stayed silent. When a full five feet of the crawlway had vanished through the fire, Protaro stopped and simply stared. The fire didn't merely burn; it evaporated the wood. The lightest caress of wood to fire brought about instant destruction.

"How does the boy live inside?" marveled Protaro.

"Might be different inside. Lenc's magicks were not often subtle, but he could do it when he tried," said Zolkan.

Kesira wobbled a bit on her feet. Protaro grabbed her around the shoulders and supported her. "Are you ill?"

"Dizzy again. Was like this when... when I got back from Limaden. Must be the effect of Lenc's death. Magicks everywhere. Got caught in some residual spell."

"Pigeon-shit idea," muttered Zolkan. "No such thing as residual magic."

Kesira sagged and Protaro caught her up in his arms. "Let's get out of here," he said to the *trilla* bird. "Nothing we're going to do for the moment. If we rest, eat and then have the chance to think on it, we'll do better."

"Good idea. Glad *someone* cares about his belly. Haven't eaten in days." The *trilla* bird hopped over to Protaro's obliging shoulder and rode out on this new perch as the soldier carried an unconscious Kesira.

"Where?" Kesira jerked erect in the bed, afraid. She didn't know where she was or how she'd gotten here. The last she remembered was the hypnotically dancing white flame encasing Dymek.

"You're all right," came Protaro's soothing words. "You slept for almost a full day. It's just now dusk—the day after our skirmish with Nehan-dir."

"The inn," she said, finally recognizing the place. "Where's the innkeeper?" When she remembered how he had died, she dropped back to the soft bed. "Lenc killed him. It's all clear now. All of it."

"Want some food? There haven't been any customers at the inn, so I've been helping myself to the food rather than let it spoil. I cook a good trail stew."

The thought of food made Kesira's stomach churn uneasily. "No, not right now. I just want to lie and rest."

Kesira drifted off to a troubled sleep, a sleep populated with a burning Dymek and a leering Lenc, gentle Merrisen turning ancient before her eyes, small children frolicking in a grassy meadow. When she again awoke, the thought of food pleased her, and she ate voraciously.

"My cooking's not that good," Protaro commented. "So you must be hungry." He leaned back and hiked his feet up to the immaculately clean tabletop. The innkeeper had done well here. His presence would be missed.

"What are you thinking?" Kesira asked.

"Things are different for me," the guardsman said slowly. "My debt of honor requires repayment, but the death of Emperor Kwasian and Empress Aglenella erases that. I owe you my life and have pledged myself to learn the teachings of Gelya." Protaro idly wiped up a droplet spilled on the table. "Never thought about running a tavern before. Don't see that the innkeeper had any relatives, and no one seems to mind that I've been running this place."

"You want to stay?"

"Being a soldier is all I know. Might be able to find a local militia that requires some leadership to fight off the brigands. No matter who's Emperor, that's always going to be a problem."

"But you don't think so?"

Protaro shook his head. "Kolya's not a bad city. Been through hard times, but haven't we all? I don't think the life of chasing across the country holds the appeal for me that it once did."

"Your commission wasn't inherited?"

"Earned it. I had risen as far as I could unless I somehow found myself elevated to nobility. Not likely, not for a beggar's son. If I died in service, then I might have made one more promotion."

Kesira knew the dilemma faced by most in the Emperor's Guard. The highest posts were hereditary offices. No one could work through the ranks and achieve more than Protaro had. If he'd died nobly, the Emperor might have seen fit to promote him posthumously to commander. There was no other way for Protaro to rise.

"Innkeeping is an honorable profession."

"Any is, as long as it fulfills a need," Protaro said. A long silence descended.

Finally, Kesira said, "You want me to free you from your vow to serve Gelya, don't you?"

"Innkeepers have little need for intricate philosophy, other than that spouted drunkenly over the rim of a frothy mug of ale. That's not the same, is it?"

"No." Kesira heaved a deep breath. "You are released. I should never have bound you. I erred. Gelya taught that promises freely given are always observed but those extorted are always regretted. Learn what Gelya taught, if it pleases you."

"The demons are dead," said Protaro. "We must stumble along our own path, without their guidance."

For the first time Kesira faced the fact that her order was gone, as were all the others. She and she alone remained of the hundreds once devoted to Gelya. She would never be able to recruit enough novices to found a new nunnery, a new order. A different path had to be found.

"The old times are dead," she said quietly.

"Yes," sighed Protaro. "Every morning offered a noble chance, and every noble chance brought with it someone willing to seize the opportunity."

"That can be again," Kesira said. "Hope cannot die this easily. The demons are gone, our Empire lacks a leader, but soon, like water seeking its level, all will settle down into a new pattern."

"I've ceased desiring to make waves in the pattern."

Kesira shook herself and knew that Protaro had changed. So had she. "Where's Zolkan? I haven't seen his green feathers since I awoke."

"He said he was going out to kill a pigeon or two. Work off his frustrations."

"I need him. If we are to pry loose Dymek from his father's infernal spell, we must get at it again."

Kesira turned and stared at Protaro when he didn't respond. She read accurately the expression on his face.

"What's changed since yesterday? Dymek hasn't been freed, has he?"

Protaro stood and began wiping at the already clean table. "The people. They've decided that no one will be allowed to even try to free Dymek. Lenc drove it home to them constantly that Dymek was his son, his successor. They don't want to release another demon on the world."

"They can't stop me from trying!"

"Right now, a dozen armed guards patrol the base of the temple. No one can enter for any reason."

"I will."

"I agree that this fanaticism on their part will fade as the months wear on. Once Kolya is again a thriving town, there'll be no reason to waste time prowling about and thrusting spears at shadows near Lenc's dark temple. But until then, isn't it best that you leave Dymek where he is?"

"What would you have answered if Dymek had said, 'Isn't it best we leave Protaro with that shaft through his guts?'"

Protaro sank down to one of the benches. He shrugged and tried to smile. Even his second attempt failed.

"What do you want me to do?"

Kesira's mind began turning over various plans, examining and discarding them, then moving on to others. Somehow, she'd free Dymek. She would!

"Bad hunting now," complained Zolkan. "No pigeons about."

"We don't want activity, we want sleep," Protaro said in a low voice. "Only two hours till dawn. I've seen sentries fresh on their post fall asleep at this time of night."

"Three of them," Kesira reported, "all in front of the temple on the square. They're sitting with their backs to the temple—seem to be nodding off."

"See?" Protaro ruffled Zolkan's feathers, and the *trilla* bird replied with a vicious clacking of his beak just inches from the offending fingers.

"How will this be different?" asked Zolkan. "We get inside, and then what? We sit about and stare at the trapped bratling?"

"I . . . it'll be different," Kesira said. "I sense that it will."

"You're still sick," said Protaro. "You're drawn, and your hands shake. Let's wait until you've had a chance to rest some more. Another day or two. That'll aid us also in getting past the guards. In only one day they've fallen off from a dozen to only three. In a week, no one will guard this place."

"Now. Let's go."

Protaro started to argue, but found himself talking to Kesira's back. "She knows her own mind," said Zolkan. "Always gets her into bad trouble."

"Us, too," said Protaro.

"I can fly away. What about you?" Zolkan appeared smug that he had gotten back at Protaro for ruffling his headcrest.

As silent as three shadows, they drifted along the black lava steps and up to the opened doors leading into the temple. The cold light emanating from within told them that Lenc's magic still fired the column imprisoning Dymek.

"Keep watch," Kesira told Protaro. She and Zolkan hurried to within twenty feet of the white fire. Through the shifting curtain of flame she saw Dymek's gently smiling face. The boy waved to her, as if preparing to go on a short trip.

Kesira moaned suddenly, then bent double. Protaro rushed to her side.

"Get back there. Don't let anyone in. I'll be all right. It's just something I ate. Still nauseated."

Kesira pushed Protaro away and turned her attention to the pillar of fire. She straightened, her mind taking control of her body. All discomfort vanished. She worked on the litanies Gelya had taught; she found the verses to her death song, now likely to run much longer. The rhythms, the flows, the urgencies all were hers.

She struggled to regain the power she'd had when she thwarted the magical barriers. She struggled and she succeeded. Kesira didn't let herself exult in it; she needed concentration, a negation of self in favor of the power. It flowed; she used it.

The white fire Lenc had used as his sigil and as his weapon flickered.

"Close. Almost. More, more!" urged Zolkan.

Sweat beaded her forehead even though the coldness from the fire chilled her to the bone. Emotions crippled her efforts. She pushed them away and concentrated totally.

For what seemed hours, Kesira fought to lift the magicks surrounding Dymek. She fought and failed. There wasn't enough left within her. She'd used it all. But the nun refused to give up. She again settled her emotions and reached within herself, but the needed energy simply wasn't there.

And then it was.

From a bright, burning point in her abdomen came a rush

of power that dazzled her. Flowing like the ocean, like the winds whipping across the world, it erupted and touched Lenc's pillar of fire.

As a candle is extinguished by a hurricane's full force, so did the white fire vanish into nothingness.

Dymek walked forward as if nothing had happened. The little boy—already waist high when measured against Kesira—held out his hand and smiled.

"Thank you," he said simply.

"Dymek!"

She dropped to her knees and hugged him. In that instant she knew the name Lenc had given him was the proper one. No other name fit.

"Kesira! One of the guards heard us. He went and fetched the others. There must be hundreds of them now. We've got to get out of here. Right now!"

Kesira jerked Dymek along by his arm, his short legs barely able to keep up. She didn't question him about his rapid growth. She had seen Merrisen age almost before her eyes. She hoped Dymek wouldn't grow old and die within weeks or months, too.

"There's only the front way out." Protaro skidded to a halt. More than fifty armed men blocked the way to freedom.

"They've freed the demon child. Kill them! Kill them all!"

"Wait!" shouted Protaro. "This isn't the demon's son. Lenc lied. Dymek is the son of peasants. He's just a child. How can one so young be a threat to you?"

Protaro's face paled when he pointed to what he'd thought would be an innocent-appearing child. Dymek's piercing gray eyes bespoke of infinite wisdom and experience, of sophistication far beyond any of the mercenaries threatening him. Only in size did he seem like a human child.

The crowd shoved Protaro out of the way in their haste to get to Kesira and Dymek.

"Stop," Kesira said, her voice almost too low to be heard. It was as if a mighty hand grabbed those in the crowd and restrained them. "You do not know me, but I am a sister of the Order of Gelya. Of all those in Kolya, I hated Lenc the most for what he'd done."

"No!" "Impossible!" came the cries.

"True," she said. Her voice carried the snap of authority. "My sisters, my order, my entire world were destroyed by the jade demons—and I destroyed them, each of them. Eznofadil and Howenthal and Ayondela and finally Lenc. I slew *four* jade demons."

Absolute silence greeted this statement.

"Believe me or not, I went into Howenthal's Quaking Lands. I met and defeated Eznofadil. I climbed Ayondela's accursed mountain and there she died."

Dymek tugged on Kesira's sleeve. "You forget," the boy said. "I'm the one who killed Ayondela. I cried and she shattered. Her entire temple came down in a rain of jade dust."

This caused the crowd to begin muttering again.

"I am beloved of demons," Kesira said, motioning Dymek to silence. "Wemilat gave me his mark. You all know Wemilat the Ugly, a good and kind patron." She exposed her breast where the lip print glowed warmly. "This mark ensures that Dymek will never be touched by evil. Lenc imprisoned him, but this mark proclaims him free of any taint of jade."

"She might be lying," came the uneasy words. "That *is* Lenc's son."

"I am," Dymek said in his unsettling voice. This created another stir.

"He is Lenc's son, but I protect him. I have fought alongside the finest of the demons. Wemilat and Merrisen. I loved and was loved by Merrisen. Lenc killed him with the jade. I cannot ever allow that green curse to happen to another."

"Kill them. Kill them all!" The cry started out as a ragged chant, then grew in volume as more and more got caught up in the power of a mob.

Dymek started to speak, to cry out. Kesira clamped her hand over his mouth to stifle his death-giving shrieks.

"Let us go!" she shouted. "Let us leave Kolya and we will never return."

The bright spot glowing within her flared once more.

The same power that had snuffed out Lenc's fire now bowled over those in the crowd. They stumbled and fell, leaving a pathway for Kesira and Dymek.

Zolkan fluttered back down to her shoulder. "What of Protaro?" he asked.

"They didn't even notice him. He'll be fine. We must find horses and ride from here, ride and find a place to live."

"Know good spot," said Zolkan. "One where you and Dymek and Suzo can live."

"Suzo?"

Kesira walked more rapidly to get away from Lenc's temple. The threat of the crowd diminished, but she felt the need for haste. The sooner they left Kolya, the easier she'd feel.

"Suzo is her name. Daughter Merrisen sired. One growing inside you."

"I'm pregnant? By Merrisen?"

Hurry, came the command within her.

"Yes, Suzo is right. Let's hurry," said Dymek.

Kesira obeyed. She could do nothing less.

Epilogue

GENTLE BREEZES laden with the sharp tang of sea salt blew across the meadow and up the slopes of the low mountain. Below, in a misty fog, rolled the blue Sea of Katad. Above, cloaked in the purple haze of distance, rose the lofty peaks of the Sarn Mountains. All around Kesira Minette were peaceful, grassy pastures bursting with the promise of warm summer and just beginning to catch spring-fire with brilliant blossoms and verdant leaves.

Kesira sighed as she sat back against a dead stump and looked downslope to the sea. It had been only three years since that lovely expanse of bright water had been frozen into viciously edged cutting waves. No more. She saw a few fishing boats working the shoals and bringing in their catch. Above drifted white and pink seabirds, wary of predators like Zolkan.

Try as she might, Kesira couldn't find the green-plumed *trilla* bird in the air. He might have tired of soaring on the thermals and come to rest. Or, knowing him, he'd gone down the coast to one of the ports to trade improbable stories with other *trilla* birds shipping on the freighters as navigators.

She plucked a juicy blade of grass and sucked on the bitter juices. Mouth watering, Kesira wondered if it were possible for life to get any better. Here she had no worry, no want; she passed the time as she saw fit and everyone was happy and healthy.

Tipping her head up to catch both the liquid warmth of the burgeoning sun and to see the puffs of white cloud, Kesira felt a lethargy creeping over her. So peaceful. She just wanted to sleep.

She did, and when she awoke it was to the sound of heavy bootsteps tramping on the freshly rain-dampened ground.

"Kesira!" A figure dressed in a crimson tunic and leather breeches waved. She waved back.

"Up here, Protaro."

Protaro climbed the slope and, out of breath, dropped beside her. "I'm not used to exertion like this. The life of an innkeeper appeals more and more to me."

"It was good of you to come and see me. You didn't have to."

"You never come to Kolya. If I want to see you, I have to come here." They sat side by side, silent, lost in their own thoughts.

"There's no need for me to leave here. I am content," she said after a while. "Such harmony not even Gelya preached. Every insect knows its place. Look." Her fingernails dug into the stump she'd used for a backrest. Termites squirmed under the sunlight, diving back down well-drilled tunnels into the heart of the rotting stump. "They know their duty, do it and live well. In a year the stump will be returned to the soil."

"It's always been that way. This isn't something new."

She noticed the man's uneasiness. "This is the way it is with *all* things now. Men do not fight men. There's harmony once more in the empire. Emperor Benniso rules wisely and well. Everyone knows his station and duty; everyone performs it."

"Are you happy with your duties?" Protaro's discomfort grew. His eyes darted around the peaceful meadow as if looking for a band of brigands. The last of the roving thieves had died over a year prior, at the request of the children, but Kesira didn't tell Protaro that. It would only add to his restlessness.

"My duties are few now. The children are mature."

"I saw Suzo but not Dymek. She looked to be eleven or twelve."

"Dymek is a handsome young man. He told me the other day that he wasn't going to allow himself to age any further. He might pass for seventeen." Kesira smiled. "That will

The White Fire

change. In a few years he'll prefer to look older. That'll give him more credibility."

"Does a god need credibility?" asked Protaro.

"Even a god," she said. Again the silence fell between them. *Trenly* crickets chirped, and flying insects intent on pollination flitted from flower to bright flower sucking nectar. "Especially a god. Being all-powerful isn't enough. Coercion is never as good as allowing your followers to . . . follow."

"Lenc tried to force worship. His son does better?"

"Dymek knows—and he cannot make the mistakes of his father. Lenc was a demon; Dymek is a god." Kesira sighed. "The Time of Chaos, they called it. The demons' name, and a poor reflection of what has actually happened."

"For them it was chaos. They died."

"And the gods were born. You know that Dymek and Suzo talk of their children? Not any time soon, mind you. Thousands of years from now, but already they talk of their successors. That was something the demons couldn't."

"Their human traits got in the way," said Protaro. "The demons were shortsighted, even more than humans, because all their traits, both good and bad, were magnified."

"That might be. I doubt it. The demons were imperfect, a steppingstone to . . . them." Kesira pointed to where Dymek and Suzo walked on the far side of the meadow. Deep in discussion, they seemed oblivious to the world around them, yet faint touches of thought brushed over Kesira's mind.

"They say hello," she said. Protaro jumped as if someone stuck him in the side with a dagger. "Don't be like that, dear friend," she said, reaching out to touch Protaro's arm and calm him. "They are gods and have a god's interest, but that doesn't mean they ignore everyone around them. They seem aloof only because we cannot understand their concerns. Would you believe that Dymek actually worries over the extinction of a single species of insect on the far side of the empire? And it won't happen for another four hundred years."

Protaro shook his head. "They make me uneasy."

"But they will not harm you."

"That bug they talk about might be us. It might be all of us."

"Yes," Kesira agreed softly. "It might be."

She took his hand and led Protaro down the slope to the small house where she lived. Dymek and Suzo had long since moved out to live under the sun and stars, to feel the elements against their skins and be that much closer in contact with their world.

"My ale suffers in comparison to yours, I'm sure, but will you have some anyway?" She poured a mug of the frothing brew and slid it across the table to Protaro.

"It's good, but you're right; that which I buy for the Stonewood Inn is better." This struck Protaro as ludicrous. "You can have *them* conjure anything you want. Why settle for second-best in anything?"

"Live like the Emperor, you mean? In a fine palace, with servants waiting on me every instant of the day, satisfying any whim I might have? It doesn't suit me. I was raised a nun and have simple tastes. Even now, I haven't changed that much."

"What of the bird?"

A loud squawk announced Zolkan's arrival. He flapped through a partially opened window without touching the frame and landed heavily on the edge of the table. Zolkan found the spot where his talons had left familiar marks and formed a rude perch.

"Saw you coming but wanted to finish hearing from Zeeka. She travels the coastline all way to Clorrisai. Need new victuals for inn? She can provide them at a discount through her humans. Rare foods. But you must hurry. She leaves soon. Hurry, hurry."

Protaro laughed for the first time. "Zolkan, you never change. No, I'm content with what I have."

"Content. All humans are only content. Is no one happy? Sad? Always content. Damn bratlings."

Protaro recoiled, waiting for the gods to strike the *trilla* bird down. Nothing happened.

"They are kind, Protaro. It is so hard to believe that after the atrocities done to us by Lenc and the other jade demons, but these are gods."

"Born of human and demon, just as the demons were born of animal and human."

"They have transcended most of the faults in humans. Only the best is there, and magnified, as in the demons. They are more than human, but only in the good ways." Kesira sipped at her ale. "And I think they have abilities unknown to humans. Even I cannot guess at them."

"How long do you stay, Protaro?" asked Zolkan.

"I am only passing through, just for the single day. I've been to the coastal fisheries to arrange for fresh catch to be iced and then shipped overland to Kolya. Good prices. I'll make the Stonewood Inn the best in the city or know the reason." Protaro took a large drink, then dropped the mug to the table with a loud, ringing bang. "Why not join me on the way back to Kolya, Zolkan?"

He addressed the *trilla* bird but looked at Kesira.

"Good change of pace. I tire of not being able to understand Dymek and Suzo. Demon talk was plain. Not theirs." Zolkan launched himself and deftly turned in midair. "Let's be off. Much distance to travel this day."

"Patience, Zolkan. How about you, Kesira? Will you join us, too?"

More than a simple request for company went with Protaro's words.

"You two go on. I may decide to join you later in the summer."

"You aren't needed here. They can care for themselves."

"Go on. If I decide I can leave, I'll see you in Kolya. Later."

Protaro nodded and quickly left, Zolkan perched on his shoulder and chattering away about the sea, about Zeeka and her pet sailors, about a thousand other things. Seeing Protaro reminded her of Molimo—Merrisen—and brought a tear to her eye. She wiped it away quickly. The past was so sad, so strange—and gone.

Kesira watched them go down the winding gravel path and finally vanish from sight in the direction of the village, knowing she'd never join Protaro. Zolkan might return someday. Or he might not. It didn't matter any longer.

Kesira Minette was content. And mother to gods.

THE EXCITING SCIENCE FANTASY ADVENTURE SERIES
by ROBERT E. VARDEMAN

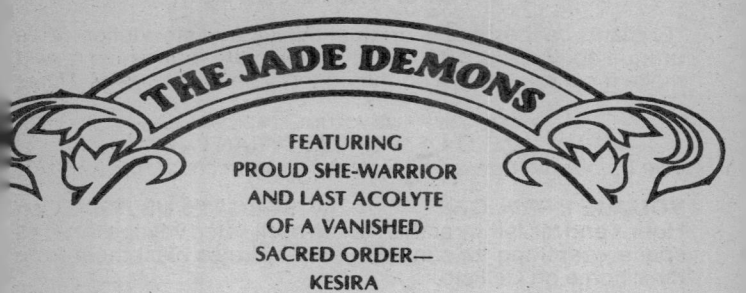

THE JADE DEMONS

**FEATURING
PROUD SHE-WARRIOR
AND LAST ACOLYTE
OF A VANISHED
SACRED ORDER—
KESIRA**

BOOK 1: THE QUAKING LANDS 89518-8/$2.95 US/$3.75 Can
With her magical bird Zoltan, the seductive wolf-boy Molimo, and her mighty champion Rouvin, Kesira challenges the loathsome Jade Demons no mortal had ever defied before.

BOOK 2: THE FROZEN WAVES 89799-7/$2.95 US/$3.75 Can
During the Time of Chaos, her world trapped under a wintry spell, Kesira and her valiant band enter the Isle of Eternal Winter to battle to free their planet from its icy doom.

BOOK 3: THE CRYSTAL CLOUDS 89800-4/$2.95 US/$3.75 Can
Kesira faces her greatest challenge as she and her loyal companions journey to the realm of the Jade Demons for a final confrontation with evil.

BOOK 4: THE WHITE FIRE 89801-2/$2.95 US/$3.75 Can
The explosive ultimate battle between Kesira's forces and the last—and most cunning—of the Jade Demons.

Buy these books at your local bookstore or use this coupon for ordering:

AVON BOOK MAILING SERVICE, P.O. Box 690, Rockville Centre, NY 11571
Please send me the book(s) I have checked above. I am enclosing $_____
(please add $1.00 to cover postage and handling for each book ordered to a maximum of three dollars). *Send check or money order—no cash or C.O.D.'s please.* Prices and numbers are subject to change without notice. Please allow six to eight weeks for delivery.

Name _____

Address _____

City _____ State/Zip _____

Vardeman 1/86

BIO OF A SPACE TYRANT
Piers Anthony

"Brilliant...a thoroughly original thinker and storyteller with a unique ability to posit really *alien* alien life, humanize it, and make it come out alive on the page." *The Los Angeles Times*

A COLOSSAL NEW FIVE VOLUME SPACE THRILLER—
BIO OF A SPACE TYRANT
The Epic Adventures and Galactic Conquests of Hope Hubris

VOLUME I: REFUGEE   84194-0/$2.95 US /$3.50 Can
Hubris and his family embark upon an ill-fated voyage through space, searching for sanctuary, after pirates blast them from their home on Callisto.

VOLUME II: MERCENARY   87221-8/$2.95 US /$3.50 Can
Hubris joins the Navy of Jupiter and commands a squadron loyal to the death and sworn to war against the pirate warlords of the Jupiter Ecliptic.

VOLUME III: POLITICIAN   89685-0/$2.95 US /$3.50 Can
Fueled by his own fury, Hubris rose to triumph obliterating his enemies and blazing a path of glory across the face of Jupiter. Military legend...people's champion...promising political candidate...he now awoke to find himself the prisoner of a nightmare that knew no past.

Also by Piers Anthony:
The brilliant Cluster Series—
sexy, savage interplanetary adventures.

CLUSTER, CLUSTER I	01755-5/$2.95 US/$3.75 Can
CHAINING THE LADY, CLUSTER II	01779-2/$2.95 US/$3.75 Can
KIRLIAN QUEST, CLUSTER III	01778-4/$2.95 US/$3.75 Can
THOUSANDSTAR, CLUSTER IV	75556-4/$2.95 US/$3.75 Can
VISCOUS CIRCLE, CLUSTER V	79897-2/$2.95 US/$3.75 Can

AVON Paperbacks

Buy these books at your local bookstore or use this coupon for ordering:

AVON BOOK MAILING SERVICE, P.O. Box 690, Rockville Centre, NY 11571
Please send me the book(s) I have checked above. I am enclosing $_____
(please add $1.00 to cover postage and handling for each book ordered to a maximum of three dollars). *Send check or money order*—no cash or C.O.D.'s please. Prices and numbers are subject to change without notice. Please allow six to eight weeks for delivery.

Name _____
Address _____
City _____ State/Zip _____

ANTHONY 7-85